The JESUS FACTORY

An Adventure Novel of the Spirit, That Reveals the Lost Message of The Hidden Apostle

The JESUS FACTORY

An Adventure Novel of the Spirit,
That Reveals the Lost Message of
The Hidden Apostle

Scott Lindquist

First Edition

Cover Art:
Graphic design by Scott Lindquist
Image of Jesus is Robert Powell, from the film
"Jesus of Nazareth" by Franco Zeffirelli

Published by Aventine Press
750 State St. #319
San Diego CA, 92101
www.aventinepress.com

Library of Congress Control Number: 2010934562

ISBN:1-59330-679-2
Printed in the United States of America

Dedication and Acknowledgements

I have dedicated all of my books to my wife, Sydney. This book is no different. She is my constant source of spiritual truth and clarity. She was invaluable not only as a support, but also as a resource for this work. What ever I become that is good and fine will be a testament to her unwavering belief in me.

I also wish to acknowledge my editor, Chris O'Byrne for his judgment and insight. Every good writer needs a great editor, and I have had one.

THE JESUS FACTORY
Contents

**There are more things in heaven and earth, Horatio,
than are dreamt of in your philosophy.**

William Shakespeare, “Hamlet”, Act 1 scene 5

Chapter One
A Godless Place

Even though the Northside State Sanitarium prided itself in a clean and comfortable environment, free from the traffic and noise of downtown Chicago, it was still a godless place. The complex of pink stucco buildings once belonged to the Catholic Church. It had been St. Mary the Divine Hospital and still bore the markings of saints and angels at the entry gate.

Here time had no value and the only allowable God lay in a bed next to you. It was the perfect place to get away from the world—and from God.

Peter sat there on the side of his bed, staring out the window. It was fall and most of the leaves had already left their branches. A godless place, there was no more depressing place than the sanitarium in Chicago when it was cold. The bone-chilling wind off the lake swept through the spires of the city and drained the color from the sky. During this time, the sun left its orbit and wandered to friendlier places.

Looking at the barren trees, he watched one last leaf fall to the ground. That was him. He had dropped away from the tree of life. His soul was gone and there was no Son for him either. He was dead inside. The only thing left was the shell that kept him moving, and it hadn't moved from this place in eight months. At five o'clock, the last medications would be given. Tonight was the night. He had hidden his sleeping pills for weeks; twenty pills, that should do it. When they gave him his nightly dose he would ask for more water to get them all down. Then he'd be off to dreamland and Hell. Hell, that's where people like him went, even if he didn't believe in it anymore. He wondered if you could go to a place that you didn't believe in. He didn't know and he didn't care. He just wanted the pain to stop.

For months Peter had sat silently in his room, staring from the emptiness in his soul into the darkness of the world. He had been God's chosen, but now his choice was to end it. He wanted no more gods in his life.

He could hear Nurse Randall's cart coming down the hall. Every night she brought her tray of pills and potions, like a peddler selling snake oil. The noise of squeaking wheels and banging trays was unmistakable. No one liked Nurse Randall, not even during the sanitarium's Catholic days. She had the disposition of an aunt that the family tolerated and the children dreaded. Perhaps it was her size, she was only four feet tall, or her elf-like manner and gravely voice that gave her the name of the Troll of St. Mary's.

Whatever it was, no one messed with Nurse Randall, not even the doctors. As Peter braced himself to face her, suddenly the door of his room opened and Wendy stepped in.

"I'm the new assistant. Nurse Randall will be here in a few minutes. I thought we might get acquainted."

He looked at her and there was something about her eyes. She looked familiar. Maybe it was the blond hair, the smile; something. Peter had second thoughts. He wasn't prepared for this. It was one thing to kill himself in front of Randall. He didn't care what that would do to her. But this new one? This girl? He felt something, some spark of a connection. Was it possible that he felt compassion? He thought that part of him had died long ago. As she got closer to him, he saw something gleam around her neck. A gold necklace flashed across his eyes. It was a cross. A sudden spike tore through his mind like a blinding light in a tunnel. Then she took out a Bible from behind her back and held it out to him.

"I thought this might bring you comfort." She said.

He screamed out in pain, throwing the Bible on the floor.

"Get that crap away from me! Garbage! God damn you! I told you I want that crap out of here!"

With that he started throwing pillows, papers and furniture around the room. Wendy recoiled in absolute terror. Then he got on his knees and started to rip the pages out of the Bible. With each page, he screamed;

"Lies——crap—garbage!"

Then he turned on her, looking into her eyes with all the hate and pain of his tormented life…

"Get the hell out of here!"

Wendy didn't have to hear it twice. She threw open the door and rushed out of the room as lamps and other objects smashed against the door. Once outside, she slammed her fist on the emergency lock button. The door bolt slid shut and locked Peter inside with his madness. She turned around and looked inside through the window in the door. Peter was like an animal, drooling and cursing the air. Randall grabbed Wendy by the shoulder and spun her around.

"You did that! You're responsible. If you think I'm taking the rap for your stupidity, you're plumb out of your mind! Well, don't just stand there, hit the emergency button."

Wendy ran down the corridor and pushed the red emergency button, which rang out on all floors. Throughout the facility, exterior security doors and wings were locked down automatically. The digital warning lights flashed 132 along with Code Red. All available attendants ran to 132. Once the attendants pushed their way into the room, Wendy watched them try to subdue him. Peter screamed and thrashed like a wild animal, throwing himself around the room, she saw pills tumble out from under his pillow.

The attendants knew what to do. The sleeping pills meant that they had a potential suicide on their hands. They had to make sure he couldn't hurt himself. Holding him down, they pinned his arms behind him, while Peter grunted and cursed at them. Wendy couldn't understand how a man of God could come to this.

Nurse Randall and Dr. Gaskin rushed in and administered 800 mg of phenobarbital to calm him down and within seconds the drug started to take effect. Peter started to breathe heavier and his arms and legs felt numb. The attendants picked him up and tied him to the bed so he couldn't move. Wendy couldn't watch any more. She turned her head away and cried. *Get the hell out of here!* The words rang in her head. What did she do wrong?

After a few minutes, Gaskin came out of the room. He was covered in sweat. It had been a hard take-down. He looked at Wendy.

"Do you think I enjoyed that? What the hell happened in there?"

"I don't know, she said, I just started to talk to him and gave him a Bible." Gaskin exploded. "Jesus Christ, what the hell were you thinking? Didn't you read the chart?"

Wendy's confidence and bravura were gone now. She answered like a seven year old child,

"No."

"In my office. Now!" He said.

As she walked down the corridor to Gaskin's office, she could feel the stares and judgment of all the nurses and orderlies that she passed.

"In here, Larsen."

Gaskin closed the door after Wendy walked in and sat down.

"I'm so sorry, doctor. I was only trying to help. I didn't mean to upset him." Gaskin tossed the chart at her.

"Read, girl."

Gaskin slammed the office door as he left. She looked down at Peter Andrew's chart and tried to read, but her eyes filled with tears. All she could think of was *Get the hell out!* The words on the chart leaped out at her. Written in red ink was the warning: Patient is to have no contact with any religious symbols, including crosses, Bibles, and especially pictures of Jesus.

What happened? What happened to him? She spent the next hour reading Andrew's chart. There were pictures of his wife, and daughter and something about a man called Jeremiah. She was shocked at what was written. When she was done, she slowly closed the cover of Andrew's chart. Standing up, she walked to the window and looked out. She wondered how a god, any god could have cursed him so.

Dr. Gaskin came in and saw her looking out the window. "Did you read it?" She nodded, not looking at him.

"Now you know. Now you know why there can't be any religious symbols anywhere near him. We've made some very important progress, but another setback like this one could put him beyond our reach."

"I don't understand." She said. "How could God do this to him?"

"God? God had nothing to do with it."

"This is such a godless place." she said

"It's supposed to be a godless place. We treat the mind with science, not superstition, Miss Larsen."

"I'm sorry—I didn't…"

"Look, Wendy. When the Catholics owned this place, God was a part of everything they did. There were saints and crosses and pictures of Jesus everywhere, but now that the state owns it, most of that stuff is gone. It has to be."

Wendy felt the whole weight of judgment and her stupidity well up inside her. Taking a tissue out of her pocket, she wiped the tears from her eyes. "When I came here, I thought I could make a difference. You know, when they hired me to use my journalism education to try to get the patients to open up and write their stories, I thought I could help. Now I don't know if I belong here."

"You were hired on a part-time basis as a favor to a friend of your family, Dr. Williams; a classmate of mine at the University of Chicago. Don't think we don't need you here. You can be of great help to these patients. You want to be a journalist, a news anchor, and one day I'm sure, in your fondest dreams, to win a Pulitzer or something, right?"

Hearing her own fantasies come from Dr. Gaskin, she had to laugh. "Pretty stupid, huh?"

"No, not stupid at all."

"He told me to get the hell out. When I was young, I stood up to my minister when the church condemned gays. I kept asking questions about homosexuality, and when I wouldn't let up, Reverend Johnson threw me out of the church. He said the same thing—get the hell out. I told him that's what I was trying to do, to get the Hell out of his church."

Gaskin had to laugh. "You see, even then you had guts. That's the kind of courage that you'll need as a reporter."

"I didn't show much courage tonight."

"You showed determination and a desire to help one Peter Andrews, but you lacked one very important thing."

"What was that?"

"You didn't do your research. If you had, you would have known what to do and what not to do for Peter Andrews."

"Research—I'll remember that."

Wendy left the office. Outside in the hall, she stopped, then turned around and went back to Andrew's room to see if he was all right. She stood outside his room and peered through the window in the door. He lay on the bed with his arms tied to the rails. They had even put a cloth in his mouth so he wouldn't bite his tongue.

As she stood there leaning against the wall, she thought hard about what Gaskin had said, that God had nothing to do with what happened to Peter Andrews. She shook her head and said, "No, God had everything to do with it!"

Sitting in the sanitarium cafeteria, she tried to eat her dinner, but her stomach felt like a Gordian knot. She had to cut through all this stuff about God and help him. She was determined to learn all she could about Peter Andrews. This was research and she was going to master it.

Wendy spent the next three nights during her dinner hours, reading all about Andrews in magazines, newspaper articles and the Internet. He had reached the top, making the covers of Time, Newsweek and Christianity Today, no small feat for a man of thirty. They were all early articles that gave no clue as to what happened to him or why he was here. He was young and blond, with a charismatic personality and the body of a California surfer. But his most striking feature was that he was a powerful speaker. He could wrap an audience around his finger with the emotional peaks and valleys that made their spirits soar. In those golden days, he had a fire in his belly. Part preacher and part rock star. The press even dubbed him Reverend Hunk. He was at the top of his game. But that was all gone now. What really happened to Peter Andrews?

The next night, about eight o'clock, she slowly opened the door and slipped inside his room. He seemed to be sleeping. She walked over to his bed and looked down at him. He was so handsome and yet so vulnerable. His head was covered in sweat. She went to the sink and wet a washcloth. She felt so sorry for him. As she started to mop his brow and face, his eyes opened. She stopped, waiting to see how he would react. When he didn't move, she said,

"I'm sorry. I didn't know. I didn't mean to upset you."

As he looked in her eyes, he felt something. As she stroked his head, his eyes closed and he drifted off. His mind didn't know if he was alive or dead, but at least he was at peace.

For the next week, she kept her distance, not wanting to disturb him. Finally after repeated requests, Gaskin finally relented and said she could have some limited contact with him.

The next day, most of the non-violent patients were allowed into the courtyard. Today it was unseasonably warm and the walls around the courtyard kept out the wind, which was always cold. As Peter sat there drowsing, he felt a warm hand on his shoulders. He opened his eyes to see Wendy adjusting a blanket around his shoulders.

"I brought you your lunch out here."

With that she put a tray of food in front of him. He looked down and saw chicken and rice. She continued to talk and help him eat, but try as she might, he wouldn't eat the rice. He said nothing, but she noticed a tear coming down his face. She reached down and touched his hand. His eyes closed and with a deep breath his troubled mind took him back to happier times and Ann.

Chapter Two
Woman, Know Thy Place

The Richland Theological Seminary was the poor man's school for young ministers. Its history developed from the Methodist tradition. In 1987, it had faced a schism between the Evangelicals and the Moderates. The Moderates won, but everyone knew they couldn't keep power for long. There was a sense that a strong fundamentalist wave was coming. Two professors were targeted. Doctor Linda Price, a perceived feminist theologian who referred to God as both male and female, and Doctor Edward Jeffers, a liberal professor who had the courage to look at the creation story in an entirely different light. His explanation that the origin of the Garden of Eden story was an ancient fable about civilization so shocked the students on the first day of class that two young girls fled the classroom in tears.

"I know this information is shocking to you students who have always, like children, believed the pleasant little Garden of Eden story, but the truth is that many historians believe the tale originated in Sumer, which is now Iraq. The origin of the story came from many stories and legends that were used to explain the creation of man and woman and the beginning of life.

Let's look at some of these stories; in one story, there was a naked primitive savage, who had been raised by wild animals. After a time, he became like the other wild beasts and could neither talk nor communicate with humans. His body, though naked, was covered with fur like an animal. Now when he came into the village to steal food, he frightened the people, so the elders determined that a young woman should be sent out to speak to him and perhaps get him to stop. But when she went to him, she fell in love with him and he with her. Their love changed him and made him tame. Then all of his fur dropped off of his body. He followed her back to the village and became a peaceful member of the village, i.e., he became civilized."

"Professor, you're not saying this was a historical fact, are you?" asked Peter.

"Of course not; this is just a symbolic tale of how ancient people explained how savage man became civilized. They believed that when the man marries and forms a family, he becomes less like an animal, less violent. I believe that the American West became civilized when women and families moved into the rural areas. Their migration eventually brought churches and schools and more permanent towns. When this happened, the saloons became less popular and the undesirable cowboys, drunks and prostitutes were eventually driven out. It is the common belief that guns tamed the West, but I think it was women and children who really brought civilization and tamed the frontier."

"What about the Devil, Professor? Isn't the Garden of Eden story a story about temptation and sin?" asked Peter.

"Peter, the serpent was never identified as the Devil until much later. In ancient mythology, serpents were gods and stood for wisdom; in fact, the serpent was also the symbol of the Goddess. When the early church fathers wanted to eliminate the appeal of the various nature cults and pagan religions, they made the snake symbol into something evil. The other part of this story is the issue of the veneration of Mary. Many pagans were drawn into the new Christian religion because they could transfer their veneration from the Goddess to Mary. The most important thing to remember," Jeffers said, "is that the Creation story is a myth and was never meant to be taken literally. If you take it as actual fact, then there are too many inconsistencies that just don't make sense."

"I have a question, professor." asked Ann

"Go ahead, Miss Parks."

"What about the story of Cain going into the Land of Nod to find his wife. If Adam and Eve and Cain and Abel were the only humans, where did she come from?"

Jeffers had to laugh. "Oh, what a tangled web we weave, when we believe the Bible literally. This is one of the inconsistencies that I spoke of. In reality, none of this matters. If you understand that it's an allegory that was written by very primitive man to make sense of how we all got here…"

Ann had to interrupt. "Then I have to ask why, if this is just a fairy tale, why has the church used this and other parts of the Bible to justify their subjugation of women."

That remark prompted boos and jeers from some of the male students. Jeffers stepped in.

"Stop that! Stop that at once. We'll have none of that in my class, do you understand? She has every right to ask the question. Go ahead, Miss Parks."

"Thank you, Professor. As I was saying, even today, when a woman feels like God has called her to the ministry, she is shut out because of prejudice and bigotry." Ann was visibly upset and on the verge of crying.

"Miss Parks, I understand you're upset. Why don't you see me after class and maybe I can explain all this to you."

"All right," she said.

"Now I want to make one final statement about taking the Bible as the literal word of God. Anyone who believes that every word of the Bible is the divine word of God and a factual reality will inevitably create ridicule from historians and people who think.

"But Professor, shouldn't we defend the Bible as the word of God?" Peter asked.

"There is no need to get caught up in defending the Bible if you really understand it. Unfortunately, most ministers today are totally ignorant of its history and its complexities, and what's worse, they have no desire to learn. That's all for today. Class dismissed."

After the students left, Jeffers closed the door and sat down to talk to Ann. She was still visibly shaking. She wiped her face with her handkerchief, took a deep breath and seemed to calm down. Jeffers went over to the water fountain in the rear of his class and poured her a glass of water. He handed it to her and sat down. "Are you all right now?"

"Yes, professor, I'm better. You see, I wanted to be a minister, too, but the administration here won't let me take the necessary courses to be ordained."

"You know Ann, most ministers and church administrators believe that the church has always kept women from ministry because

Jesus wasn't married, and then there's the scripture from Paul in First Timothy." Jeffers thumbed through his Bible until he found the verse:

Let a woman learn in silence with all submission. And do not permit a woman to teach or to have authority over a man, but to be in silence. For Adam was formed first, then Eve. And Adam was not deceived, but the woman being deceived, fell into transgression.

"With all due respect, Professor, Paul was misunderstood. He was influenced by the Greeks, and the Greeks under Aristotle believed that a female was nothing more than a deformed male. Aristotle's ideas about women had colored all of Greek society and eventually found their way into the foundations of European culture. If we really understood the history and the culture of that time, Paul's time, we would know that he was really not prejudiced against women at all. But we take Paul's writings out of context, and besides, who knows if he really wrote all those things anyway."

"I can see you have some very strong views on this subject. You've done your research, haven't you?" said Jeffers

"Yes, I also know that the Jewish society, as well as much of the ancient world, with the exception of Egypt, was also against women having any power at that time. You know, it really makes me mad to think that in most churches, it's women who do the bulk of the work. If it wasn't for them, these churches would fail, and yet for all their devotion and work, they are still second class Christians."

"Ann, I must say you're absolutely right, but unfortunately it doesn't make any difference. There's no way that this denomination is going to change their views of women, not with the fundamentalists taking over."

Ann thought for the longest time. She was trapped in an organization that refused to change. In her heart, she knew it was all a waste of time. "I suppose you're right, but it still makes me mad."

"You know, there are other jobs in the church for women: education, music, church administration…"

"You don't understand, do you? I was called to be a minister, just like you or any man out there. God made me a female, and God called me to preach. Now you explain that!"

With that, Ann stormed out of Jeffer's classroom. As she left, he thought long and hard about her. She was right, and he knew it. He walked over to the window and watched her walk across the campus.

Jeffers had to admit it. “This is why Christianity is in trouble. When we continually keep talented, thinking women like that out of ministry. God help us.”

Peter had heard Ann’s remarks, but didn’t really get a good look at her. When he thought about her remarks, it did make sense to him. The information about the Garden of Eden made him feel a little empty as his childhood story of creation and the birth of sin seemed to get smashed against the footstone of logic and historical reality.

The turmoil that surrounded Jeffers was nothing compared to the downright hate that some students felt toward Dr. Price. What was most shocking to Peter was how there were just as many women as men that were angered by her reference to God as being as much female as male. It was hard to argue with her logic that since God was a spirit; how could we state that a spirit was a male?

The resistance seemed to form along male/female lines. The men were adamantly opposed to any new feminist theology and although some women opposed her, on the grounds that she was trying to turn them into radical feminists and lesbians, others realized that she made sense.

A group of female students formed to support Price, but it wasn’t too long before Price went too far. When she tried to change the male references in the Bible to female, the faculty stepped in and fired her for heresy.

It was a huge scandal; one that tore the students apart. As for Peter, he just tried to stay above all the turmoil and politics. He had enough trouble with his studies, let alone protesting or organizing against fundamentalists. Most of the professors had privately laughed at the hard liners and fundamentalists, and that was easy; because they were content to be ignorant of Biblical history.

Jeffers withstood the outrage at his lectures, but did agree not to introduce alternative views of the Garden of Eden story again. But when Dr. Price was fired, the moderates knew that the handwriting was on the wall, and that they had best keep their mouths shut and not question.

After that, the days were uneventful and dull at the seminary. Each day and night was filled with unending research and endless study. On April 5th, however, Peter’s life changed. As he walked to the cafeteria, he felt especially alive. Perhaps it was the weather; an unusually warm spring day in Chicago. It was a gift that made the air feel almost magical.

Peter looked up from his tray and tried to juggle his books, Bibles and papers as he shuffled through the cafeteria line. Today was fried chicken and rice. He loved the chicken, but could do without the rice. There's something so Christian about fried chicken, he thought. It seemed every minister's ordination came complete with a recipe for fried chicken with biscuits and gravy. There was even conjecture among the students that had Jesus and the Apostles served fried chicken for the last supper, they never would have lost Judas. And that was when Peter first saw her.

"Do you want rice?"

As usual, he didn't look up. "No thanks, not today, he said." It was an automatic response that he'd said a hundred times before, but this time he looked up and saw there was a smile attached to this offer that was too hard to resist.

"On second thought, I will have some rice."

She was gorgeous, that was a fact. Her name was Ann Parks and she was a blonde Navajo. Her blue eyes stood out against her caramel colored skin. She was statuesque and vibrant and no matter what she served, no student could say no. Ann looked at Peter for a long moment and then smiled and put an extra helping of rice on his plate. He smiled back at her and in that moment, nothing else mattered.

The general thought was that she could lead a man to heaven or hell, just by smiling at him. They were right, he thought. She was something to behold. If the mere thought of sex was a sin, then they were all sinners in need of a baptismal font or a cold shower.

"What's your name?" he said.

"Ann. Ann Parks".

He remembered her. She was the one who challenged Professor Jeffers. Word had it that she was also involved in the whole Dr. Price affair and some of the guys had spread the rumor that she was probably a dyke. As Peter thought about it, he dismissed it all because most of the male students thought all feminists were either gay or of the Devil. But Peter knew better. There was something about her, something in her eyes that he had not seen in any other girl at the seminary.

She was different and he couldn't get her out of his mind. She was the kind of woman who knew her own soul. It was like she had been here before and part of her was laughing at the limited ideas and stupidity of the men around her. Each day he came back and whatever she was serving, he'd always have seconds or thirds or more. After a while, when he started to gain weight, she caught on to his methods.

"You don't always have to eat what I'm serving, you know… and the answer is yes."

"Yes?" he said.

"Yes, I'll go out with you. That's what you're thinking, isn't it? That's why you come in here everyday and eat this stuff. You want to ask me out, don't you."

Peter couldn't respond. She saw right through him.

"No? Then you really do like three helpings of rice at every meal? Okay, how about four?"

Peter couldn't hold it in any longer and laughed. "Wait! No, I hate rice!" She laughed at him and said, "Me too. So when do you want to go out?"

Her assertiveness startled him. He wasn't used to women being that aggressive, especially not Christian women. The fact that she spoke right up thrilled him.

"I don't know, the sooner the better," he said.

"How about tonight?"

"Sounds great" He instantly condemned himself for being so ordinary. Surely he could have come up with something wittier, but in reality, in her presence he was lucky he could remember his own name. She looked at him and locked his eyes.

"Seven o'clock; I'm in Babbott Hall."

"I know. I'll see you tonight."

With that she turned and walked away. He couldn't take his eyes off her. He walked over and scraped the rice into the trash. He was in love, but he would never eat rice again.

That night he arrived forty-five minutes early. He wanted to be early, but this was ridiculous. He paced back and forth in front of her building. The other female students went in and out of the hall, each one eying him as they passed.

Ann was just about ready, when two of her roommates told her there was a strange guy lurking in front of the building. She went over to the window and looked out. There he was, walking back and forth like a soldier guarding the entrance. She smiled and called out to him.

"Peter! You're early."

He looked up at her and said, "I know."

"How long have you been down there?"

"About half an hour"

"Are you eager or just bored?

"Eager!"

She had to laugh. For the first time she was thrilled to go out on a date. He seemed different, and that appealed to her. "I'll be right down."

It was a beautiful night, so they decided to walk to the restaurant. As he looked around, the campus was bathed in a teal blue moonlight, but it paled next to the red silk dress that Ann wore. She seemed to radiate a kind of Earth-mother warmth that dissolved the cold night air.

They decided on Chinese food because it was the one food that they never served at the seminary. Song Chow's was the only Chinese restaurant near campus. It was small and dark with the traditional red walls and golden dragons. Few students or faculty ate there, so it would be a nice hide-away from prying eyes. When they sat down the waiter immediately brought water, tea and two bowls of rice. Peter looked at it and then looked up at Ann, who burst out laughing.

"Oh my god, rice again!" he said.

They took their time getting to know each other. He was enormously attracted to her, but then who wouldn't be. She enjoyed his sense of humor and witty elegance. As he talked, she could tell that he was a cut above the other students. There was something special about him, she thought.

As the night wore on, the table got smaller and their hands found each other. She told him that she had read an article in a magazine that said that holding hands was the most intimate thing two people could do and that it meant more than sex. He wondered if she was telling him that her hand was as far as she was going to go. He hoped not. She liked his hands and examined them as if she was going to do a palm reading.

"You have nice hands, Peter. They're gentle and graceful."

If there was one thing Ann was set against, it was hands that were stubby and rough. Peter's hands were easy to hold. The warmth they shared in the booth was palpable. It was a night they would long remember. As their relationship developed, they took many long walks at night around the campus. The hand holding soon led to hugs and kisses and caresses, but always out of view. On one Sunday afternoon after opening her picnic basket, she asked him what he wanted.

"I'll take anything you've got," he said, with a slight smile that toyed with her.

"Anything?" she said. She looked in the picnic basket. "Are you sure? That could be dangerous."

He found himself staring at her instead of listening. She had a mouth that perpetually smiled, even when she was sad. He wanted to play with her now.

"I can handle that kind of danger. Can you?"

She smiled, then laughed. She knew what he meant. It was a veiled invitation for sex, a kind of flirting innuendo that tickled her mind. She loved that about him. He wasn't obvious like the other guys. He knew how to use words and turn a phrase to get the most impact. It was to be his greatest asset in ministry.

She looked at him, smiled, and then reached into the picnic basket, trying not to let him think she was on to him. "Let's see, what do we have that would satisfy Peter… ah, here it is."

With that she suddenly brought up a huge dill pickle. He laughed and she joined him. They both new what they meant, but neither had the courage to say it out loud. They walked and talked and studied together. She was the only woman he'd ever seen who was as pretty in the morning sun as she was in the moonlight.

Like most men, he didn't always listen to her words. But unlike the others, it wasn't because he was self-absorbed, it was that he was too captivated by her. As he studied her, his mind raced through all the words that might describe her and found himself constantly writing poems about her. Despite his best efforts to concentrate, his thoughts turned to her during classes. Their relationship was getting to be a real distraction. He told himself that the only solution was to marry her when the time was right.

One night at his apartment, after a watered-down spaghetti dinner, the conversation turned to the Catholic Church. Ann had read a book about Pope Joan and that led to her favorite cause, women in the ministry. Peter was sympathetic, but skeptical about the story.

"Ann, this is nonsense; Pope Joan could never have existed."

That was a big mistake. He knew it the moment the words left his mouth. She was furious. "What do you mean nonsense? She was one of the most extraordinary women in church history. She sacrificed her femininity to gain knowledge. She had to disguise herself as a man. They wouldn't let her read or write, so it was the only way."

Peter tried to placate her, and asked her how could Pope Joan or any woman have gotten away with it?

"Look, Peter, when her brother died she took his identity. She studied at a monastery at Fulda and became Brother John Anglicus. He or she became a great church scholar, went to Rome and was ordained Pope."

Peter looked at her and said nothing. It was obvious that she was extremely upset.

"Are you upset?" he asked.

"Yes, damn it!"

She couldn't look at him now. Walking over to the window, she was caught up in her own desperation to make something important of her life.

"Look, I'm sorry Ann; I didn't know this meant so much to you."

"It means so much to me just like it means so much to you."

Now he was really confused. "I don't understand."

"Ministry. I'm talking about ministry. Just like you, Peter, God called me to ministry, but I can't just because God made me a woman. Does that make any sense?"

He looked deep into her eyes. How could he argue with her; she made perfect sense. "No, it makes no sense. So, what happened to Joan?"

Ann tried to dry her tears and compose herself. "She had a baby. She was either stoned to death or she went into a convent, but the point is that Pope Joan, just like all of us women, had to fight this crap about men running the church and not letting us have any power. Look, the Catholic Church either destroyed or hid all the records of Pope Joan, but they can't kill the truth. Just like they can't keep women down, and neither can you. You can't keep me down."

Peter held her in his arms and stroked her hair. Resisting his comfort, she fought back, and pushed him away.

"That doesn't cut it. It's condescending to try to sooth my anger with a few caresses and sweet words.

Peter knew he was in trouble just because he was a man. "I would never hold you down."

After a long pause he said; "You know, I must admit that women would make much better ministers. That kind of fire belongs in the pulpit, besides… I think women's personalities and temperament are more suited to ministry, but most people just aren't ready to accept women."

Looking up at him; "No, Peter, it's men who are not ready. I just don't understand why there is still so much resistance to women in ministry."

"Power; it's about power," he said, "everything in this world is about power, and the church is no different, and unfortunately for you, right now men have the power."

Ann thought about it for a moment, and then said; "Right now? It's always been that way, but someday - someday, it's got to change."

Peter looked at her and sighed. "You're right. Someday it will change."

Peter became very popular with the other students, especially the female students. He had a dimpled chin and a winning personality that was worlds apart from the other ministerial students. Instead of being solemn and dour, Peter was always ready with a joke or a clever phrase that would disarm even the most uptight woman. He could always be found with a swarm around him. Like moths to a flame, they couldn't help but be attracted to him. He burned with a larger than life countenance. It was like being in the presence of an Apostle and that's what more than one young girl whispered to her friends. He didn't exactly fool around, but he enjoyed their attention. He was careful not to go too far with any of them; a touch of the hand, a rub of a shoulder and a hug, but no more, at least not while Ann was around.

She watched them fawn over him and part of her understood the attraction. She, too, was captivated by his personality and good looks. As their relationship grew, she knew it was going to be a problem, but she didn't want to think about it now. They became the ideal couple—blonde, attractive and intelligent.

On the weekends, most of the students spent their time in the library studying, but Peter and Ann generally worked together in a small church next to campus. They enjoyed working with people and getting things done, like building a new basement for a pastor's parsonage or a new food pantry for the poor. This was God's work, simple and good, and it made them feel good about themselves when they accomplished something.

That's when his first media exposure came. A local newspaper took some photos of him working on a church basement and ran an article on his community service. The photographer posed Peter next to the local pastor of the church and spent the next hour interviewing Peter about his ministry and his plans after seminary. Unfortunately, they forgot to interview Ann and actually cut her out of the picture because they didn't know they were together. Peter was so caught up in the adulation of the interviewer that he totally forgot Ann was even there.

It wouldn't be the first time that the media would celebrate him and ignore her; she didn't have the charisma that Peter had. She knew she would have to get used to him being in the spotlight. He could forget her when he was full of himself, especially when the accolades were coming in, and there would be many accolades to come. She was going to mention it to him, but he was so excited that she just dropped it.

On one day, the tension in the classroom grew intense. Peter had crossed the line and everyone knew it. Dr. Carlisle, Head of Religious Studies, and an imposing force, approached him.

"Mr. Andrews, it's not appropriate to question God. You must accept the teachings of the Gospel as it is written."

"But Dr. Carlisle, I'm not questioning God. I'm questioning the scriptures. There are so many inconsistencies in the writings."

Carlisle interrupted, "We don't talk about these things. We must accept the Gospel on faith." Carlisle had to make a larger point here in order to quiet the thoughts of the other students. "There are those of our flock who will never understand the complexities and inconsistencies in the scriptures, so it is best that they just accept what we tell them and let it go at that."

This time Peter interrupted. "But Dr. Carlisle, wouldn't it be better if we educated them to know the history and why the scriptures were written?"

A murmur rose up in the class. The other students were starting to have doubts, and Carlisle had to put a stop to it.

"You assume that most people want to know the entire truth about God. They don't. They only want a simple truth so they don't have to think. The vast multitudes are searching for simple answers in a black and white world. It doesn't matter whether the answers are actually the truth or not, only that it satisfies them for the moment. Think about it. Most of the people know nothing about religion. They are illiterate about their own faith, let alone other faiths, and they have no wish to complicate their lives with historical knowledge!"

Carlisle had lost his temper. Peter knew it and the class knew it. No one had ever questioned Carlisle about church doctrine before. The bell rung and class was dismissed. As everyone was leaving, Carlisle asked Peter to stay for a moment. This was not good. Peter knew he had pushed the envelope and challenged Carlisle, but he couldn't help but question what was being taught. After the other students left, Carlisle closed the door and sat down next to Peter.

"Look, my boy, I may have come across a little harsh today, but I want you to know that there is a great difference in being a student of faith and being a minister of the Gospel. Here it's all right to question. Out there, when you face five hundred souls each Sunday, you have to remember that you're dealing with children; ignorant, stubborn children. Remember Pandora's Box. She opened it up and all of the sickness and pestilence came into the world. For us as Christians, our Pandora's Box is the Bible."

Peter looked up at him in confusion. "I don't understand. We teach the Bible every week in our churches."

Carlisle looked at him with a wisdom and seriousness that Peter had never seen before.

"We don't teach the Bible. We talk about it and tell people what it means, but most ministers don't know enough about the Bible to even discuss it. It's not what we teach in the Bible that's the issue. It's what we don't teach that's the issue."

Now Peter was totally confused.

"Don't worry about it. Someday you'll understand what I'm telling you."

Peter thought about what Dr. Carlisle said. It bothered him that most of his studying would, in reality, never be used. If this were true, then he would never get to use all of the historical information on the Bible and the growth of the church. The people weren't interested in anything but simple truths, a black and white world. He was bothered by this.

That night, after dinner at his apartment with Ann, he brought it up. Looking at his Bible history concordance and the table filled with papers, he was frustrated.

"What's the use of studying all this stuff, if I'm never going to use it?"

"What are you talking about?" she asked.

"Carlisle, in his class today, said that it's a waste of time to teach Bible history, and that most Christians are ignorant about their own faith. What's even worse, they don't even want to learn."

"Well, that's true, isn't it Peter?"

"I guess, but I just wonder if it's all worth it, you know—ministry"

"Are you starting to have second thoughts?"

Looking around his apartment and then at Ann. "Something's got to change."

Ann looked at him and for once, she was seeing a different side of him; a side that really questioned things. He had always just gone along and never wanted to buck the establishment. Things had always come easy to him. Maybe it was because he was blonde and handsome, or maybe it was because he had never cared enough about anything to fight over it.

The question was; would he fight now? In that moment, Ann was proud of him. She wanted a fighter; someone who would not always go along just to be accepted. She recognized that if he fought back, maybe it would give her the courage to be what she really wanted. She loved him more now than before.

He sensed it. Maybe that was the impetus he needed. "Look, Ann, I can't go on this way."

This was it, she thought. He was going to give up the ministry. She hoped he would. She worried that he would be too successful and that it would tear him away from her.

"I know you've been unhappy. Are you thinking of leaving the seminary?"

"Hell, no!"

"Well, what are you talking about?"

"I'm talking about us. I want to marry you."

All other thoughts went out of her mind. She loved him and he loved her. That was all that she could think of, in the moment. "Peter, you know I love you, but are you sure?"

He put his arms around her and looked deep into her eyes. Her eyes always took him places; to other dimensions and times. Maybe they knew each other in another life. What was he thinking? He didn't believe in reincarnation. He kissed her. With all his might he wanted her here and now.

"I've never been so sure of anything in my life. I want you. I want to share my life with you."

She spent the night with him talking. Finally they fell asleep. The morning sun streamed through the windows and warmed them while they kissed and made love. He worshiped her body with as much reverence as any deity. She was his God and he adored her, her face, her shoulders, her back and every inch of her young body. They happily broke all the rules, but didn't care.

At that moment they were not Christians or anything else but just two human beings making the deepest connection possible. She didn't tell him that she would marry him. She didn't have to. Her body spoke for her. Every inch of her flesh said yes to him. She wrapped herself around him and they were one. After several hours, they lay together naked, just talking about their future and what God had in store for them.

Peter was starting to make a name for himself at the seminary. His grades were only average, but his personality and power of delivery were so outstanding that it was obvious to most of the faculty that he would be an outstanding minister. At the end of the term, Dr. Carlisle called him into his office for a conference. Peter had a four o'clock appointment and got there twenty minutes early, just to make a good impression. As Peter entered the office it was as impressive as any he'd ever seen.

Carlisle was a small bespeckled man; however he made up for his lack of stature with an impressive office. He also had his desk built on a raised platform, so that when he sat behind his massive desk it gave him much needed height and importance. It also put anyone on the other side of the desk at a distinct disadvantage. This all came from an article Carlisle had read about Louie B. Mayer at MGM Studios. Mayer also had his desk built on a raised platform, which gave him a real advantage over his actors. As they were always looking up at him, they never had the courage to question his decisions. Carlisle thought it was a great idea and had his office built the same way. As president of the seminary for seven years, his credentials were unquestioned in the denomination.

The room was paneled in dark mahogany and octagon in shape, with bookshelves that reached two stories. As Peter sat down he couldn't help but notice how small he felt. This was power, he thought. This was what it looked like and felt like. He closed his eyes and imagined himself with this kind of power and it felt good.

Peter looked around the office and saw the numerous textbooks that Carlisle had written. There were volumes on the Old Testament, New Testament and a series on the history and lineage of Jesus. There were also pictures of Carlisle with Ronald Reagan, George Bush, Sr., and Pope John Paul II. The longer Peter sat there, the more nervous he got.

Was he in trouble? Was it his grades? Or was it his relationship with Ann? He wondered if she had talked about their affair. It was strictly forbidden for ministerial students to have any kind of sexual relations with another student, not that it was particularly uncommon. Students had to sign a pledge to remain chaste, but most had physical relationships and just kept it undercover. It was all part of playing the game and pretending that they were all celibate. It was common knowledge among the faculty that things went on. Most of the faculty knew but looked the other way, for if the administration found out, it would mean instant dismissal. Peter and Ann had both vowed to tell no one, but he wondered if she had slipped up and told one of her friends. Most of their friends assumed that they were sleeping together; after all, they were young, attractive and in love. He could feel the perspiration run down his back as he nervously squirmed in his chair. He had to get up and walk around.

As he browsed through Carlisle's books, he saw a strange black lever along the side the bookcase. It didn't seem to belong. Curious; he pulled it. Suddenly another room opened up. It had been hidden from the main part of the office. He looked around to discover that this was a collection of books that he'd never seen before. These were all the books that Carlisle said had been banned from the Bible and seminary years ago, hundreds of volumes of rare theology from reincarnation to pagan cults and ancient European history. There were books about Buddhism, Islam, Hinduism, Judaism, Theosophy and every other obscure faith and belief. What was going on here? Peter realized that Carlisle was a great deal more knowledgeable than he let on about the world's religions. He was obviously a very learned man caught in a rigidly simplistic institution. Suddenly, Peter heard Carlisle's voice in the hallway, so he closed the hidden room and took his seat in front of the desk. He decided he would not mention it.

Finally, Carlisle walked in, his black professorial robes flowing behind him. "Thank you for coming Peter. I'm glad you could find time for our chat. Sorry for the delay, but I had to dismiss a student for an ethical violation".

"Not a problem Dr. Carlisle." Peter felt a knot in his stomach. A student had been dismissed. That could mean anything from drunkenness or cheating or sex. Suddenly he felt guilty. What if Carlisle asked him about their relationship? Would he lie, or would he have the courage to tell the truth? He could feel his entire future fading away. Carlisle leaned back in his chair.

"I wanted to talk to you Peter, about your future."

This was it, Peter thought. It was all over. He felt sick and caught like a child waiting for his punishment. His emotions immediately took him back to when he was ten years old. He had been playing with his dog and in a moment of wild enthusiasm, the puppy pulled a carpet square from under a table. Peter's mother always put protective carpet squares under the furniture legs, and when Peter lifted the table leg to put the carpet square back, a lamp on the table came crashing down. This was no ordinary lamp, but a double ball hand-painted chimney lamp that had been his grandmother's only prized possession. It was an heirloom from a dying mother to Peter's father. Peter screamed at the dog and then spent the entire afternoon crying. He was sure to get a whipping from his father when he came home. When his father finally did come home and saw what had happened, he felt so sorry that Peter had spent the whole day crying that he figured Peter had been punished enough. His father had a violent temper and a voice that could shake the trees, but unlike most men, he could never bring himself to ever hit his boy. Peter looked at Carlisle and swallowed. He might as well face up to it, he thought. "Dr. Carlisle, I must confess that…"

"Peter, I didn't call you in here for a confession. I wanted to tell you that many in the faculty, including me, feel that you have a great future ahead of you. We have been watching you and we're not alone. There are several churches that have petitioned for your services as an interim minister. Tell me, what are your plans after your graduation?"

Peter breathed a sigh of relief. "Well, I'm not really sure yet, except that Ann and I want to get married." "

"Tell me, what kind of church do you see yourself in?"

"I don't know. We've been volunteering in a couple of churches near campus, and they seem comfortable."

"Comfortable, that's an interesting word. Do you think that the Lord wants you to be comfortable in your ministry?"

"I don't know, Dr. Carlisle, I've seen large and small churches, and I think I'd be more comfortable in a smaller church; maybe a couple of hundred members in a rural area."

Carlisle got up and walked around to the front of his desk. It was clear he was troubled. "Peter, I'd hate to see you waste your gift on a small, comfortable church. You have a great deal of God-given talent. Remember that the larger the church, the more souls for Christ and the more successful you are."

"I understand, but with a larger church comes more problems and more responsibility."

"Yes, Peter, but to be blunt, you'll also have a larger paycheck." With that, Peter was forced to laugh.

"That would be good. I know Ann would like that."

"And you, Peter, wouldn't you like a more comfortable income?'

"Yes, of course." As Peter left he said he'd think about it and let Carlisle know.

The conversation continued that night with Ann, although whenever he tried to bring up the subject, all she wanted to talk about was their wedding plans after graduation. After dinner, they both sat around the kitchen table in Peter's apartment. He finally got her to think about their future beyond the wedding.

"We need to talk about this, Ann. Carlisle said he's got a couple of churches that are interested in me."

"That's good news, Peter."

"Well, I'm a little apprehensive about a big church."

"Why don't you want to serve in a large church?"

"I don't know. It's just something inside of me. There's a kind of dread about a huge church with all its problems and responsibilities."

"But Peter, it would be grand to see you at the head of a great congregation and maybe on the radio and on television. You know you have to think about the fact that a larger church could afford a better salary."

"I know. Carlisle said that too. The money thing; I didn't get into this to make money. You know that. I want to make a difference. To make the world a better place through Christ. That's why I chose ministry."

Ann looked at him, and with sadness in her voice, "I know, that's why I chose the ministry, too."

"I'm sorry, Ann; I know how much you've always wanted it."

She came over to him, sat on his lap, and wrapped her arms around his neck.

"We both heard the call, but only one of us can do it, so you'll have to do it for both of us."

He looked into her eyes and had never loved her more. She was more than his woman and lover. She was his partner in ministry and in life. He kissed her and told her how much he loved her and that he could never succeed in ministry without her. She stroked his face and said;

"As the Father and I are one, so Peter, you and I are one."

Spring came and Peter and Ann both graduated. Peter was now a minister, but Ann had to settle for a degree in Church Administration, which she hated. The wedding followed two weeks later. It was a simple affair. Peter's mother came in from Rockford, but his father had died several years earlier from multiple myeloma, a form of bone cancer. Ann had no family left anymore. She had talked fondly about her mother and her losing battle with a bad heart five years earlier, but any talk of her father was off limits. Whenever the subject was brought up, she would say that he was gone and not part of her life anymore. Peter suspected that maybe Ann's father had walked out on them, but try as he might, he could never get her to talk about it.

For the ceremony they both wrote special vows in which they not only promised fidelity and love to each other, but also to Christ. It was a marriage steeped in missionary zeal. There was little time for a honeymoon other than a weekend at the Holiday Inn on Chicago's North Side. As he carried her over the threshold of their room, they both looked around and were immediately disappointed. They sighed together. Peter kissed her and told her that one day he would carry her across the threshold of a mansion on a hill and she would be his queen.

She wrapped her arms around him. "This is enough, Peter. You are my life."

After unpacking, Ann went into the bathroom to change. He looked around at the shabby surroundings and shook his head. After a few minutes, the bathroom door opened and Ann stood there in an elegant lace negligee. The light behind her made her body shimmer in the shadows. Peter looked at her and silently thanked God for her. As he embraced her, Ann reached down and opened the dresser drawer. Peter looked at her and then down at the dresser. There it was, the Gideon Bible. They both looked at each other and smiled. Peter put the Bible in the drawer. In that moment, they each knew that they had found their God in each other, and the only prayer would be that the weekend would last forever.

After their all too short honeymoon, it was back to the Lord's work. Peter had been hired as a new pastor of the First Church of the Open Bible, about three blocks from the seminary. It was a growing church with about three hundred members. Ann wanted to work at the church as well, but they had no need for an administrator. She volunteered part-time at the church and worked for minimum wage at a local drug store.

They moved into a small house near the church. Thank God the church paid for their lodgings as part of the manse, because money was tight. It was a fact that no matter how well the church did financially, there never seemed to be very much left over to pay the minister. Some on the Board of Trustees and in the congregation still held onto the old idea that ministers were supposed to get their reward in heaven. Peter reminded them that just like the church's other creditors, his bill collectors expected their money on this side of the veil.

Peter and Ann were happy in those early days. Life seemed to unfold easily for them. He was successful in his sermons and the church attendance was increasing by a comfortable rate. Ann watched him from the balcony and in her heart she, too, wanted to feel the thrill of giving sermons and counseling people in need, but her needs would go unfulfilled.

About a year after Peter's first anniversary at the church, Ann had a baby girl. Although Jennifer Ann, as she was called, wasn't planned, she was a welcome companion for Ann. Peter spent more and more late nights at the church, going from one meeting to another or counseling.

It was during this time that rumors started to spread about young women who were spending too much time around the minister. Ann started to suspect that maybe Peter was having an affair. She didn't know who, or when, but there were just too many counseling sessions at night with women in need. She tried to force the thoughts from her head. It was crazy. She loved Peter and she knew he loved her, but after the baby came, she was too tired to give him all the attention that he wanted. He always seemed to brush off her rejections, saying that he understood and that they'd make time for love later. But with all the church responsibilities, later never came.

In June, Ann started to receive anonymous phone calls. The first one came on a Saturday morning. Peter had already left to play tennis with a couple of friends when the phone rang at ten o'clock. Ann heard the phone ring from the shower and had no intention of answering it, but it kept on ringing. She hurriedly dried herself and put on a robe.

"Hello?" There was no response, so she asked again, "Hello, who is this?"

Still no answer, then a woman laughed.

"Who is this?"

The woman laughed again. Ann felt a chill run through her blood and she slammed the phone down. She walked around the apartment and felt cold and alone. She checked the doors and windows to make sure that she was locked in and everyone else was locked out. She tried to put it out of her mind, but the laughter bothered her. Who was it? Maybe it was just some kids. That was it. It was just a prank. There were three more phone calls that morning, but she wouldn't pick up the phone. Each call rang three times and no more, then silence. About an hour later, the phone rang again, but this time it rang three, four, and five times. Finally the phone woke up the baby. Ann was furious. She finally picked up the phone and held her breath. She heard the voice.

"Ann? It's Peter, where have you been? I've been calling all morning."

"Peter, thank God it's you. There was a call. Some woman just laughed and hung up."

When Peter came home, she had to talk to him. Peter hardly had time to catch his breath, when Ann came in from the bedroom with the baby.

"What's going on Peter? Who was that on the phone? You don't know what I've been through. These calls—I heard this woman laughing or breathing. I've got to know, are you having an affair?"

Peter tried to calm her down, but she was shaking with fear and rage. "Look, I don't know who's calling you, but as God is my witness, I'm not having an affair. You know me better than that." Ann started to calm down a little. "Just breathe. I'm here now and it's going to be all right."

Ann walked around the room trying to calm herself. Finally sitting down; "Look Peter, I want to believe you that you're faithful, and in my heart I know that you are, but it's hard with you being at church all the time."

" I admit that I've been doing a lot of counseling at night, and that it might look suspicious, but I swear—nothing is going on."

She couldn't let it go now. "Peter, these women at the church can get you in a lot of trouble. You've got to be careful."

He walked around the room trying to think. "You're right; I've gotten too close to some of them. Maybe they've become too dependent on me."

She was calming down now. "Peter, it's probably some crazy woman trying to break us up. Maybe some of the requests for counseling are not really what they seem. Maybe it's just an excuse to get you alone. You've got to be careful."

He hugged her and smiled. "I know. I'll start referring some of my counseling to the Chaplain."

Ann was relieved. She knew in her heart that he was faithful, but her mind needed convincing. "Look, Peter, I need you more now than before the baby came. I never see you anymore."

"The church is too demanding, I know. I promise to spend more time at home with you and the baby."

He did keep his promise and the church's demands on his time seemed to slow down for a while.

Chapter Three
The Golden Family

The years passed and things got better. Jennifer was growing up and the church attendance grew to over eight hundred. On his tenth anniversary, the church gave him a nice raise. Ann was now the Church Administrator and things couldn't have been better. In the spring they moved into a small house with a yard.

One Sunday, Peter delivered a sermon that startled and excited the congregation. He called it, *Finding the God That Will Change the World.* It was a fiery sermon which challenged people to find the God of courage and resolve inside them. He told them that it was time to throw away the passive loving God and find the warrior God of the Old Testament. He said the world was on a collision course with sin and it was time to martial all our resources and fight back. It was the first time that the congregation was so moved and they forgot their rules and church protocol and gave him a standing ovation at the end of his sermon.

The Trustees were shocked, but they were also shocked at the offering. Donations tripled and forty people came forward to accept Christ and join the church. The sister of a reporter for the Chicago Sun Times was in attendance and she immediately called her brother and told him that she had just seen a new fire-breathing evangelist that would knock him down. The paper interviewed him, and it was the beginning of Peter's rise to prominence. The newspaper featured a large article on Peter and named him, "The New Voice for a New Generation of Christians".

The Chicago paper had long tentacles and it reached into the caverns of the most important people in the country. One such cavern was the Queen Anne-style sandstone and red brick mansion at the foot of Lincoln Park. Just two blocks from Lake Michigan, it had been the home to seven Catholic Archbishops since 1885. Even though Pope John Paul II and FDR once spent the night in its splendor, its historical value couldn't save it. Cardinal Fitzpatrick sold the place to the Temple Christian Church for 15 million dollars. Although many of the 2.3 million Chicago Catholics picketed for weeks to stop the sale, Cardinal Fitzpatrick said the church needed the money to keep the deficit-laden archdiocese from closing more schools. It also helped pay sexual abuse settlements, but that wasn't talked about. Now, one man stood sipping his morning coffee on the very same balcony where the Pope had waved to thousands of adoring children in 1979.

He looked around at the morning sunlight streaming through the trees. It was a good day to make a decision. Jeremiah had read the article about Peter Andrews in the Chicago paper when he first got up. He had circled Peter's name. There was something special here, he thought. Over and over Jeremiah paced the ornate sitting room where he had his breakfast. He always walked while he thought. That was his way. Take a thought and tumble it over in your mind until it feels right. It might take him a long time to make up his mind about something, but once he had come to a decision, it was carved in stone. Nothing or no one could change it. He finished his coffee, put the newspaper in his briefcase and told his butler to order his car. Jeremiah walked into his closet and thumbed through his three dozen Fioravanti custom-made suits. The $10,000 super merino 220 wool would make the appropriate power statement. As he selected the very best red silk tie in his collection, he stepped back to enjoy the view. There he was, seven feet tall, jet black hair and alabaster skin; a majestic Lincoln without the humanity, The most unusual thing about Jeremiah, though, wasn't his height— it was his eyes. His pupils were pink, until he got angry, and then they turned red. He was a sight to behold, and he knew it. The bell rang to tell him that his car was ready. As he waited for his limousine to pull around the front of the drive, he smiled. Yes, the idea was brilliant, but would the board go along with it? Jeremiah laughed at the question. *What choice do they have?*

As the limo sped through traffic, Jeremiah picked up his car phone and talked to his secretary.

"Rachael, I just read an article in the Chicago Sun Times. Get me everything you can find on Reverend Peter Andrews. I want everything, the good and the bad; any scandal that could prevent us from using him. Get all the information on his family, friends, associates, lovers; anything you can find. I want his tax records, bank account balances, credit reports, criminal history… leave nothing out."

"When do you need it? Tomorrow?" she asked.

"If I needed it tomorrow, I would have called tomorrow. Also, find out if he has any secrets, anything that we might have to use in the future. You know what I'm looking for."

"Yes, sir," said Rachael.

He hung up the phone and asked his chauffer what he thought of the name, Peter Andrews. The Chauffer told him that the name was significant and that it was a combination of the names of two of the Apostles.

Jeremiah smiled and said, "Excellent, I hadn't thought of that. That's even better."

As the car pulled through the Chicago traffic, the wheels of Jeremiah's organization moved into high gear. Hundreds of people scurried around the Temple Christian Church computer research room going through phone records, tax information and medical records for even the smallest piece of information on Peter and Ann Andrews. Once the information was compiled, it was then fed into a computer analysis system that generated a code number. Then the code was entered into a special security computer. At once the computer screen flickered and the FBI and CIA seal came up. A special 15 digit password was then entered to finish the analysis. Within a few minutes, every scrap of information on Peter and Ann was all part of a new, very private dossier. A young woman put the file into a black leather briefcase and walked to a private elevator.

Jeremiah's car eventually pulled up to the side entrance of the Temple Christian Church. This was no ordinary church, but a mega-church, the size of a football stadium. Jeremiah got out of the car and walked into the foyer of the church, past the thirteen fountains. He walked down the long hallway toward the elevator. Just then the doors opened and a young secretary handed him the black leather case. He nodded and then walked past a suite of offices to the Board of Trustees meeting room. The room was quietly elegant with dark paneling and what appeared to be brass lamps and brass trim around the door; but it wasn't brass, it was 14 karat gold.

When Jeremiah entered the room, the nine white-haired men in dark suits stopped talking and stood. There was a solemn air in the room and no sunlight. This was the death watch. Jeremiah quietly put his briefcase on the table.

"How is he?" asked Jeremiah.

The chairman of the board looked at all the members and gravely stated that the doctors have told them that there wasn't much time left. Jeremiah stated that they should start thinking about the future.

"Dr. Remington has been a great prophet and pillar of Christ's church. Now we must get ready for a new leader."

One of the other men asked about the Assistant Minister, but Jeremiah abruptly interrupted him, stating that the church would never accept a female as head of the church.

"No, we must find someone new; someone young and fresh—with fire in his belly."

With that, he opened his briefcase and put the newspaper article on the table.

"Gentlemen, meet Peter Andrews."

* * *

The following Monday would start out like any other day off for Peter and Ann. After a busy work-week, Monday was always a day off for the minister. They were planning to take the day and get away from the city. Jennifer was watching television that morning when the door-bell rang. Not interested in leaving the TV, she let it ring. Peter called out from the bedroom.

"Jennie, get the door!"

With a good deal of reluctance, she opened the door to see a young man in a red and yellow uniform standing there.

"It's some guy with a package. He says you gotta' sign for it."

Peter came into the room and signed for the package and gave the man a dollar tip.

"What's that, Dad?"

Peter opened the package and it was a letter. By this time Ann had come into the room.

"Who's it from, Peter?" said Ann.

He looked at the return address on the envelope and his mouth dropped.

"It's from Temple Christian Church." said Peter.

Ann looked at the envelope that contained a picture of the church on the outside.

"It looks big, Peter."

Peter was overcome with fear. He sat down holding the unopened envelope. Temple Christian was one of the biggest churches in the country.

"What do they want from you?"

"I don't know."

"Well, why don't you open it?"

Peter gave it to Ann to open. She tore the envelope open and read it silently.

"They want to talk to you about being a minister there." Peter read the letter, took a deep breath, looked at Ann and then walked out of the house. Ann ran after him, not understanding what was driving him.

"What's the matter, Peter? This is good news isn't it?"

Peter walked over to a tree and sat down, holding his head in his hands.

He looked up and asked Ann, "What do you know of Temple Christian?"

Ann thought it was a strange question.

"Not much, really."

Peter grabbed her hand, pulling her down beside him.

"I know all about it. It was started thirty years ago by Dr. Matthew Remington. The news is, he's dying. They have over 200,000 people."

Ann looked again at the picture on the letter. "That's not a church, it's a city."

Peter crumbled. "I think I'm going to be sick."

With that, he ran back into the house and slammed the bathroom door. Ann sat under the tree, holding the letter, then folded it and put it in her pocket. As she looked back at the house, she saw Jennifer standing in the doorway.

Jennifer walked over and sat by her mother. "What's wrong with Daddy?"

"Oh, I think he's afraid."

"What's he afraid of?"

"Honey, I think he's afraid of the future. The future can be a frightening place."

Ann held Jennifer close, but hid her tears. Ann felt a cold wind come over her, like a foreboding cloud of doom. Ann's mind raced back to when she was Jennifer's age. Her father looked at her with tears running down his face, then turned and walked out of her bedroom. She tried to stop him, but all the screaming and crying couldn't stop them from taking him away. She watched him go down the stairs and saw the police officers put handcuffs on him. They walked him out to a patrol car and placed him in the backseat. She screamed out for him, but the social worker held on to her and tried to comfort her by telling her that it would all be all right. It was a lie and Ann knew it. She knew she'd never see her daddy again. As they drove off, he looked back at her. She was so confused. Her feelings went from sadness to anger to a sense of relief.

It had been going on for years and she had to tell someone, but she never thought it would come to this. It was her fault. He loved her, maybe too much, and maybe in the wrong way, but he loved her and that was all that mattered. Now he was gone and it was all her fault. She never should have said anything. The secret should have stayed inside. These were the little girl thoughts that she'd fought against all her life. The adult Ann told her that he was wrong; that he had robbed her of her childhood and ruined her for life. That was true, she knew it, but she couldn't help believe that he still loved her. She fought the tears and the sense of aloneness, but it would be with her always.

Ann and Jennifer walked back into the house. As she walked by the bookcase, she picked up a book of poetry called The Prophet. As she did, an old faded black and white photograph of her and her father fell onto the floor. She picked it up and looked at it. There she was when she was only six, sitting with her Daddy on the Ferris wheel at the county fair. She looked with sadness at the picture. Turning it over, she read her father's words.

"Remember, honey that you can be anything your heart desires."

He was wrong. He had robbed her of that. She wanted to be a minister, and the church had robbed her of that, too. Now, as Peter was about to get the chance of a lifetime, what was there left for her? She had to be there for him. He would need her now. Maybe she could find a way to serve. Maybe God would find a place for her. She walked into the bedroom and Peter was sitting on the bed.

"Are you all right?"

He looked out the window and his mind was a thousand miles away. Ann sat next to him and put her arm around him.

"This is a great opportunity, isn't it?"

"Yes, I guess so, if it happens—if I'm ready."

"Peter, this is going to change everything, isn't it?"

He turned and looked at her face that was filled with worry.

"I suppose so, Ann. I feel like I just got asked to play Carnegie Hall, and I just remembered I can't read music."

Ann smiled and laughed a little. Jennifer called out from the den.

"Hey Mom and Dad, you should see this church on the Internet. It's huge!"

They all spent the rest of the afternoon investigating Temple Christian. It was a massive campus of buildings, gardens and statuary. The more they read, the more excited they all became. They got swept up in the thrill of having their dreams come true.

Peter called the church and scheduled his meeting for next Saturday and was told that a car would pick him up at 2:00 pm. When he hung up the phone, he had a massive headache. That's when he heard the voice. It was a gentle whisper that sounded like a brook tumbling over rocks. *Be at peace. Your path is given. All things work according to my plan for you.*

Then as quickly as it came, it was gone. He dared not tell Ann or Jennifer. He didn't know if he was hearing something divine or just going crazy. He had been under a lot of stress lately and this whole thing was about to push him over the edge. He held his head in his hands as the headache returned. Ann looked at him and asked if he wanted some aspirin.

"I'm all right; I just need to lie down for a while. He closed his eyes and rested for a while. After a time, his thoughts and worries faded and he opened his eyes. He stared at the cracked and broken ceiling. Slowly, he breathed. After a long sigh, some measure of peace came over him. He could barely see Ann in the doorway.

"Do you know what they call it?"

"Call what?" Peter asked.

"The church; they call it the Jesus Temple."

The words rolled over in his mind as he drifted off to sleep.

* * *

Jeremiah studied the reports on Peter Andrews. There were massive computer readouts of credit history. The amount of personal information on him was staggering. There were pictures of him and Ann as children and pictures of Jennifer when she was born. Analysts were consulted as to their physical attractiveness and behavior and whether they would be suitable stewards of the church. As he met with his advisors, Jeremiah asked for a presentation. The next day at eleven o'clock, he sat down in a screening room to watch what amounted to a film on their life story. Everything was revealed, even Ann's father's sexual abuse of his daughter and his subsequent arrest.

At the conclusion of the film, Jeremiah asked his team for a rating. The team rated Peter as an 84, while Ann was rated at a 73. Jennifer was rated at a 65, because she was only sixteen and there was no guarantee as to her level of resistance to church teachings and being controlled. Jeremiah asked if they thought Ann could be controlled. They told him that she was an ideal physical candidate for a minister's wife, although she was a little too beautiful to be content with being in the background for long. Was there a concern for any sexual issues between Peter and Ann? All of the members of the team were somewhat concerned as Peter was very attractive to young women. The issue with Ann was that she was fragile due to the abuse and could have some problems with her figure.

"What do you mean?" asked Jeremiah.

"We might have an issue with her breasts. They may attract too much attention. The suggestion was to have a committee of church women talk to her about toning down her figure with more conservative attire. Jeremiah recommended that she be given a selection of colors and fabrics and some photos of acceptable attire for a minister's wife. The idea was to take a page from the first lady's handbook, in being sweet, sensible and subservient, but not in an obvious manner. It should not be apparent that she or any of them is being manipulated. Be subtle, until we know where we stand with them. Above all, we must groom them for successful church leadership. They must be the ideal family; wholesome, gentle, attractive and white. Do you all understand?"

With that the team went to work. Like Moses in the wilderness, they would fashion a new idol for the church. Like the calf beneath Mount Sinai, Peter, Ann and Jennifer would become the golden family.

Chapter Four
To Everything There Is A Purpose Under Heaven

Peter didn't feel Wendy's hand wipe away the tear that ran down his cheek. But when she stroked his hair, Peter jerked his head. Ann had done this. For a moment, he forgot where he was. He looked around the cold grey walls of the sanitarium courtyard. He was back. Oh, God, if he could only forget. If only he could start over. Wendy was determined to get him to open up.

"You really should eat, you know. Is it the food? Do you want something else, something besides chicken and rice?"

Wendy adjusted the blanket around his shoulders.

"Are you cold?"

Peter looked up at her and with a vain attempt at a smile of gratitude said, "Thank you, no, I'm not cold, not now."

She had made contact. Her thoughts raced; *I mustn't go too fast, she thought. Don't push it. Let him open up at his own pace.* "I'm glad to hear you talking. You have a nice voice."

Peter looked at her and wondered just how interested she was in him. He didn't trust her. He couldn't. He had had too many women in his life. They had been his salvation and his curse. He had loved them and destroyed them. Sensing he was lost in his thoughts, Wendy touched his hand.

"Mr. Andrews, how can I help you? I really want to help, if you'll let me. I've read about some of the terrible things that have happened to you. I can understand how painful it must be to think of them."

He looked away. Did she say too much? Did she go too far? Wait now, she told herself. Wait to see if he responds.

"You must stay away from me. I'm not safe. You're in danger. Don't you understand? I've killed. I'm a killer."

Wendy's mind tried to remember what she had read in his chart. She couldn't remember any mention of a criminal case or him being on trial.

"What do you mean; that you've killed?"

He looked up at her with tears streaming down his face.

"I killed them. I killed my wife and daughter. There is no hope for me now. I'm going to hell, where I belong".

In an attempt to comfort him, she touched his shoulder. It was enough to break him. He slumped over in his chair and wept. She backed away from him. She had opened a wound and now, she couldn't help him. She turned and walked away from him, but she knew this was a beginning; a painful beginning. Every day for weeks, she would walk with him and talk to him. He rarely said much; nothing of any consequence.

Then one day his past crashed through the gates of the sanitarium. It came innocuously enough in a newspaper. At first no one noticed the article, but later in the day an orderly laid it on a bench in the garden. Peter picked it up. He hadn't read a newspaper in six months. He thumbed through the headlines and advertisements. Nothing touched him anymore. Then, just as he was about to discard it in the trash, he noticed the name of Parks. Something told him not to look, but he couldn't help himself. He scanned the columns, shuffling page after page until he found it. He looked down at the paper and his face turned to stone. He started to shake and then, he let out a scream like a wounded animal in the death-throws. Orderlies and attendants rushed over to him. Wendy ran from the kitchen when someone said that Peter Andrews was having another attack.

By the time she got there, he was slumped over in his chair, unconscious. They picked him up and put him in a wheelchair and tied a towel around his waist to keep him secure. After they got him back to his room, Wendy asked the attendants what had caused the relapse. One of them said that Andrews was reading the newspaper when it happened. Wendy turned to look for the newspaper. Maybe she could find what had set him off. The paper was crumbled in a ball where Peter had been sitting. She tore through it, but didn't really know what she was looking for.

Then, suddenly there it was; an obituary for Ann Parks Andrews. This was no ordinary obituary; two columns a photo and the headline: Missing preacher's wife dies of cancer; burial services to be held today. As Wendy read the article, she saw Peter's name scattered throughout. According to the writer, the fact that Andrews was missing and didn't attend the memorial services last week was a testament to the fact that either he didn't care enough to attend or was lying dead somewhere. Wendy thought about Peter. It was ironic that the sanitarium was only a few blocks from the funeral home and cemetery. She looked at the picture of Peter's wife. Yes, she was beautiful—blonde—the kind of woman men always went after. She rushed back to Dr. Gaskin's office and knocked on the door, but he wasn't there. She quickly went to the filing cabinet and pulled Peter's files. Just then, Gaskin walked in.

"What's going on here?"

"Dr. Gaskin, I'm sorry to be in here, but I think I know why Peter Andrews had a breakdown."

"Why, what do you know?"

"It's here. Look." With that, she dropped the newspaper onto Gaskin's desk. He bent over and read.

"Ann Parks Andrews, Peter's wife, here in the obituary column. That's why he screamed." Gaskin sank into the chair. "Well, now we know."

Wendy's mind was clouded in confusion. "But he told me he killed his wife and his daughter."

Gaskin shook his head and sighed. "Peter Andrews is no killer, except in his mind."

Wendy left Gaskin's office and walked out into the streets for several hours. She couldn't stop thinking about Peter and the funeral. Peter tormented her mind as she walked down the street. It helped to get away from the sanitarium. She passed stores and shops and empty lots. Her thoughts went from Peter to her own life. Her mind told her, that as a journalist, she should be objective, but she couldn't. She pulled out the obituary again and looked at it. The cemetery was only a few blocks from the sanitarium. She started to run. She had to see it. Maybe there would be a clue as to what drove Peter to break down.

The gates of the Parkdale Cemetery were rusted and twisted barely able to open or close due to years of neglect. She stopped in the caretaker's office by the gate and showed the grizzled old man the newspaper. He didn't say much, but then walked out of the office and pointed toward the far end of the cemetery.

"That's were you'll find 'em, but I think it's almost over."

Wendy looked at a sign that the caretaker placed on the shack. Help Wanted Caretaker

"It's my last day. I'm leavin'. If you come back this way later, it'll be all locked up."

Wendy walked quickly through the grave stones, not wanting to look at them. She never liked cemeteries. It always made her think of her high school boyfriend, Bill Jennings. He could have been the one. She did have feelings for him, but his father was a funeral director and Bill always smelled of the dead. Bill was destined to take over the lucrative family business, but Wendy just couldn't get beyond it. The thought of her being a mortician's wife was too much to bear.

Peter was different. What was it about him that intrigued her? Yes, she was attracted to him, but there was more. He was certainly handsome enough. Perhaps it was the caretaker in her. She'd always been the one for taking in strays, to the constant exasperation of her mother. But, this was different. Andrews was troubled, that was obvious, but his trouble wasn't just emotional or psychological, it was spiritual.

As Wendy approached the section of the cemetery where the burial was taking place, she saw a long black limousine pull away from the canopy. One tall man stood by the grave. No one else attended. There were no flowers, no mourners; just a solitary minister who talked with the strange, tall man. She tried to hear what they were saying, but they were too far away. After a few moments the minister left. Wendy was careful not to let herself be discovered, hiding by an elm tree.

The tall man looked around to make sure he was alone. Then he did something that shocked her. He took out a piece of paper, looked at it and crumpled it up and tossed it in the open grave. He looked around, then back at the grave, smiled and walked to the waiting limousine. After he left, she walked over to the grave. This was it—Ann Parks—Peter's wife. There was nothing on the tombstone but her name, birth date and date of death. Wendy looked in the grave. There it was, the crumpled up paper. It looked like a letter. She could barely see Peter's name on it.

She knelt down and struggled to pick it up off the coffin. She was about to read it, when it started to rain, so she quickly put it in her pocket and left.

After she got back to the sanitarium, she found a secluded place in the library. Once she was certain she was alone, she picked the crumpled letter out of her pocket and read it. It was the saddest letter she'd ever read. Just then, she heard herself being paged by Dr. Gaskin. She put it away, wiped the tears from her eyes and left.

For the next two weeks, she stayed away from Peter. He spent most of his time in his room and occasionally could be seen in the garden. As the weeks and months passed, she gradually spent small amounts of time with him, and he began to gradually open up with her. Then one day, he saw Wendy sitting in the garden reading the Bible. He tried to hide so she wouldn't see him. She read a page here and there, then flipped the page in disgust, then read some more.

Finally, after shaking her head and blurting out, "Oh, for God's sake, I can't understand this. It just doesn't make any sense!"

He couldn't keep quiet any longer. He had to speak. "I know. It doesn't make sense to me either."

Wendy heard his voice behind her but didn't turn around. He came around and sat next to her. "I understand that I caused you some problems."

"No," she said, "It was no problem, but I have to ask you, why do you hate the Bible so much? If you don't want to talk about it, I understand."

Peter looked at her. It was obvious that she did care for him. "Call me Peter."

His mind trembled—a sudden headache.

"I used to believe. I used to think it had all the answers. Not now. Not now. Now I can't even look at it. Sometimes I think it's a hateful book."

Wendy watched him as he spoke. She didn't think he really believed what he said, but it was obvious that the Bible had caused him great pain. As she looked at him, she felt the beginnings of a real connection.

"Well, I'm no minister, but I've always had lots of questions about God and the Bible, in fact, I had so many questions that I got thrown out of my church."

Peter looked deep into her eyes and smiled. Then they both laughed. Wendy touched his arm and he smiled. He missed the warm touch of a woman and gently put his hand on her hand.

"Don't ever stop asking questions. Believe what your mind and heart tells you, not what any self-righteous minister or self-appointed prophet tells you."

"Is that why you hate God so much?" she said.

He looked up at her and smiled. He hadn't thought about his real feelings about God in a long time. "I don't know whether I hate God or whether I hate what I made of God. But I do know that God hates me. And I know that you won't find God in any huge church or fancy cathedral."

"Where do you find him?" she asked.

Peter looked away from her. "I don't know where you'll find him or her or it, but I know now where not to look." He reached for the Bible in Wendy's lap and picked it up.

"This book is not the only answer," he said, "there is more, there has to be."

Wendy looked at him and knew at that moment that he was going to be well. He wasn't lost. He wasn't found yet, but he wasn't lost anymore. Taking his hand in hers, she was drawn to him.

"Peter; what's driving you?" He rubbed her hand and closed his eyes.

For a moment he was with Ann. He looked down at Wendy's hand, and in a flash, he was back in time. All he saw was Ann's hand with the engagement ring on it. He kissed her hand. Looking up at her beautiful face, she smiled at him and nodded her head. Then, in a flash, he was back at the sanitarium. He stared into Wendy's face. She was more cute, than pretty. Her face was young and not yet wise, not like Ann.

"I'm not sure, but I know that it's not finished, not yet," he said.

Inside, he knew that he'd just made a decision to live. He held on to her as they walked through the courtyard. They talked and got to know each other. She finally made contact. In her closeness to him, Wendy realized that he was no longer a story, he was a friend. Maybe someday, she would be more to him, but not now. Now he had to get well. She couldn't get the letter out of her mind. She read it over and over, but every time she thought of giving it to Peter, she hesitated. He wasn't ready yet. It would tear him apart. She thought about showing it to Gaskin, but something inside her told her to keep it a secret. Something inside her – was it her mind? Was it God, or was it her feelings for Peter? She couldn't deny the fact that he had become the most important thing in her life.

From the end of the courtyard, Dr. Gaskin was just finishing his rounds. He looked over and saw the two of them walking. At first he was upset. He had told her to let Andrews alone, but when he saw that Peter was carrying a Bible, it was a good sign.

One morning, three months later, Dr. Gaskin walked around his desk and sat on the corner. Peter never liked these impromptu talks, too much like a test. He used to hate tests in the seminary. It made him feel like he was always on trial. His apprehensions exploded when Gaskin dropped a Bible in his lap. Peter looked at it and then slowly picked it up and put it on Gaskin's desk.

"What was that?" Peter asked

Gaskin didn't respond.

Again Peter pushed the point. "Why did you do that?"

Gaskin looked at him and then sat down and made some notes in Peter's chart. "No response. That's good, Peter."

"What do you mean no response?"

Gaskin put his pen down and finally looked at him. "A month ago if I had dropped that in your lap, you would have had a very violent episode. Today, you hardly reacted at all. That, my friend, is a good sign."

"I still don't like it." Peter said.

"Yes, you don't like it, but you don't hate it. Why?"

Peter opened the book and thumbed through the well-worn ornate pages. "Because, it's just a book." Peter paused for a long time thinking. He looked at Gaskin and then glanced out the window at the wind-blown trees. "Because if it's just a book, it can't hurt me anymore?"

Gaskin smiled and with a deep sigh said, "Peter, I've been waiting a long time for you to say that. I think it's time for you to find your life again on the outside."

"My life? I don't have a life."

Gaskin took the Bible from Peter and thumbed through it to a well-marked passage.

"To every thing there is a season, and a time for every purpose under the heaven: a time to be born, and a time to die; a time to plant, and a time to pluck up that which is planted; a time to kill, and a time to heal; a time to break down, and a time to build up; a time to weep, and a time to laugh..."

Peter picked it up from there. "... a time to mourn, and a time to dance; a time to cast away stones, and a time to gather stones together; a time to embrace, and a time to refrain from embracing – Gaskin joined in, reciting the verse along with Peter. –"A time to get, and a time to lose; a time to keep, and a time to cast away; a time to rend, and a time to sew; a time to keep silence, and a time to speak; a time to love, and a time to hate; a time of war, and a time of peace. – Ecclesiastes, 3."

Peter didn't have to think about it; the verses were deep inside of him. Gaskin nodded and closed the book. He looked at Peter in a different way now.

"Look, Peter, I'm no preacher, but I think you've been at war with yourself and with God. Maybe it's time to know some peace."

Peter felt alone and unsure; the sanitarium had been a refuge since the breakdown. He knew he couldn't go back. That was impossible.

"I wouldn't even know where to start."

Gaskin reassured him as much as possible. "I know it can be frightening. We're here for you if you ever need to talk."

"When do I leave?"

Gaskin looked at the documents in Peter's file. "In about two weeks. It'll take that long for the paperwork to get approved for us to sign off on your release."

"Any suggestions as to where I go or what I should do?"

Gaskin put his hand on Peter's shoulder and patted it. It was something he rarely did, but he felt a special warmth for Peter, like a lost son.

"Well, I think I'd stay away from the ministry, Peter."

Peter looked up at him. "Too many memories," said Peter.

Gaskin nodded. It was rare that he saw this kind of recovery and renewal in a patient, but he was grateful. Peter walked out of Gaskin's office. He had done this hundreds of times before, but this time it was different. This time he knew he was going to leave, but where would he go? He had reached the pinnacle of success and fame and lost it all. Now he was a nobody. But, at least he wasn't dead, and maybe he could start again. Maybe he could be born again. He smiled at his own habits. Born again; he had used that phrase so often and so trivially that it didn't mean anything anymore. But now, for the first time in his life, it had a new meaning.

The next day, Wendy knocked on Gaskin's office door.

"Come in." Gaskin had his back to the door and was going through his files. There were files and papers scattered all over his office.

"I'm determined to clean up this mess and get organized."

Wendy walked toward the desk, picking up a file from the floor.

"Dr. Gaskin, can I have a moment of your time?" she said.

Gaskin turned around, seeing the file in her hand, "Thanks, I was looking for that one. What's on your mind, Larsen?"

"Dr. Gaskin, I wanted to ..." She was about to hand over the letter, but changed her mind. "Ah, after Peter's breakdown, I went to the grave where his wife was buried. After the funeral, there was a man standing next to the open grave. When he was sure he was alone, he looked in the grave and then smiled. It was so strange. He acted like he was glad she was dead." Gaskin sighed and sat down. Wendy pressed him.

"Who was that man, Dr. Gaskin?"

Gaskin walked over to the filing cabinet and pulled Peter's file. Thumbing through it, he read for a moment. "It could be a man called Jeremiah. Was he tall, black hair?"

"Yes," she said. "It must have been him. He was very sinister looking."

"Wendy, you care for him, don't you? Peter, I mean."

She hesitated. "Yes, I guess I do."

"Have you discussed your feelings with him?"

"No," she said.

Gaskin leaned back in his chair. Suddenly he felt old and out of touch. "Wendy, I've never said this before, and you and I know it's against the rules here, but I think that if there's one thing Peter Andrews needs, that would help him heal, it is to know that someone cares about him."

"Really?" she said.

"Yes. He's very lonely and I doubt that he could accept a relationship at this point. He's got to find himself again, and that may take some time." Wendy was indeed troubled.

"Dr. Gaskin, why is Peter's recovery so difficult?"

Gaskin turned to his bookshelf for a book. Thumbing through the pages until he found what he was looking for;

"Wendy, people like Peter Andrews see the world in terms of black and white. His values, like many ministers, come from what they believe is 'divinely revealed scriptures'. People like him, who get caught up in this pattern of thinking tend to ignore his own conscience and common sense to follow what he's told or to conform to the beliefs of the group."

"The group?" Wendy asked.

Gaskin continued, now reading from the book.

"The church – the congregation – whatever has the strongest pull. He buried his own common sense and authority to submit to the "higher power".

"Are you talking about God?" she asked.

"Yes, and no," Gaskin said. "When Peter or anyone gets so wrapped up in their belief system that they lose all sense of whether it's right or wrong, then they're out of balance. They don't hesitate to inflict physical, psychological, financial, social, or other forms of harm on anyone who threatens their belief system. Conformity also feeds their sense of themselves as being more moral and righteous than others -- a perception that's usually buttressed by the use of magical absolution, or forgiveness of one's sins, techniques that they use to get rid of guilt, in John Dean's words. Because they confessed, or are saved, or were just following orders, they can commit heinous crimes and still retain a serene conscience and sense that they were or are still righteous people. On the other hand, when it comes to outsiders, there is no absolution. Their memory for even minor transgressions is nothing short of enormous."

Gaskin placed the book on the desk in front of Wendy. "Here, read it. It will help you understand where Peter came from and how his mind has been taught to function."

Wendy looked at the book. *Conservatives without Conscience* by John Dean. "I didn't know he was a medical doctor." she said.

"He's not. And it's not a medical book or a religious book, but it's a good read and it'll help you understand the abyss that held Peter captive."

The next week Peter spent as much time with Wendy as he could. They had become close friends. She was special to him and he needed her friendship. As for Wendy, she was at cross-purposes. Part of her was glad Peter was leaving, but there was another part of her that felt empty and alone. He had become much more than a friend to her, but she never revealed her feelings or the contents of the letter. He wasn't ready for that or a relationship. Besides, it was strictly forbidden for interns and patients to become involved. But, they were involved. They were connected on a level deeper than either of them could have imagined.

As Peter packed up his belongings into a suitcase, he felt empty. Where was he supposed to go? What should he do now? He couldn't go back to ministry; that was unthinkable. He had no home or job now and no reputation to build on. He would have to start over, but where? He looked out the window at the grey Chicago sky. It didn't give him much to start on. He sighed and looked down. The Bible that had brought him so much pain, should he take it? He reached down and opened it. This was no ordinary Bible. It was his Bible, the one that Ann had given to him on his first Sunday at Temple Christian. He opened the leaf and read.

In an instant, his mind took him back to his debut Sunday at Temple Christian Church. Jeremiah had arranged an elegant reception in the main fellowship dining room. Everything was decorated with yellow roses and cut glass plates of hors d'oeuvres. Hundreds of people stood in line to welcome the new minister. One by one, they came to shake his hand and wish him well. Ann and Jennie were stunned at the vast numbers of people that waited to greet Peter. It wasn't until several hours later that they had a chance to be alone. Ducking into Peter's office, Ann threw her arms around him and kissed him.

"I'm so proud of you. Here, I got you something."

Peter smiled and told her he loved her. Opening the package, he knew at once what it was. "Beautiful Ann, thank you." He opened the gold-embossed Bible to read the inscription. *To my beloved husband – May God always give you the truth to know your path. Love, Ann."*

The memory faded and he was back at the institution. He struggled to comprehend what his mind was trying to tell him. Path. There was something familiar about that, something in his past. What was it?

Suddenly there was a knock at the door. It was Wendy. She stuck her head in and with a smile that belied her true thoughts.

"I wanted to say goodbye."

Peter walked over to her and put his arms around her. She was warm and sweet and willing, and it felt good to hold her next to him.

"I'm so glad you came. I was worried that I wasn't going to see you before I left."

Wendy touched his face and stroked his hair. "I wouldn't let that happen, Peter. She paused in her emotions to gather her professionalism. "You're leaving today?"

"Yes; to what or where, I don't know."

Wendy reached into her pocket and handed him the obituary page from the newspaper.

"I thought you'd like to have this."

He looked down at it, winced and folded it into his pocket. "Thanks."

Wendy saw the Bible on the bed and picked it up.

"What's this?"

"Oh, it's the Bible that my wife gave me when I started at Temple Christian."

Wendy opened the leaf and looked up at him.

"Mind if I read this?"

"No, go right ahead."

After she read it she knew what she had to do. "Peter, would you get me a drink of water from the hall?"

"Sure." When Peter left the room, Wendy slipped the letter inside the Bible. As he returned, she quickly turned around and wiped a tear from her eyes.

"Look, Peter, I'd like you to keep in touch with me."

Peter smiled and said, "I don't know where I'm going to be or when I'll return."

Wendy playfully slapped him on the shoulder. "I hope you never return here. Here's my phone number and address. If I leave here, I'll give Dr. Gaskin my address. Please write me or call if you can."

Peter took the slip of paper from her hand and kissed it. Wendy stroked his head and more tears flowed down her cheeks. She tried to regain her composure.

"Boy, I'll never be a hard-bitten news journalist if I can't control myself."

Peter smiled and patted her cheek. At that moment, Dr. Gaskin walked in. Peter hugged Wendy.

"Goodbye Wendy, ah—Miss Larsen," said Peter.

Peter shook Gaskin's hand. "Thanks, Doc."

Gaskin patted Peter on the shoulder.

"Take care of yourself Peter." Wendy said.

Gaskin looked both at Wendy then at Peter and smiled. "Goodbye, Peter."

Handing him his Bible, he said, "Please write if you can."

"I will." Peter said.

"Oh, and one more thing, I almost forgot. After you were committed, a woman came here asking for you. She refused to identify herself, but I think it was your wife, Ann. I must say she didn't look like herself. She must've been very sick at the time. Anyway, she gave this to me to give to you if you were ever well enough to leave".

Gaskin handed Peter a velvet bag containing an old necklace with a strange cross attached. "I asked her what it was and she said you would know. Then she left and I never saw her again. Does this have some meaning for you"?

Peter nodded, looked down at the cross and then put it in his pocket. He walked over to his suitcase and started to put the Bible inside, but changed his mind and carried it under his arm. As he walked toward the door, he turned to look at Wendy. He smiled a sad smile and said;

"Don't forget me."

And with that, he walked down the hall for the last time. As she watched him go, she asked herself over and over if she'd done the right thing by not telling him about the letter. Her heart told her that he wasn't ready to see it now – maybe later when the time was right, he'd find it and then it would give him comfort. The echoes of his footsteps reverberated against the hospital green walls. He opened the door, looked up and saw the sun breaking through the clouds. He nodded and closed the door.

Peter walked out of the sanitarium for what he hoped was the last time. He couldn't even remember the day he arrived. It was all a black hole in his brain. The warmth of the winter sun broke through the daily overcast, and it felt good on his face. He walked through the streets, past stores and shops, and glanced at children playing in what was left of the grey, Chicago snow.

Chicago's North Side wasn't what it used to be; empty stores, back alleys and vacant lots now. It was all so depressing, but then so was his life. He wasn't what he used to be, and like the vacant lots all around him, he also felt abandoned. As he walked he glanced around the streets for something familiar, but nothing looked right anymore. His mind had been through too much. He couldn't seem to connect with the real world anymore.

Then he saw a street sign and something clicked. "Charles Avenue". Where had he seen that? Suddenly his brain was clear. He pulled out the obituary from his pocket. Charles Avenue, yes, that's where the cemetery was. Ann was there. He walked and walked, faster and then he started to run, following the numbers until he reached the top of the hill. There it was; Parkdale Cemetery. He checked his watch. He had to go in anyway. He passed the caretaker's shack and saw that it was empty, so he had to wander around looking for something that would seem familiar. He had no idea where to go. The old cemetery had dozens of old paths and roads that lead to one section of graves after another. After about a half hour, something guided him toward a new grave on the hill. That must be it. He walked over to the grave. He'd found it. Standing there motionless and rigid, he looked down at the tombstone, but all he could see was Ann; his wonderful Ann. So many memories flooded back to him. How could she be there? How could his life have come to this? He felt a great wave of sorrow come over him as he sank to his knees and wept. He wanted to be dead too; to lie in the dark, cold earth with her. It was too much to bear. He dropped his suitcase and sank to the cold earth and wept. After what seemed like hours, he opened his eyes.

He reached for Ann's Bible. For months, the book was nothing to him; just a lot of words and judgments from the past. But now, it was more than a book, it was Ann. What she believed—what she felt—what she meant to him—and how much he'd hurt her. He opened the book to see the inscription once again. What was this? A paper? He hadn't seen it before. It was a letter from Ann. He held it as though it were a fine manuscript, thousands of years old. He started to read.

My darling Peter;

By the time you read this letter, I will probably be dead. I don't blame you for anything, as I'm sure you've blamed yourself for all of us. I remember the day we met and our life together before Jennifer and before the church took you from me. So many times I've sat in my chair and wished our lives together could have been different. Your calling took you from me and from the world. Did you ever think that it also took you from Christ as well? In all your success and strivings, I only wish you hadn't lost your soul along the way. There was once such a sweet spirit in you. I loved you so, but Jeremiah took all that away. After Jennie died, I couldn't bring myself to visit you. I'm sorry for that. I know you were all alone in there, but I was all used up. My life, if it is to have any meaning, will be what you do with what you have left. I have left this letter at our house. I suppose it ended up with Jeremiah. Imagine that? The one man who took everything; the one man I hate. I can only hope he has enough compassion to give it to you. Someday, when you get out, I hope you are free of him and find that spirit inside you that I always loved. There is goodness inside you. I hope you find it and find a reason to live again. I will always love you. Remember me. – Ann

Peter's soul was gone. He curled up in a ball on the winter ground and wanted to die. Ann's words were like a blanket of warm memories that flooded over him. The cold wind whipped through the cemetery leaving only loneliness and desolation. Several hours passed. When he finally stirred, the falling leaves had covered him. They had kept him warm on the cold ground. He looked up at Ann's tombstone to see a small cross engraved above her name. It was a simple stone; the kind that someone supplied who didn't really know her. She deserved more than this. She didn't deserve this. She didn't deserve to have the life he gave her—and the life he took from her. He looked again at the cross. The cross… the cross... His mind faltered. He remembered the cross around Wendy's neck and the gold cross engraved on the Bible that Ann had given him at his ordination.

There was something else. What was it? He thought. He reached into his pocket and remembered the small velvet bag that Gaskin had given him. He opened it and smiled. It was Jennie's cross; the Cross of

St. Philip. All of the pain and memories of Jennie's death came flooding back. Did he ever apologize for slapping her? He couldn't remember. The tears flowed down his cheeks as he knelt on the cold ground. He looked up and saw the other cross on Ann's tombstone. His mind was torn by the meaning; the cross, the symbol of Christ and the symbol of death and pain. His twisted mind told him that if they'd killed Jesus with a knife, we'd all be wearing little golden knives around our neck. He wanted to throw Jennie's cross into the open grave, but couldn't bring himself to do it. The symbol carried so much baggage with it. Then he remembered another cross, the one that changed his life and destroyed it.

Chapter Five
Two Apostles For The Price Of One

Peter peered out of the window of the limousine to see a huge cross extending above all the other buildings in the city. Its massive presence towered two hundred feet high and changed colors from white to red each night. This was Temple Christian Church, or the Jesus Temple as it was called, and he was on his way to be interviewed to be their minister. It was a once in a lifetime opportunity, and he knew it. But there was also that foreboding feeling deep in the pit of his stomach. He tried to shake it off as butterflies, but couldn't. As the car pulled up the long driveway, he sank back into the rich black leather seat and closed his eyes.

"We're here, sir," said the chauffer.

Peter took a moment and just sat there. After a moment, the car door was pulled open and he got out and looked up. In front of him swept a huge, stone staircase to the front entrance. Each step was engraved with the name of a book in the Bible; all sixty-six of them. The front of the church was glass and stone; so massive that you couldn't see the sides or top of the building when you stood at its front door. He felt like he was about to enter the gates of Jerusalem. As he slowly walked up the steps, the top of another large wooden cross became visible. He stopped and looked at it. A small, gold plaque on the base of the cross proclaimed that the wood was Cedars of Lebanon from Israel. Peter remembered what professor Jeffers told him at the seminary; that the *Sumerian Epic of Gilgamesh* designated the cedar groves of Lebanon as the dwelling place of the gods. Peter felt very much like he was entering that same place; and it all made him feel very small.

As the doorman held the massive front door, Peter cautiously walked inside. The lobby shimmered with glass and marble. It spelled success like nothing he'd ever seen. The Lobby floor was inlaid with a stone walkway. Chiseled on the path was *The Way;* this was the name that early Christians used to identify themselves during their time in the catacombs. On each side were six great stone fountains, each one containing a huge bronze statue of an apostle with bubbling streams pouring down in all directions. All of the statues had their arms raised in praise, all except one. This held a figure crouched in shame. Peter walked over to it. He didn't need to read the plaque; *Judas Iscariot; The Betrayer*.

Towering above all the others, was a massive fountain and great bronze statue of Jesus. Peter stopped, not in reverence, but in shock. Unlike the other fountains, which flowed with water; this one flowed with blood. The large sign on the fountain made his heart sink. *Bathe yourself in the blood of Jesus*. Of course it wasn't really blood, just red water, but the effect was the same. It was meant to shock the non-believers, and it worked.

It was all too much. Peter was overwhelmed, and had to sit down. As he tried to gather himself; a middle aged woman dressed in white approached him.

"Mr. Andrews?" He looked up.

"Yes?"

"The Board of Trustees is waiting for you."

Peter sighed. "I'll be along in just a minute. I've got to catch my breath."

The woman looked peeved. "Very well, when you're ready, it's the fourth door on the right."

With that she turned and walked back down the hall. Peter breathed in and out, again and again. That old feeling was back. He told himself that he was just nervous. This was a great opportunity. For God's sake, don't blow it, he thought. He got up and slowly walked down the hall. As he approached the door, he was amazed to see that the door was covered with gold leaf. He had never seen such opulence. All this was done with donations, he thought? It was hard to believe. He opened the door and walked in.

He passed the secretary's desk and walked down another long hall to a carved wooden door that was eight feet high. He knocked, and from the other side he heard; "Come in, Reverend Andrews, Jesus is expecting you."

Peter winced, took a breath, then opened the door and walked in to what was a large cavernous meeting room. Twelve old, white men stood around the table, each one dressed identically in a dark blue suit with black ties. Peter smiled and looked up. The entire ceiling was a massive oval with a fresco of the heaven painted on it. He closed his gaping jaw and then looked down and introduced himself around the room. They all seemed polite and cordial, but he was reminded of those decrepit Lords of Parliament in the film, *The Ruling Class*. Like them, these Lords of the church were all ancient and wizened.

Peter spoke first. "I would like to say that I'm thrilled to even be considered for the position of…"

He looked up at the huge, black, crepe-covered portrait of Dr. Remington which hung over the fireplace. At first, the old men around the table seemed like they weren't listening to him at all.

"I know I'll never take Dr. Remington's place." His remark drew an instant unanimous response from the group. "Yes!"

Peter stopped short. He didn't know what to say. Suddenly a door burst open and a tall, thin man with ink-black hair came in. As he did, all the men bowed their heads. Flashing the men and Peter with burning eyes and a commanding voice, he said,

"Thou art Peter, and upon this rock I will build my church."

Peter was stunned.

"Peter Andrews, I am Jeremiah. Just Jeremiah."

"I am not the Peter of whom you speak."

Jeremiah smiled and shook his hand. Placing his other hand on his shoulder, he laughed and said, "Not yet, my friend, not yet."

With that, the secretary closed the heavy door, but try as she might; she could not hear the muffled voices coming from the Board Room. They talked about everything from the Bible to the mission of Christ in the world. After about two hours, it was agreed that Peter would give a sermon in two weeks to the entire congregation. If they were impressed, he would be hired. When the meeting was about over, Peter reluctantly brought up the subject of salary and housing. Jeremiah smiled.

"Don't worry, my friend… God will provide, and in this place, He provides very well."

Peter thanked them all and turned to leave. He was genuinely scared and convinced that he was in way over his head.

"Pray for me," he said.

Jeremiah looked at Peter, then at the old men and smiled.

"We already have. That's why you're here."

As Peter left the room, one of the old men at the table turned to Jeremiah and said,

"He seems too young, to me. I think you've got the wrong man, Jeremiah."

Jeremiah suddenly turned on the old man and with the eyes of a demon, said;

"Everything is too young to you, Benjamin. A word to the wise, my old friend; never question me again!"

The old man cowered like a child and sank into his chair. Suddenly, Jeremiah's demeanor changed to one of good cheer.

"Gentlemen, Peter Andrews will do just fine. I tell you that Jesus has given me a sign. After all, his name is Peter Andrews; Peter and Andrew—two apostles for the price of one."

With that, Jeremiah laughed and left the room.

Ann was busy cleaning the living room when the limousine pulled up. As Peter got out, she went out on the porch. He looked natural getting out of a stretch limo, like he was a politician or head of state. Ann couldn't wait any longer, and ran to greet him.

"How did it go?"

Peter didn't answer her, but just threw his arms around her and hugged her. Finally he said, "I love you. God, I hope…"

"What", she said. "What happened?"

They both went into the house. For the next hour they sat at the kitchen table and talked about what he'd seen and heard and about his fears and excitement at what this could mean for them.

"I have two weeks to prepare the greatest sermon of my life," he said.

Ann kissed him. "I'm sure you'll do just fine. It's just one sermon. Yes, it's a big church, but it's just a church, and after all, they're just people, like you and me."

Peter turned his head away from her. "Peter? What's the matter?"

He sat back down and after a long silence, looked up at her. His face was strange, like there was a cloud over his eyes.

In a whisper barely audible, he said: "This is not a church. These are not people like…" His voice trailed off. Ann was startled.

"What? What did you say?"

Suddenly, the old Peter was back. In an instant his face changed. "What?" he said, and then he looked up at Ann with a smile.

"Peter, you said it wasn't a church and that these were not people… and then you stopped. What did you mean?"

Peter was confused. He had no idea what Ann was talking about. "I don't know what you mean. Did I say something?"

Ann looked at him and embraced him as hard as she could. Something happened, and it scared her. She wanted to hang on to him and never let him go. In a moment of precise clarity, she said; "Peter, I know you will get this job, and…" she took a breath, "and I know our lives will never be the same."

He looked at her and they both knew everything was going to change. He felt like he was adrift on a raft in heavy currents. There were forces at work and try as he might, he couldn't stop them. But then again, he didn't want to. This was his moment in time and he knew it.

For the next two weeks, she didn't see much of him. Every day he spent his regular time at the church, but his mind really wasn't on his work. He couldn't concentrate on his classes or meetings, and he found his mind drifting off when he listened to people during his counseling sessions. The next Sunday, he gave a rather ordinary sermon that was anything but inspired. When one of the congregants yawned, he got angry. His voice changed and he slammed his fist on the podium. When half a dozen heads popped up to attention, he said, "I know you weren't praying, but perhaps I was the one who was asleep."

They laughed. He sighed and took a deep breath. The rest of the sermon was more energized. He seemed to have caught his wind. This was a term he often used to explain the effect of speaking through the spirit. Whenever this happened his sermons would soar, but the words would not be his own. In fact, it was often the case that he would have no idea what he said after an inspired sermon. After church that day, he ran home to work on his next week's audition sermon. As he came in the house, Ann was startled to see him.

"Peter, why are you home so early?"

He barely noticed her as he rushed past into his study.

"I got the wind!" was all he said as he quickly found his typing paper and jammed it into his typewriter. It was an old Smith Corona that he'd had since high school. He never did trust computers ever since he lost a sermon when the power went out. Ann came into the room to see what all the hurry was.

"What's with you today?"

He looked up and blew her a kiss.

"I'd rather have the real ones," she said."

"I've got it. My sermon title for next Sunday, 'Will you be asleep during the Second Coming?'"

Ann smiled. "Good title; where'd you get that?"

"It came to me today when I put the congregation to sleep."

"You did what?"

"I put 'em to sleep. Isn't that great? I was just awful."

At seven o'clock in the morning that next Sunday, two black limousines pulled up into Peter's driveway. Two chauffeurs got out and pulled open the doors. Jeremiah, dressed in his typical black suit walked to the door and knocked. When Jennifer unthinkingly opened the door in her slip and saw him standing there, she screamed and slammed the door. Peter rushed in from the bedroom.

"What's the matter? Why did you scream?"

Jennifer covered herself with the living room drapes and shouted.

"There's a ghost at the door!"

Peter looked out the window in the door and laughed.

"That's Jeremiah. I told you about him."

Peter opened the door as Jennifer ran into the bedroom.

"Good morning Peter, are you ready?"

Peter looked at his watch. "You're a little early."

Jeremiah smiled and said, "Yes, I know. I've brought two limousines. You and I will ride in the first limousine and your family will ride in the second."

Peter thought that was a little strange. "Is that necessary?"

Jeremiah looked around and then at his watch. "Quite. There are things I must talk to you about on our way to the church. Your family will be more comfortable in the second car."

"Very well, whatever you say, Jeremiah."

Peter smiled, but Jeremiah's sullen expression never changed.

"We'll be out in just a minute."

As Peter closed the door, Jennifer came into the dining room to use the iron.

"You're right, Jennie, he does look like a ghost."

After a few minutes, both Ann and Jennie were ready and they all grabbed their coats and walked out onto their driveway. They were startled to see the two limousines.

"What's this?" Ann said.

Jeremiah was quick to answer. "This is customary for us to take two cars on the first Sunday. I need to talk over a few contractual things with Peter on the way. You both will ride in the second car."

Ann was a little bothered by this. "Peter, I wanted to ride with you, to give you moral support."

Peter looked at her and smiled, then looked at Jeremiah, who showed no signs of changing the plans. "Well, it's just for this one time, right Jeremiah?"

Jeremiah didn't say anything, but did nod. Then he walked Ann and Jennie to the second car. As he took Ann's arm, he gave her a look that sent a shudder through her entire body.

"You both look lovely today, especially you Ann."

She knew what he meant. She could feel him examining her body with his eyes. Suddenly, she felt a chill like she was naked. Jennie was oblivious to all this. She thought it was cool that they were riding in a limo. After Jeremiah had done his duty, he got into Peter's limo and told the driver that they were ready. As they drove out of the drive, the street was cluttered with curious neighbors staring at the procession of black limousines.

As the limos pulled out into traffic, Jeremiah could tell that Peter was nervous.

"Don't worry," he said. "I'm sure you'll do just fine."

As Peter watched the passing scenery, he fidgeted with his notes.

"How many people… ah... you know…?"

Jeremiah laughed and patted Peter on the back.

"Speaking before our church and yours is really not that much different, just bigger." Peter looked back inside the car and looked directly into Jeremiah's eyes.

"Bigger. How much bigger?" asked Peter

Jeremiah smiled. "You have how many people on an average Sunday attendance at your church?"

"We have about 500 people on a good day."

"Well, that's a good size church. All you have to do is add a couple of zeros."

Peter swallowed hard. "Are you saying that your average attendance is 50,000?"

Jeremiah sighed and continued. "Our attendance fluctuates between 50,000 to 80,000 for all of our combined services."

Peter didn't know what to say. "Combined services? What do you mean by that?"

Jeremiah was eager to get through this moment. "Look. Peter, we have one senior pastor, that's the job we're interested in you for. However, we also have four Associate Pastors and twelve Assistant Pastors. They take care of the other eleven services each Sunday, but you'll only be doing the 11:00 service today. Now listen—I'm sure everything is going to go well, and after the service you'll be hired. But just so you know, if the congregation doesn't like you or if the board rejects you, you'll still be paid for today's sermon."

Jeremiah handed Peter an envelope. Peter opened it. It was a check for $5,000.

"That's more than I make in two months!"

Jeremiah laughed again.

"Like I said before, God provides. Now, if all goes well, and I'm sure it will, the board is prepared to offer you a very nice home, two automobiles, all your expenses, and a salary of $250,000 a year for the first three years, and if your contract is renewed at the end of that period, an increase of $150,000. That would give you and your family $400,000 a year. After that, your income would remain the same, but you would receive an additional Christmas bonus of 25% of your yearly income. That's an extra $100,000. So, what do you think?"

Peter hadn't heard a word after Jeremiah told him he'd be making $250,000 a year.

"I can't think about this right now. I just have to get through this day."

Jeremiah smiled. He had done well. Peter was hooked; he could tell. His thoughts took a sarcastic turn. *I will make you fishers of men.* Jeremiah laughed to himself.

Ann tried to be comfortable riding to the church, but it wasn't easy. Jennie was caught up in the grand luxury of the moment, but Ann couldn't help but worry that Peter was alone – trapped in that car with Jeremiah. He gave her the creeps. She couldn't say anything but there was something about him that wasn't right. Perhaps it was the coldness that she felt when he shook her hand. Jennie said it was like shaking the hand of a corpse. It was all part of the package, so she had to keep silent. The ride to the church was quiet, except for Jennie's constant chatter about how rich they were all going to be. Ann tried to ride the wave of excitement for Jennie. Today, she had to be the good wife.

As their car followed Jeremiah's limousine into the main gate of Temple Christian, Ann glimpsed out the window.

Jennifer immediately said, "Wow!".

Ann was too shocked to say anything. She had never seen anything like it before. The size of the church was so immense that she felt like she did when she was a teenage girl. During a European vacation, while walking through Geneva, Switzerland early one morning, she turned the corner to see the immense slope of Mont Blanc towering above her. She had been there several days, but had never seen it because it had been covered by clouds. The size so shocked her that her knees buckled and she had an anxiety attack. It all passed and eventually she got better. This time however, she wondered if her sense of foreboding would pass at seeing the enormous Jesus Temple.

Chapter Six
Lawsie, We Sure Is All Rich Now!

There was nothing like Temple Christian Church. It dwarfed every other mega-church in the country. From its 85-acre campus, 35 buildings and 9-level parking garage; it was an entire city. It had restaurants, stores, schools, gymnasiums, parks, a roller rink, and a Christian theatre and movie house. It also had its own security force of 300 officers; affectionately knows as Cops for Christ. Its main temple had 30-foot-tall stained glass windows, 14-karet gold-plated door stops, and security cameras everywhere. The carpets were two inches thick and cost hundreds of thousands of dollars. The floors in the lobby were all covered in imported Rosa Aurora marble, shipped all the way from a quarry in the Estremoz region of Portugal. It all dripped of money; the result of hundreds of thousands of TV and radio contributions. It was an immense cash cow feeding on a constant supply of un-taxed funds. Each Monday, four Brinks armored trucks made their way into the complex to take the money to the four banks that housed all of the church's many different accounts. If money was needed for a new building, TV network or other improvement, it was easy to get. Even when the Board of Trustees balked at the new spending, all Jeremiah had to do was to say it was God's will and they all buckled. No one had the courage to stand up to him. He was a force unto himself.

On this most special of Sundays, Peter was to give his inaugural sermon. For weeks, the church had promoted Peter as the next Billy Graham. Someone had put up posters calling him God's New Prophet. When Ann saw them in the lobby, she quietly told Jennie that maybe they really meant God's New Profit. As Ann and Jennie stood amidst the tumultuous crowds milling about the lobby, Jeremiah took Peter off to prepare him for the service. Everywhere they looked, they were stunned at the immense power of the edifice. Thousands of people rushed past them towards the main auditorium. This football-sized sanctuary could seat 100,000 people or more. As they made their way toward the main entry doors, a young woman approached them. She looked like an usher, all dressed in white.

"Excuse me, but aren't you Ann and Jennifer Andrews?"

"Yes."

"Please follow me; we have special seating arranged for you."

They all walked down the hall toward a bank of twelve elevators. The woman walked to the only elevator without any buttons. She put a key in a lock and turned it. The elevator door opened and they all got in. Another young boy ran over to get in with them, but the usher stopped him and told him that she was sorry but this was a private elevator and he would have to take one of the public elevators. Ann and Jennie looked at each other with amusement. The elevator doors closed and they were surrounded by mirrors. Jennie looked around and then dropped her purse. As she bent down to pick it up, Jennie looked at the ceiling. The top of the elevator contained a painting of Jesus ascending into heaven.

"Mom, look at that!"

Ann looked up and couldn't help but laugh.

"Who did your elevator, Michelangelo?"

The usher wasn't amused, but just groaned and looked forward. Finally the elevator stopped and the doors opened. This was the Grand Mezzanine. It was all decorated in various shades of purple and gold. Ann saw several groups of men standing and talking. From what she could hear, the conversation seemed to be about Peter.

To announce the beginning of service, church bells started to ring out a familiar Christian hymn, *Shall We Gather At The River*. The doors to the seating area all automatically opened and everyone immediately went into the main auditorium. Both Ann and Jennie's jaws fell open as they entered. It was the largest and most impressive church they had ever seen.

The main auditorium was immense. It was a grand horseshoe stadium-like room with ten massive TV screens hanging to give every one a good view of the platform. The choir had over 300 voices dressed in scarlet robes with gold glittered crosses across their chests. Each one sounded like they could have been a professional singer. At the center of the room, there were three giant angels, each one with a spotlight in their hands. As the lights dimmed, the angel's lights focused on the back of the platform. The platform then separated so that the choir was split into two sections, each section moving away from the center. As the choir separated, white smoke started to drift onto the platform. The orchestra started to play *Turn Your Eyes Upon Jesus* as the choir joined in. Everyone in the auditorium, all 75,000, stood up as a giant stained glass window rose behind the choir. It had to be at least 150 feet tall and had a massive picture of Jesus on the cross.

Ann and Jennie had never seen anything like this. It was like the Ringling Brothers and Barnum and Bailey Circus had come to town and its main attraction was Peter Andrews. Ann looked around and saw people weeping and sobbing.

Several women even screamed, "Jesus! Oh, Jesus!" and then collapsed.

Ushers were waiting nearby to scoop them up and get them to the infirmary. Apparently this was a common occurrence. This was all too much for Jennie.

"I think I'm gonna throw up, Mom."

Ann tried to comfort her, but Jennie's threshold for grandiose Christianity was low.

"I gotta get some air."

With that Jennie ran up the steps into the hall. A few minutes later, she found herself outside the temple in the Garden of Gethsemane, a grove of trees and benches where people could find peace amidst all the chaos of Sunday mornings. She sat down on a bench and pulled out her cigarettes. She sighed as she took the first drag. "Now that's what I call salvation."

A young teenage boy came over to talk to her. He introduced himself as Rod and told her he couldn't take the church services, either. He was close to Jennie's age, maybe a year or two older. They talked and laughed and shared her smokes. Maybe it wasn't such a bad day after all. Maybe Jennie had found a friend and fellow skeptic.

As Jeremiah strapped Peter to the speaker's pedestal, he could hear the choir above him finish the hymn. Jeremiah told him to hold on tight and remember to make this the best sermon he'd ever given. Peter assured him that he would. Jeremiah then told him that as the pedestal rose, the floor above him would separate, and not to get off until the pedestal came back down to the platform and the attendants came to unhook him. Peter stood there feeling like he was about to get shot out of a cannon. Suddenly the orchestra stood and played a shimmering transition. The choir all stood and started to sing the Halleluiah chorus from The Messiah. With a jerk, the pedestal started to rise. Peter grasped the railing with all his might. Slowly it rose up until he could see the hole above him. Going through the hole in the platform, Peter expected the pedestal to stop, but it kept going, up and up until he was fifty feet above the platform. As he reached the top, the choir sang the last part of the *Halleluiah chorus* "*… and He shall reign forever and ever, and ever, and ever, Halleluiah!* With that Peter was struck silent as he looked out upon the massive crowd. All was silent. He didn't know what to do. Should he say something? Should he gesture? He looked down at the platform. Everyone was looking up at him waiting, but waiting for what? The silence seemed eternal as he searched his brain for the right words, then it came to him. In a voice as loud as he could muster, he yelled out;

"I am the resurrection and the life, he that believes on me shall not die, but have everlasting life."

At first there was shock in some faces. People turned to their neighbor in confusion. Was this new preacher talking about himself, or Jesus? Then, all of a sudden, the choir broke into the Halleluiah chorus. Some in the crowd screamed for Jesus, and others lifted their arms in praise. As for Ann, she just couldn't believe what she was seeing. She had to sit down.

The pedestal vibrated as it took Peter back down to the platform, where he then began his sermon. It was a rousing sermon filled with fire and passion. It was a welcome change from the sedate sermons of Dr. Remington. Peter talked of love and faith and a new spirit of compassion. As he talked, Ann could see several men, all dressed in black, working on computers in the back of the auditorium. How rude they were, she thought. They could at least pay attention to Peter's sermon on his first Sunday.

The service lasted about an hour and a half. At the end, the collection was taken and a call for Christ urged people to come forward for prayer and salvation. When Peter gave the benediction, Ann made her way up to the exit doors of the mezzanine. As the doors opened, Jennie stood leaning against the wall.

"Can you dig all these pictures of Jesus?"

Ann hadn't noticed, but now that Jennie mentioned it, there were a lot of pictures of Jesus everywhere. No wonder they called this the Jesus Temple, Ann thought. As Peter made his way out of the church to greet the exiting congregants, Ann joined him. She tried to get Jennie to stand with them and shake people's hands, but she would have none of it.

"I'm not a politician," she said, "and I don't kiss babies."

For the most part, the congregation was very enthusiastic. They liked his sermon and seemed to like his personality as well. The teenage girls hung around the procession and traded smirks and giggles, while they watched Peter and Ann. After the reception, Jennie signaled Peter to come into a private classroom. Peter walked in smiling, but somewhat confused.

"Dad, I know I've been a pain in the… lately, but I'm really proud of you."

"Thanks, Jennie. That means a lot to me."

"Here, I got this for you, a present for you to wear."

Peter looked at the velvet bag and smiled as he looked at Jennie. She had never given him a real present before, so this had to be very special. He opened the bag and found an ancient gold symbol.

"It's beautiful, Jennie, what is it?"

"It's called the Cross of Saint Philip. It's supposed to be an ancient symbol of the apostle. He was called the Greek and was known for his healing."

Peter was really touched. "Where on earth did you get it?"

"A couple of years ago, when the school choir went to Greece, I found it at a little shop off the Omonoia square in Athens. If you wear it always, it will bring you understanding and power."

"Well, then Jennie, I'll wear it from now on. Thank you sweetie; I love it and I love you."

"Love you too, Dad."

They hugged for a long time, then Ann finally came in.

"Hey you two, they're out here asking, Where's the minister?"

Peter and Ann walked out on the steps of the church. Jeremiah walked onto the balcony of the church grand mezzanine and looked out the window. Dr. Peterson and Mr. Robertson, both board trustees, joined him. Jeremiah looked down at Peter and Ann greeting the many thousands of congregants leaving the church.

"We have the report, sir." said Dr. Peterson. "It was a good day. The attendance was 83,000. The preliminary count on the offering was $934,000; not our best Sunday, but respectable; considering it was his first day."

Jeremiah never looked at them, but continued to look down at Peter. Mr. Robertson stepped forward to Jeremiah.

"There are some concerns…"

"I know," said Jeremiah, "but we have him now."

After the service, the church held what they called a small reception for Peter and Ann. But like everything else at Temple Christian, the reception was anything but small. There must have been 7,000 people that mingled about with champagne and cake. As for Peter and Ann, everyone wanted a piece of them as well. The women swarmed around Peter and the men surrounded Ann. In truth, she had never been so popular since high school. After a couple of hours, Jeremiah came to rescue them. He told them that he wanted to show them the parsonage that the church would be providing.

The long ride with Jeremiah was a relief. Peter was exhausted and could barely concentrate on what Jeremiah was saying. Ann listened intently as Jeremiah told them that the board had decided to validate the contract with Peter. As for Jennie, she was still bored. The car finally entered the church's parsonage grounds. In reality, it was a 45-acre well manicured estate. After the car stopped, they all got out.

Jennifer looked up at the white Georgian columns and massive second story veranda and immediately thought of *Gone with the Wind*. "Lawsie, we sure is all rich now!" she said aloud.

Jeremiah gave her a look; he didn't appreciate her humor. Turning to Peter, he told him that they should relax and get to know their new home. Jeremiah then got back in the limousine and left. They all stopped, took a long breath, and then opened the massive front door and walked through the main foyer and stopped dead in front of a white, circular, grand staircase to the second floor. Walking through the dining room and living room, they were amazed at the opulence. Everything was decorated in various shades of white. Each room was twice the size of their house. Ann was thrilled. Peter grabbed her around the waist and kissed her.

"This is God's payback, Ann, for all the hard work and sacrifice you've made for me over the years."

She loved him more than she had ever loved him. "I'm so proud of you Peter; after all your hard work and dedication to your people, now its time for your reward." They held each other in quiet gratitude.

Jennie's scream pierced the moment. Peter and Ann rushed upstairs and down the hall.

"Jennie, where are you?"

"I'm in here!"

Peter and Ann threw open the bathroom door.

"Look; look at that!" Jennie stood there next to the commode, staring at a menacing picture of Jesus. "I can't go with him looking at me."

Both Peter and Ann laughed. Peter took down the picture and put it in the closet. There were a lot of pictures of Jesus in every room; pictures of the nativity, the crucifixion, the resurrection. He was everywhere.

The next few days were filled with packing and crating up the furniture for storage. As the new parsonage came with everything, there was no point in moving their old, tattered second-hand furniture into their new home. When the last box was moved, Peter and Ann sat down in the living room to enjoy a Chinese dinner and several glasses of wine. It was a special night and even though it wasn't their anniversary, they decided to make it the start of a new life together. These would be the good times, filled with prosperity, success and fame. One thing led to another and soon they were kissing on the carpet in front of the fire.

Deep in the bowels of the church at the far end of the basement behind the archive storage area, there was a secret room. Only a handful of people knew about it; Jeremiah and a few assistants. On this night, a lonely figure sat inside surrounded by TV monitors; each one recording a different scene at the church parsonage. Nothing was hidden; nothing too personal. Jeremiah sat there with no expression just staring at monitor #7.

Like a seventeenth century inquisitor, he sat there watching Peter and Ann make love in their bedroom. He heard every word, and saw every naked touch. It went on for over an hour. When they finished, he pushed the record button on the console and the machine squealed as it did its work. Then with a click, the tape popped out of the machine. He labeled it and stuck it in a cabinet. It was as graphic as any pornographic film could be, but you'd never know it to look at Jeremiah's face, for he took no pleasure in what he saw. This was business. This was something to be used one day, if necessary to control Peter and Ann, and that made him smile.

Chapter Seven
The Power In The Word Je-Sus

Ann felt on top of the world as she stepped out of the limousine. They had always been poor as church mice and now that Peter was in the chips, she was determined to have some fun. She went through one shop after another down Chicago's Miracle Mile, and tried on shoes, coats, dresses, and put it all on the church credit card. Jeremiah had given Peter the card and told him to use it to beef up their wardrobe. Ann had always scrimped on her own clothes to make sure Peter looked good. After all, he was the one in front of the people on Sunday. But now it was her turn. When she threw down the American Express gold card with Temple Christian's name on it, the clerks jumped like jackrabbits. Nothing was too good for the preacher's wife.

When Ann got back to the estate, she saw three black cars parked in the driveway.

"I don't recognize those cars, do you Jimmy?"

The chauffer walked around to the front of the vehicles and then called out to Ann.

"They're from the Women's Auxiliary Committee. Mrs. Andrews, I'd advise you to watch out. They may smile like cats, but word is they're snakes, and everything they do is reported back to the Board."

Ann put her hand on Jimmy's shoulder and said, "Thanks Jimmy, I really appreciate the advice."

When Ann opened the door, Jennie was waiting for her. Talking in a whisper, she said; "The witches are in the living room."

Although she was worried, she decided to face the devil and walk into the living room smiling. "Welcome ladies; so nice to have you drop by."

Ann looked at the three elderly, white women and had to admit that Jennie was right. They did look like witches. All dressed in black with black straw hats and white ruffled blouses, they looked like they stepped right out of the 1930's. All three women stood up and spoke in unison, "We're the Church Women's Auxiliary Committee."

Miss Winslow spoke for the others; "We're here to welcome you, Mrs. Andrews, and help you make adjustments to becoming an appropriate leader for the women of the church."

"An appropriate leader?, Well ladies I can only hope that I'm able to serve as a beacon for all the women in the church."

As soon as she said it, Ann had trouble keeping the sarcastic comment down. It was so much blather and she knew it. She also knew that the church ladies would never catch her meaning. The three women sat down and opened up a large bag of cloths and pictures.

"My dear, my name is Miss Winslow, and I'm the Director of the Auxiliary. We brought you some samples of the types of cloths and colors that we feel are appropriate for a pastor's wife. You know we must be conscious to portray the right kind of woman to the young girls of the church."

Ann couldn't believe what she was hearing. Every word dripped of condescension and judgment. Holding down her mounting anger, she looked at the swatches and photographs.

"These colors seem all right, although they're rather conservative. But the women in these pictures… they look like they've stepped right out of the 1950's.

"Yes, we feel that the wife of a pastor should set the example by wearing styles that were of a more wholesome time."

Ann bristled at the arrogance; "Miss Winslow," Ann sighed and got up. "I hope you won't take this the wrong way, but there's no way I'm going to wear styles that even my mother would have refused to ware."

Miss Winslow got up, followed by the other two.

"We quite understand your reluctance. It was only meant as a suggestion. By the way, one more thing that has come to our attention; I, ah, hesitate to mention it, but could you tone down your figure a little?"

Ann's mouth dropped open. "What?"

Winslow glanced at the other ladies and indicated Ann's breasts.

"Well, you see, we have had some concerns that your... bosom may be a bit too noticeable. We wouldn't want our young Christian men distracted by your figure during your husband's sermons, now would we?"

Finally Ann could take no more. She burst out laughing. "Well ladies, I think I've heard it all. First you want me to dress like a spinster, then you want me to act like June Cleaver, but the final blow is that you think my breasts are too big! Tell me, do you think I should have them altered, just for the sake of our Christian boys?"

Winslow was quick to respond. "Well that could be arranged, and of course the church would pay for it."

Ann had had enough. "Good day ladies. Thanks for coming by, and may God bless you in your search for the perfect pastor's wife, but she doesn't live here."

All three stormed out and immediately got into their cars and left. Ann was furious. How dare they tell her what to wear and the crack about her breasts; she just couldn't believe they had the nerve. As she sat there in the living room thinking about what had happened, the phone rang. She answered and it was Peter telling her that he had several meetings that would last until late and not to expect him for dinner. Ann didn't mention the three women and just said okay and hung up. After the call, she went straight to the French provincial cabinet in the study and got out the bourbon. This called for a drink, a nice tall glass to help the hypocrisy go down.

Several hours later, as Peter waited outside Jeremiah's outer office for what was to be their weekly meeting, the three women from the Auxiliary Committee came out of Jeremiah's office. Peter smiled, but none of them smiled back. As he entered Jeremiah's office, he was amazed at the decor. The office was all trimmed in ebony with crimson accents. The windows were covered with thick, black curtains that cut out the sun. The only light came from a small lamp on Jeremiah's desk and a light that illuminated a huge picture of a rather stern looking Jesus behind Jeremiah's large, burgundy, leather chair. The whole effect was one of foreboding power and spiritual darkness. Jeremiah however, was all smiles as he asked Peter how he liked his new house. Peter had to admit that he'd have to be pretty ungrateful not to like their new home.

"Peter, we are very pleased with your sermons. In the past several weeks you have moved our congregation many times with your mastery of the language, the Bible, and the Gospel of salvation. In fact our researchers at my institute have analyzed your sermons and found that you've scored an average of 78 in our satisfactory category."

Peter was a little confused. "A 78, what is that? And what is your institute?"

"Peter, we score each sermon on a graph of suitability of words, as well as speaking style, and the ability to move the congregation. As to my institute, in due time I will let you know more about me and my grand plans for your future. Now, there is one area that we need to discuss; and that is the terminology that you use."

Peter sat up in his chair to get closer. "What do you mean by terminology?"

"According to our analysis, you used the term God, 10 times; Christ, 23 times; and Jesus, only once."

"So what are you getting at?"

Jeremiah got up and came around the desk and sat on the corner. It was his attempt to be more personable. "We have found that very few Christians ever say the word God. Some in mainstream Christianity still say Christ, but we've found that the word 'Jesus' has a certain cadence that releases the inhibitions of our people. Lord is also good; but the word 'Jesus', especially if you split the word into two syllables and elongate the first 'Je' part, has a tendency to be magical. This is extremely important if it's used just before the offering. Je-e-e-e-e… sus, or Ja-a-a-ae… sus as some have come to use it, has increased our offerings by over 40%. So from now on, we'd like you to use Jesus at least 30 times in your sermons. Anything less than 30 shows up as a drop in giving. Other than that, everything is fine… oh by the way, you might tell Ann to tone down her attire just a little. Some of our ladies are quite conservative and aren't used to the new styles of today."

Peter swallowed hard and said he'd try and do better next week. He also said he'd talk to Ann. As he left, he felt like he'd just been to the principal's office in grade school. He walked out into Temple Christian's Garden of Gethsemane and sat under the trees. His mind was spinning. He'd never heard of this kind of analysis of a minister's sermons or heard about the use of Jesus over Christ. He had to ask himself; was there a difference? He remembered the other seminary students discussing the back woods churches and how they would get caught up in an almost trance-like state when they used the word Jesus. No wonder they called it the 'Jesus Temple'.

What was going on here? Is this a church or a business? It was a question that would haunt him in days to come. Peter stopped in and told his secretary that he'd be out for the afternoon, but would be back for the meeting later that night. Before he left, she gave him a manila envelope. He didn't think much about it, but after he got in the limo, he opened it.

The cover sheet said Sunday Sermon Analysis. He couldn't believe what he was seeing. Each word had a small blue number by it. The numbers represented the strength of terminology and likelihood to produce revenue at the offering. Words like Christ and Lord were fairly high, over 70 on the enclosed chart, but the word God scored only 45. When he came to Jesus, it was a 95. At the end of the sermon was an analysis of his talk and the suggestion that he incorporate the word Jesus a minimum of 30 times.

It also recommended that he refer to Christians as being victims and not as victors in life. The report went on to explain that people who identify themselves as being persecuted are more likely to band together and follow the leadership from the pulpit. It also said that sermons that talk about how Christians are being persecuted, whether true or not, result in a significant increase in offerings. It was also suggested that even though Christians made up the largest faith group in the world at 33%; it was unwise to mention it, but to rather talk about incidents where Christians were persecuted.

Peter stared out the window of the limo as it made its way across town. He felt numb, like he'd just entered another world; a world that he didn't understand. What had he gotten himself into? Where was the heart? He always knew Jeremiah was cold, but now he wondered about whether the Jesus Temple had any heart at all. It was too much. He had to bury it deep inside his mind until later.

That afternoon, Jennifer and her new friend Rod went upstairs to her room and listened to music. Jennie was already pretty fed up with church people, and couldn't wait until she was 18 so she could be out on her own. Rod told her that his dad was on the Board of Trustees, but that they didn't speak much anymore. He too was sick to death of church and couldn't wait until he was old enough to take off. Together, they got to know each other and fantasized that they would one day leave together and never come back.

They smoked cigarettes and laughed and shared their loves and hates. One thing led to another and it wasn't long before Rod was sharing more than just his dreams. Jennie smiled as he produced a plastic bag of pot. This was a first for her. She had been sheltered for most of her life and drugs were definitely not part of her history, however Rod showed her how to get the most out of each joint. Together they lay on the bed, laughed and sang and eventually drifted off to sleep.

About an hour later, Peter came home and immediately went into the living room to relax. Ann came in, and seeing the mood he was in, walked over to the cabinet and poured him a glass of wine. She asked him how his day went, but she was reluctant to tell him about the visitation she had that afternoon. It was difficult for him to begin. Walking around the room, he was visibly upset. Ann went over to him and tried to get him to sit down, but he was too agitated to sit.

"What's going on Peter?"

He took out the manila envelope and dropped it on the sofa. "Here it is. It's all in there, and you won't believe it."

Ann took the envelope and opened it. As she read she could scarcely believe what she saw. "What is this, about Jesus?"

Peter took another drink. "I'm supposed to say Jesus thirty times, do you believe it?"

Ann laughed and poured herself another drink. "What nonsense."

Peter sighed and then plopped down on the sofa.

"What are you going to do, Peter?"

"I guess I've got to find a way to comply. I mean, if it makes such a difference in the Sunday offering, with what they're paying me… it's the least I can do."

Ann was disgusted. She'd hoped Peter would fight back and stand up to Jeremiah. "So that's what you're going to do? For the money, it's always the money, isn't it? What happened to the simple itinerant preacher that wanted to help people and make a difference in the world?"

All of a sudden Peter was furious. "Look, Ann, I'm doing this for you, damn it! For you and Jennie; I can't very well be an itinerate preacher and give you this kind of house and all those fancy clothes you're wearing, not to mention the big salary and chauffer-driven limousine, on a poor preacher's salary! And by the way, they want you to tone down your wardrobe a little."

"They want me to get a breast reduction! Did you know that? They want me to have surgery so that I'm not a distraction to all the virginal, young boys." Ann walked over to the cabinet and poured herself a tall glass of bourbon. "Let's not kid ourselves, Peter.. You're doing this for you. Jennie and I are along for the ride, but it's your roller coaster and this is your amusement park. That's what it is, a Jesus amusement park, and sweetie, you're the main attraction in this show."

When Ann went to bed that night, she and Peter were barely speaking. She looked through her closet for something 'appropriate' for Sunday. Then she saw it, a flaming red dress that would set the church bells ringing. Low cut and sexy; she was determined that no one, not even Peter was going to make her into a little church lady.

Chapter Eight
Everything Belongs To Me!

That next Sunday would prove to be a pivotal moment for Ann. They left the house at the normal time and arrived at Temple Christian about an hour before the main service at eleven o'clock. Jennie refused to go once again, which only fueled the church gossip about the pastor's absent teen. That day, Peter left early because he was uncomfortable with his new instructions from Jeremiah about saying Jesus over and over again to increase the donations. Ann, however was even more of herself than ever before. Maybe it was the spirit of Pope Joan or a thousand other feminine martyrs that gave her the courage to flaunt herself before Jeremiah and all those closed-minded church ladies.

As she walked to her special seat in the front of the first balcony, she stood for a moment and gazed at the thousands staring up at her. Her mind raced. Did she really have the guts to do it? She hesitated for a moment and then saw the church ladies all turn in unison and look up at her. Ann smiled and waved and then took off her dark topcoat. Her crimson dress caught the sunlight and seemed to glow as if it were on fire. There was a stunned silence from the crowd, followed by a cacophony of murmurs. She could imagine what they were all saying. As the service started most of the people turned to face the pulpit and Peter's dramatic entrance, however a good number of young teenage boys continued to stare at Ann. She had never looked more radiant and sexy, and for once she enjoyed all the attention she was getting.

Peter struggled that day and it was clear to Ann, at least, that he looked and sounded like a fish out of water; like he was fighting to find enough air to speak. Despite her defiant attitude to stand up for herself; her only thought now was to go to him now that he was in trouble. She'd never seen him in so much torment when he spoke. Sermons had always come easy for him, but when she heard him stutter and saw his hand tremble as he took out a handkerchief to wipe his brow, she knew he needed her. She quickly stood up and left the balcony. Making her way along the many corridors and hallways towards Peter's office; she wanted to be there when he came in after the service.

The office was empty and cold. She paced around the desk and chairs, stopping to look at the books of Dr. Remington and paintings of Jesus, but she didn't find a single picture of her or Jennie. Jesus was everywhere; Jesus at the Last Supper, Jesus at the well, Jesus in the temple, and Jesus on the cross. It was all too much, she thought. How could any man, preacher or otherwise feel good about himself when everywhere he looked, the perfect Christ was always looking down upon him and judging him. Ann walked over to Peter's desk. On the top of the desk were several Bibles and his private calendar. She stooped over to get a better view and saw that he was scheduled to attend over twenty-five meetings that week, along with teaching four classes and holding two workshops. On his desk there were two golden crosses with the words 'Positive' and 'Negative' inscribed on each base. Stuck on these spindle-like crosses were comments and complaints from the congregation. She couldn't help but notice that the 'Negative' cross had dozens and dozens of complaints on it, while the 'Positive' cross had only a couple. Sitting down in Peter's chair, Ann could feel the whole weight of ministry cascading down upon her shoulders. She never really understood the level of responsibility and stress that Peter had been under. She had always wanted to be a minister, but today she finally realized that what she fell in love with was the idea of ministry; the prestige and the cloak of religious dignity that only a minister could wear. Now she understood how immense Peter's burden had always been, especially now. She gazed up at the painting of Jesus on the cross.

No wonder it killed him. She couldn't help but wonder if it would kill Peter too. With that thought, the door opened and Peter came in. He looked terrible. His shirt and robes were stained with sweat. He looked at her and winced, then without a word he came over and took out of bottle of Scotch from his desk and poured himself a drink. Then, collapsing on the Italian leather sofa, he closed his eyes, tilted his head back and sighed. "Oh God, that was awful!" As Ann was about to go to him, a dark shadow appeared in the doorway.

"I couldn't agree more," said Jeremiah.

His sudden appearance startled Ann. "Where'd you come from?"

"Oh, I get around. Peter, why don't you take the rest of the day off and Monday as well. Let's get together on Tuesday for lunch. I'd like to show you something."

With that he walked around behind Ann and put his hands upon her shoulders. She could feel the coldness of his hands reaching all the way down to her feet.

"Ann," he said, "I just love your dress. It's so… Christian."

With that he squeezed her neck so hard that she thought she was going to pass out. Then in a split second, he was gone. Ann didn't know whether or not to tell Peter about Jeremiah's touch. After a moment, she decided to keep it to herself.

Peter said he wanted to get away for awhile and not go home. They both decided that they needed to go back where life was simpler, and made the long drive to Richland Seminary. They had both been happy there, and life was simpler when the future was unknown. On the way over, Ann called Jennifer and told her that they would be out late and to go ahead and fix herself dinner. Jennifer said that Rod was there and that she'd fix something for him too. Ann told Peter that Rod was at the house and that he and Jennifer had been seeing each other for some time. She wondered if he was good for her, but Peter assured her that Rod came from a good Christian family and that there was no cause for concern.

After the call, Jennifer ran upstairs to her bedroom and told Rod that they could order pizza and listen to music for awhile, and that her folks would be out late. Rod had only known Jennie for a few weeks, but already they both felt the chemistry. His father, Dr. Robert Anderson, was a significant member of the Board of Trustees of the church. What made him significant was the amount of money he contributed to the church every month. What made him insignificant, however, was his total lack of interest in his son.

They had one thing in common; a mutual distaste for everything their parents stood for. For Rod, it was his father's Christian values and demand for absolute obedience. For the most part, Rod ignored his father, spending most of his time in his own world of music, computers and drugs. For both of them, it was really about freedom. Neither he nor Jennie found much interest in the church, but what they really hated was Jeremiah. They both laughed and tried to come up with a description for him. Finally, in a burst of creativity and marijuana, they had it—The Black Ghost. That's what he was, a slithering creature with death in his eyes and a cross around his neck.

That Sunday afternoon was filled with laughter, drugs and sex. Both Rod and Jennie were all too eager to make the most of their freedom. If they couldn't be physically free, at least they'd be free in their minds, and the drugs would take them there. It didn't take long for both of them to find what they were looking for; an end to their loneliness in each other's arms. Jennie was young, but not naïve. She knew a thing or two about sex, but that day, she learned a whole lot more. Rod insisted that they get it on in only one room; the vacant apartment over the garage. When Jennie asked him why, and that it would be a lot more comfortable in her room; he said it was because the house was bugged. Rod told her that he'd heard his father talking on the phone about a secret room in the basement of the church. He'd never seen it himself, but he'd heard that it had video monitors that recorded everything that happened in the big house.

Jennie would have normally been shocked, but she was too high to really comprehend what he was talking about. That day, she was fortunate. Although she put up a good front, it was obvious to Rod that this was her first time. He took time for her and was sensitive and patient as they explored each other's bodies. It was obvious that he really cared for her. The sex would last only a short time, but the pot would last for hours.

When Ann and Peter finally drove onto the Richland seminary campus, they both felt a sense of relief. As they walked the long tree-shrouded walkways and felt the cool moonlight on their faces; they felt closer and more in love than they had in a long time. Peter said he felt more at home at Richland than at Temple Christian, and Ann confessed that she wished they could trade it all in, and go back to that little church with a couple of hundred people. Peter held her close and said that although they had been happy there, he also reminded her how much they struggled during those years. Ann agreed, but also admitted that life was better before "he" came into our lives. Peter stopped and sighed.

"I'm embarrassed to say it, but I've got some real doubts about..."

Ann finished his thought. "Jeremiah?"

"Not just Jeremiah, but the whole church. There's something wrong and I don't know what it is or what to do about it." Ann squeezed his hand.

"I know, they've got a lot of people and money, but something's not right. As far as Jeremiah is concerned, I, ah…"

Ann couldn't finish her thought. She didn't dare tell him that Jeremiah frightened her and that maybe, just maybe he was not who he said he was. Peter looked at her and held her close. "I know Jeremiah is not like anyone we've ever known, but he did give me the greatest job any minister could ever hope for. We've got more money than we ever thought we'd have. This is the kind of opportunity that could really launch me into a national platform."

Ann stopped him. "Platform… you sound like a politician running for office. Are you?"

Peter laughed. "Don't be silly; of course not."

No matter how much he denied it, Ann could tell that Peter was trapped in a web of his own ambition. As they walked to Song Chow's Chinese restaurant, all Ann could think about was The Devil and Daniel Webster. Had Peter sold his soul to Jeremiah? Was he lost? Were they both lost? The sidewalk was dark and Peter was blind to her fears. As she entered the restaurant, she quietly wiped the tears from her face. Not noticing her pain, Peter smiled when the waiter remembered them and ushered them to their favorite booth. They sat there for the longest time, not saying anything, just holding hands; each one deep in their own thoughts.

The next day, Ann was off to Jennifer's school for a PTA conference, but Peter left to go fishing at Lake Glenview; something he hadn't done in years. After he rowed the boat to the center of a cove, he just sat there thinking. It was not really the fish he was after but a handle on his own soul. He questioned whether he should have ever gone into the ministry.

There were many things that he loved about it, but the burden of dealing with everyone's expectations was getting to be enormous. Everyone had an agenda for him. The members each had their own idea of how and what a minister was supposed to be. More often than not, you had to be a cross between Mother Teresa and Billy Graham. Half the time, people still resented the fact that you got paid for preaching.

Peter couldn't count the number of conversations he'd overheard where someone would say that the preacher should preach for nothing and get his reward in Heaven. It was all so insane, and it all had to do with Jesus. Jesus this and Jesus that; it seemed that these people believed in Jesus, but they didn't believe what Jesus was all about. His message of love and compassion seemed to just fade away amidst the dollars and sermons and building projects. Jesus said he'd make them 'fishers of men', but all he felt like he'd become was a fisher of money and power. His mind was torn between who he was and who he thought he should be. After he rowed the boat to the pier, he walked toward the lodge. It was then that he heard the voice again.

"Be at peace. All things work according to my plan for you."

Peter turned around; looking for someone, anyone, but there was no one near. For the first time, a sense of peace came over him. It was like a calm breeze that gently flowed in the early evening. Had he witnessed something? Had God actually spoken to him? Maybe he was on the right path after all.

On that Monday, Ann came home alone after the PTA meeting. Jennie was no where to be found. As she walked into the house, Jeremiah stood in the kitchen drinking a glass of wine. "What are you doing here? You're not supposed to be in here. This is our house."

Jeremiah slowly drank his wine and turned to her. "This is MY house, and don't you ever forget it. This is mine. This church is mine, this house and everything in it belongs to me."

"You're drunk. Get out!" Ann brushed past him in a fury, but he grabbed her by the hair and twisted her back. Holding her arms behind her, he ripped off her coat.

"Wearing the God damned red dress again, I see."

Ann winced as he twisted her arms behind her. "Let me alone, you bastard!"

"You are so naïve. When I said everything belongs to me I meant everything; Peter, and Jennifer, and YOU!" With that he kissed her forcing his tongue down her throat. She felt sick and tried to get away but his power was overwhelming. Finally he stopped and getting her arm free, she slapped his face with all the strength she could find. She looked up at him, and it had no effect. Then she saw his eyes turn red. Like a demon, he slapped her sending her tumbling across the kitchen floor crashing into the cabinets. Ann was barely conscious and couldn't see anything but a blur. He stepped over to her and reached down and lifted her up off the ground. Then, with his face next to hers and covering her with his hot breath, he grabbed her breast and squeezed it. The pain shot through her and radiated into every part of her body. It was so intense that she collapsed on the floor. As he left, Jeremiah turned and said, "Now you have seen a small sample of my power. Holding up his silver cross from around his neck, "Don't you ever cross me again! You will do what you're told and be the proper minister's wife or else. Do I make myself clear?"

Ann could only nod and whimper as Jeremiah slammed the door. Clutching her breast, she staggered upstairs to the bedroom and passed out on the bed. That day, the dreams came back; little girl dreams of her father's molestation. She silently cried the rest of the day. Peter finally came home and although Ann made some small talk at the dinner table; neither Peter nor Jennie had any clue that she'd been assaulted.

Ann vowed she would never tell Peter. She couldn't, not now. While Peter slept that night, Ann spent several hours in the bathtub, crying and thinking about her life and what the future held for her. One thing was sure, she had to get away from Jeremiah somehow, some way. She was also sure that Peter was not strong enough to go with her. He was trapped by his own ambition and self delusion.

Chapter Nine
The Jesus Factory

The next morning, Peter's appointment with Jeremiah was at 10:00. As he was ushered into Jeremiah's private inner office for the first time, he couldn't help but look around. The room, like the outer office, was very dark and ornate. The walls were covered with religious paintings. One very extreme work was a disturbing painting of Dante's Inferno. There was one large painting of Jesus over Jeremiah's desk. It was a strange picture of the Last Supper. Although at first it appeared like it was a reproduction of DaVinci's famous masterpiece; on closer inspection it was sinister in the most subtle of ways. The faces of all the disciples were strangely contorted so that they looked almost evil in appearance. The entire painting gave Peter a cold feeling that he couldn't quite shake. As he was about to reach up and touch the painting, Jeremiah swept into the room like a cold wind.

"It's Spanish in origin, the fifth century I think. I got it in Mexico many years ago. Do you like it?"

Peter turned away from the painting and sat down next to the large desk. "It's very different, isn't it?"

Jeremiah came around the desk and sat down. "Yes, the artist's view of our Lord is most unique. Now let's get down to business. I thought your sermon on Sunday was— troubling. You seem to have had a great deal of difficulty concentrating. I don't blame you. Your wife's appearance was impossible to ignore."

Peter interrupted him; "It wasn't about her, I just had trouble with the structure that you've given me for my sermons."

Jeremiah was quick to respond; "The Jesus thing?"

Peter nodded. "I've never had to worry about what I said in a sermon. As long as I didn't stray too far from the Gospel, I was in safe territory, but now..."

Jeremiah put his hand on Peter's shoulder. "But it all feels so technical, doesn't it. You must understand that my organization has done a great deal of research into what makes a church successful. We represent over a thousand churches in our network, each one growing from 25% to 50% per year, with the average donation of $56.00 per person per week."

"Your organization.. I'm a bit confused. Do you work for more than this church?"

"Look, Peter, we could sit here all afternoon and I could tell you about the network, or I could just show you. Let's take a ride."

Peter smiled, "Okay. Is it far?"

"It's about an hour's drive from the church. While we travel, I'll tell you how I got started. You'll be surprised to know that, like you, Peter, I too came from humble beginnings."

As they sat in the back of Jeremiah's limousine, he told Peter of his humble beginnings in Romania and how his first ambition was to be a priest.

"What stopped you?" asked Peter.

"The war. When the Germans marched into my country in October of 1940 I had to make a choice, either join them or fight them. Since I was only 19, I couldn't very well stop them, so I joined them."

"You became a Nazi?" asked Peter.

"No, of course not, I was a member of the Iron Guard; a very elite group of soldiers assigned to protect Ion Antonescu, the conducator, or leader, as you would've called him. After the war, Romania fell behind the Iron Curtain, and I fled the country."

Although Peter didn't know it at the time, he would later learn that the Iron Guard was originally called the Legion of the Archangel Michael. It changed its name to the "Totul Pentru Tara" party, which meant "Everything for the Fatherland". It was a very fanatical religious organization whose anti-Semitism was so extreme that the violence of its pogroms had to be restrained by the Nazis. Its members were called Legionnaires and were required to perform fanatical and violent actions that would condemn them to damnation, which was considered the ultimate sacrifice for the nation.

Ignorant of Jeremiah's true nature, Peter sat there listening to him talk about the good old times in Romania during the war. It was a good story, but something wasn't right. If Jeremiah had been 19 in 1940, that would make him 87 years old. Although it was difficult to tell his age, as his skin was stark white with no wrinkles or imperfections; there was no way Jeremiah was that old. Peter sat there, deep in thought. His questions about Jeremiah were mounting, but he couldn't tell Ann. She was more than a little skeptical of Jeremiah's motives, and besides, the money they made took a lot of stress out of their relationship; so why risk derailing the gravy train now. He'd just have to keep up a good front and bury his feelings about Jeremiah. He could do it. He'd had a lot of practice hiding his feelings. It was a basic requirement of ministry, and he'd become a master at it.

As the limousine pulled off the Dan Ryan Expressway to the Edens and then to the Tri-State Tollway along Lake Michigan, Peter took time to see the changing leaves. Eventually the car turned off the main highway onto an isolated paved road that led into the woods. Peter was fascinated with all this. Ahead of them loomed a large wrought-iron gate and a 20-foot-tall chain-link fence. A guard all dressed in black approached. Jeremiah waved and the guard smiled and let them pass.

"This is my small enterprise, Peter—J.F. Industries."

The road led to a huge complex of black buildings with guards and guard dogs everywhere.

"J.F., what does that stand for?" Jeremiah smiled.

"It's my name, Jeremiah; Jeremiah Faust."

Peter felt a cold chill run down his spine. In all the time he'd been at Temple Christian, he'd never heard anyone refer to Jeremiah as any thing but his first name. Faust. The name carried the weight of history and of a legend of Dr. Faustus who'd made a pact with the Devil to sell his soul.

Jeremiah could see that Peter was troubled. "Faust, my boy is just a word. In Latin it means 'lucky' and yes, I know about the historical references to Faust's pact with the Devil." Jeremiah laughed. "It's all just a pleasant bedtime story."

As they made their way into the main building, Peter was amazed by the look of the place. Everything was black—walls, ceilings, floors. The lack of windows only enhanced the feeling that you were in a very elegant underground bunker. All of the doors and furniture were brightly polished chrome and it had the feeling of hidden elegance. They walked down a long hallway toward a massive security screening system.

Peter chuckled. "An eye scanner? You must be very concerned with security here."

"Yes", said Jeremiah, "and you will see why."

The large metal door opened and they both entered the main information gathering center. Jeremiah kept walking, but Peter had to stop to take it all in. The center was the size of a small football stadium with at least five or six hundred people all dressed in black, working at computer terminals. There were dozens of huge computer screens on the walls, each one playing a video of some minister giving a sermon. At the bottom of the screen was a computer analysis of what he was saying and some kind of rating system display.

"This is our main terminal room. Each computer terminal monitor on the wall is analyzing the sermon from one of our one thousand ministers. We analyze the length, strength and composition of the talk. We not only count the number of times he says Jesus, but we can also tell how his sermon is affecting the congregation".

"What do you mean?" Peter said.

Jeremiah walked over to a man sitting at a computer terminal. "Robert, pull up 3150 center section for last Sunday."

Instantly Peter saw a section of a church congregation. Then the display zoomed into a single man's face to analyze his eyes, mouth, and facial expression. Numbers and codes flashed on the screen next to eyes, mouth, forehead, and body. All of these figures were instantly being analyzed by the computer to assess the success of the sermon.

"We can tell if this man is feeling fear, joy, comfort, discomfort, anger, or even boredom, just by analyzing his facial composite. Based on the ratings generated by our data, we can predict to within five dollars, the amount of money that this man will give in the offering. Of course our goal is to always make him slightly fearful or angry, uncomfortable or even jubilant. We must always keep him in an emotional state. You see, the basic emotions of fear, guilt, and anger are motivators for what we call Submissive Christians.

Peter was, more than a little intrigued. "What do you mean by Submissive Christians?"

"Well, Peter, there are two kinds of Christians, one kind studies the Bible, asks questions, is well-read and has a curious mind. This kind of Christian gets their news and information from many sources. They tend to be open-minded, inclusive and tend to not be too judgmental of others. That sounds like Jesus, doesn't it? Well that's the worst kind of Christian for us." Jeremiah looked at Peter's face, which was a roadmap of confusion.

"I can see that you're very troubled."

"Yes, I am" said Peter.

Jeremiah put his arm around his shoulder. "Let me tell you about our kind of Christian. The Submissive Christian is not well-educated, not inclusive, and they tend to believe whatever they are told, especially if the source is one they trust. In short, they are submissive to authority. They tend to come from very patriarchal families where the father rules. When they are children, they learn to obey and not question. As the Bible says in First Peter:13, *For the Lord's sake accept the authority of every human institution...* and of course the Fifth Commandment, *Honor thy Father and Mother...*For centuries these people have made the church very powerful. They obeyed the priest and Holy Mother Church with complete faithfulness and fear. They couldn't read or understand the Bible and the priest told them what it said and meant. It's that way today, nothing much has changed."

Peter interrupted. "Yes I know... even today, even though people can read the Bible, they don't read it, and certainly don't study it or understand it. They..."

Jeremiah interrupted. "They memorize it, just like children. Peter, don't you see, this is why Submissive Christians are the source of great churches."

Peter felt like a cloud had been lifted from his mind. "You're looking for followers, not leaders. You want people who you can control." Jeremiah interrupted him again.

"We want people God can control. Peter, we want them to give when we need them to give; be frightened when we want them to be frightened, and to be angry when we need them to fight. These are our Christian Soldiers... marching off to a very real war."

Peter was exhilarated; "a war with the Devil!"

"Yes Peter, now you've got it!"

They walked around and talked with various members of Jeremiah's staff.

"Peter, there's one more thing I want you to see."

With that, they walked down another hall to a room that was anything but black. It was decorated with American flags and covered with posters and pictures of patriotic scenes.

"This is our American Manifesto room. I bring you here to give you our dream. God is in control of our world; but He is not like some mythical Greek god who amuses himself by tampering with our fate and makes life difficult for us for no particular reason. Far from it. Instead, the Bible shows us very clearly that our God—the God of the Old Testament and of the New—has His own political agenda. He has planned the ultimate final solution for all the problems of our world, and it is for that perfect remedy that every true Christian should pray.

The Bible tells us that God, the Creator of this earth, has had one specific purpose in mind for it from the beginning of time, and tells us quite unequivocally what that purpose is. The time is coming when God's laws will be enforced throughout the whole earth. The Word of God contains this divine political manifesto for the planet's future. It is a manifesto full of promises which God himself will deliver and towards which He is constantly at work in our world. Moreover, He gives us an absolute guarantee that what He has promised, he will deliver."

"I'm very confused, what does all this have to do with me?"

"Peter, you are the chosen one. Do you think your only purpose is to be a preacher in a church? We have much bigger plans for you. You will continue to preach for five years. All this time we will be grooming you for political office. You will run for the Senate and win; we guarantee it. Once you've fulfilled a term in the Senate, you will then run for president."

Peter had to laugh. He'd never heard of anything so absurd. "What are you talking about? I don't have any political ambitions, and even if I did, politics cost money."

Jeremiah walked over to a man standing by a large steel vault. "Open it up." With that the guard opened the vault door. "Look inside Peter."

Peter hesitatingly walked over to the vault. Inside were stacks of money and gold bars from floor to ceiling. "Where'd all this money come from?"

Jeremiah smiled, picking up a gold bar, he handed it to Peter. Inscribed on it were the words: 'For God and Country'.

"Each church tithes 10% of every dollar they make to us each month. That's a thousand churches, each sending us about $50,000 per year. If you know your math, that's fifty million dollars per year, and we've been doing this for over ten years. By the time you run for president, we'll have all the money we need for a national presidential campaign. Now you see why you're here and why we need you. We will bring forth God's law and change the course of history."

Peter was speechless. He could hardly breathe. He knew that he couldn't tell Ann. She'd never believe it. As they walked back to the car, Peter was silent.

Peter looked around. Everywhere he looked he saw the initials J.F. He wondered if there wasn't something else here. Yes, it stood for Jeremiah Faust, but could it also be...? Yes, that's what it was. It all made sense now. It all came together. The Jesus Temple – JF, Jeremiah Faust, That's what Jeremiah had built—not just a Jesus Church, or a Jesus Temple, but a Jesus Factory.

Jeremiah had a business; a manufacturing business; with a product... and the product he was selling was Jesus. Jeremiah had built a Jesus Factory and he, Peter Andrews, stood on the threshold of his own greatness. It all sank in now—his place in the cosmos—Senator Peter Andrews—President Peter Andrews. This is what the voice meant, *Be at peace, your path is given. All things work according to my plans for you.* The long ride back to Temple Christian was like a dream. There was a new inner resolve in him. He had a new mission. He would do whatever Jeremiah asked of him, and nothing would get in his way, not Ann, not Jennie, nothing.

* * *

The weeks passed and with the passage of time so grew the chasm between Peter and Ann. Although there were no fights or disagreements, there was a widening gulf between them. Peter spent more and more time at the church, while Ann tried to busy herself helping Jennie with school and shopping. The church continued to grow and the offerings came in larger than ever before. It was during the one year anniversary celebration of Peter becoming Temple Christian's pastor that Jeremiah announced that they had been contacted by Christianity Today. It seems that Peter's reputation had spread nationwide. Everyone was excited at the recognition and national prominence that Peter had obtained—everyone except Ann.

Ever since her encounter with Jeremiah, her breast had continued to bother her. At first it was just an occasional ache, but as time passed it developed into an intense throbbing at night. After weeks of trying to ignore it, she finally decided to see a doctor. The normal clinic and medical staff that the church provided as part of Peter's insurance policy, was less than three blocks from the church. However, Ann didn't want the church to find out about her condition. She worried that it would reflect upon Peter's standing and definitely didn't want to reveal Jeremiah's assault. To keep it all quiet, she chose a doctor in a Hispanic clinic on the other side of town. Doctor Rodriguez could not have been kinder. He examined her and asked her how long she had felt pain in her breast. Ann told him about Jeremiah and the difficult situation she was in at the church. After numerous x-rays and blood work-ups were performed, Rodriguez called one Saturday morning. Jennie picked up the phone, and had a hard time understanding Rodriguez.

"I'll get it, Jennie," Ann said.

Jennie was about to run upstairs, when she saw the color drain out of her mother's face. Ann hung up the phone and sat down.

"What's up, Mom?"

Ann looked up at her with tears in her eyes and immediately ran into the den to get a drink. She poured a tall glass of wine, gulped it down and turned to face Jennie.

"Mom, well what's going on? Why are you so upset?"

"Jennie, Dr. Rodriguez wants to see me today. It must be serious because he never sees anyone on Saturday. Will you go with me?"

"Sure, when's your appointment?"

Ann poured another drink. "Two o'clock."

They drove across town in silence. Neither talked, but both knew what the other was thinking. It was the foreboding feeling that something bad was coming. But whatever happened, they had each other.

Jennie sat in the empty medical office waiting for her mother. After about 45 minutes, a nurse came out and got Jennie. "Your mom wants you to come back." Jennie hurried to the back of the hallway and was ushered into an examination room. Ann was lying on a table, propped up talking with Dr. Rodriguez.

"Jennie, this is Dr. Rodriguez," said Ann.

"How you doing, Mom?"

Ann didn't answer her, so Rodriguez spoke up. "Jennie, your mom has a lump in her breast."

Jennie felt like someone just punched her in the gut. Tears started to well up in her eyes.

As they looked at the x-rays, Rodriguez explained that the position of the tumor was difficult to reach but that they needed to take a biopsy to determine if it was malignant.

"When do you want to do it?" asked Ann.

Rodriguez didn't hesitate. "I'd like to do it right away."

Rodriguez explained that he was going to refer her to Dr. Palatine for the surgery. After their appointment, Ann and Jennie decided to walk around the corner to a small restaurant for lunch, but neither could eat. Silently they stared out the window and sipped on a cup of coffee. Jennie could remain silent no longer.

"What are we gonna tell Dad?"

Ann sighed with tears in her eyes. "We tell your father nothing."

"Why?" Jennie said.

Ann took hold of Jennie's hands and stroked them. "Your father is in a delicate situation with the church. Any scandal or bad publicity right now would damage his career."

"So what? Who cares about his damn career?"

"Jennie, please… I can't get into my reasons now, but just trust me. Your father is not to know, not yet."

Chapter Ten
Thou Art Woman

It wasn't hard to keep things from Peter in those days. He was enmeshed with Jeremiah's plans and meetings, and his ego was flying so high, that he barely noticed that Ann was cold and withdrawn and spending long hours away from home. He just chalked it up to moodiness and an unwillingness to embrace his future.

A week after Ann's appointment with Dr. Rodriguez, she was referred to Dr. Palatine, an oncologist and specialist in treating breast cancer. Ann's experience with Palatine was as different as it could be. Whereas Rodriguez was kind and sensitive, Palatine was cold and distant. Palatine's waiting room was filled with women only, all on the edge of an emotional collapse; each one waiting for the surgical biopsy that would either relieve them or condemn them with the dreaded word—cancer.

As Ann waited in Palatine's waiting room, she could hear the anguished screams and whimpering of a woman in the back room. The more the woman cried and whimpered, the more she could hear Dr. Palatine's frustration. It was as if he had no sympathy or compassion at all.

After about an hour, Ann was ushered into the surgery examination room. Palatine came in after a nurse had cleaned her breast. Ann asked whether they would use some kind of anesthetic to deaden the pain, but the nurse said that Palatine didn't use it because it might affect the outcome of the pathology report.

"So, I've got to suck it up?"

At that point, Palatine walked into the room. He immediately went to work preparing Ann for the cyst aspiration. Ann jerked when a small needle was inserted into her left breast. While Palatine looked at the computer screen which guided his hand; the intense pain in Ann's breast became almost unbearable. Not since Jeremiah's assault, had she felt that kind of pain. It was like Jeremiah was in the room with them, stabbing her breast to make her pay for the unconscionable sin of having an independent mind. She looked up at Palatine, hoping to find some kind of emotional connection, some empathy and caring, but his face was as cold as his instruments. He was nothing but a detached mechanic with a job to do. Finally the pain became so intense that Ann passed out.

The nurse, noticing her, told Palatine; "She's unconscious, doctor."

"Good," he said. "If there's anything I can't stand it's a whimpering female". This makes my job easier."

After the procedure, the tissue sample was sent to the pathology lab for analysis.

Seven days later, Ann received a call from one of Palatine's nurses, saying that the sample was malignant and that they wanted to schedule her in for surgery as soon as possible. When Ann asked whether it was serious, the nurse told her it was a Stage Two, but they weren't sure if it had spread to the lymph nodes. They wouldn't know that until the surgery.

Ann asked, "What would it mean if it spreads to the lymph nodes?"

The nurse told her that it might mean a mastectomy. Ann hung up the phone. She was devastated. She went to the bathroom and immediately took off her blouse and bra to look at her breasts. Looking at them, she burst into tears and quickly covered herself with a towel. As she laid there on the bathroom floor sobbing, all of her faith in God evaporated.

There was something so frightening about the word cancer that drains the color out of you. The eyes are the first to tell you that mortality threatens. She remembered the faces of all the women who sat motionless in Palatine's waiting room. They all had that look. It was a look that said that no matter how many people loved and supported them, they were basically alone to face the darkest night of the soul. She, like most of them had prayed day and night for a positive test result, but now she felt like God had deserted her. Not since they took her father away when she was eight, had she felt so abandoned.

Now, all those feelings flooded back over her, the loneliness, the darkness, the anger and then the deep, deep sadness. The feeling persisted that somewhere in her past, she had sinned a great sin against God, and that was why this was all happening. Where did that thought come from? Now she remembered – watching her father being taken away by the police. She knew it was all her fault, that God was punishing her by taking her daddy away because she was bad. Of course, these were little girl thoughts and Ann knew that they were illogical and wrong, but there was something primal about her pain that made her connect with that same little girl who was left alone that traumatic night.

Although she had resolved not to tell Peter, she now knew she had to. She just couldn't go through this alone. She could only hope that his love for her was stronger than his ambition and obsession with the church.

The lumpectomy was scheduled for a Saturday morning two weeks from that day. Each day, Ann woke early before dawn and started her prayers. Each day she read the Bible and asked for forgiveness and then understanding. All of her background in the seminary and church history had told her that if Christians did all the right things, obeyed God, lead a good life and believed in Jesus, that nothing bad would happen to them. That was what she was taught over and over again. God punished the wicked with disease and misfortune and rewarded the faithful with health and joy. Yet in all her childish training, she knew deep down that it didn't make sense, not really. Bad things did happen to good people. Was it God's curse? Or was it just part of life and death? She didn't know.

Jennie handled the situation in a very different manner. Of course she cried and held her mother while she cried. They had done that many times, but she also took action. She got on the Internet and asked her friends to pray for her mom. She didn't know if it would make any difference, but she had to do something. She also decided that she would also be the one to tell her father.

It was a Sunday afternoon and Peter was in the middle of a Board of Trustees meeting with Jeremiah. Jennie stormed in and seeing her father deep in conference, threw her mother's medical records at him and screamed.

"She goes in for surgery next Saturday! Read it, God damn it!"

With that, she stormed out. She had never spoken to her father like this before, but she couldn't help it. She was mad; madder than she had ever been, and right now she hated the church for what it had done to them.

Of course, the board was shocked at Jennie's language. Peter apologized while he glanced at the medical papers. His face turned white as he saw the prognosis.

"I've got to leave. My wife needs me."

Jeremiah tried to stop him, insisting that the situation at home could wait, but Peter would have none of it. He immediately drove home, all the while whipping himself for his own insensitivity and emotional distance.

When Peter got to the estate, he could see that Ann's car wasn't there. First things first; a tall glass of Scotch in the library, then he had to take some time and figure out how he should approach her. He picked up the Bible from the bookcase. Opening it, he found the perfect verse. Suddenly the door opened and Ann walked in. When she saw Peter, she just stood there. He walked toward her holding out the medical records.

"Jennie threw these in my face today."

Ann sighed. "Well, what did you expect?"

Peter took a drink and walked back toward the bar area. "I would have thought that you would have been the one to tell me."

Ann took off her coat and walked over to the bar area to pour herself a glass of wine. "You're never here."

Peter snapped back in his own defense. "I've been doing the Lord's work."

That was too much for Ann. "Don't give me that!"

With that Peter shifted into his preacher role. "As the Bible says: *Therefore I say to you, whatever things you ask when you pray, believe that you receive them, and you will have them*; Mark 11:24."

Ann spun around in a rage and threw her glass at Peter. "How dare you quote the Bible to me, you sanctimonious…"

She couldn't finish without bursting into tears. She screamed, then turned and bolted upstairs to the bedroom, slamming the door. Peter was tempted to follow her, but stopped to get another drink. The front door burst open and Jennie walked in. Peter couldn't help himself. He had to take it out on someone.

"Jennie, how dare you burst into a board meeting like that!"

Jennie stopped and just stared at her father with contempt. "Screw you!"

Peter lunged at her and slapped her face. Jennie burst into tears and ran upstairs. As Peter took another drink his mind collapsed in confusion and self-loathing. What had he become? He'd never hit her before. He'd never hit anyone before. Two drinks led to three and then four, until he sank into the sofa in a drunken sleep.

It was very difficult for Peter to talk to Ann in the days that followed. She was cold and distant. Their eyes never met. Peter tried to understand her anger, but her silence left him grasping at the source of it all. "I know I've let you down, Ann. I've been way too involved at the church, but I didn't see… I should have been here when you found out. I should have been with you when you went to the doctor, but I didn't know." Ann had no response. "Look, I promise I'll be here for you from now on. All you have to do is call me and I'll come right home, no matter what I'm doing."

Ann looked at him, trying to find the Peter she once loved. After a long pause, she finally spoke. "I needed you Peter. This thing with Jeremiah; it's tearing us apart. You've got to be with me when I go in for the surgery. I need you to be there."

Peter came over to her and hugged her. "I promise. When is it?"

"It's a week from Saturday. I don't know the time yet, but it's some time in the morning." Peter kissed her on the forehead and held her close. "I have nothing on my schedule that day. So there's nothing to interfere."

"I need you to be there whether it's on your damned schedule or not!"

That week Peter and Ann got close again. He seemed like the old Peter that she fell in love with. They laughed and cried and just held each other. He told her over and over that she was his whole world and that he couldn't make it with out her.

The gulf between Peter and Jennie, however, remained uncrossed. They barely talked. Peter was still angry about her bursting into the church meeting, but he tried not to show it. Jennie couldn't forgive her father for not being there for her mom and for slapping her, and she did show it—every chance she got.

Jennie was there for her mom, but spent most of her time away from home staying with Rod. They had been close, but now a common contempt for their fathers increased their feelings for each other. There was lots of sex and drugs and talk of how religion was so corrupt and hypocritical.

Saturday came too quickly. Peter paced back and forth in the hospital waiting room, while Jennie kept to herself in the corner. When an older woman started to cry, Peter couldn't help himself and asked her how he could help. She said her daughter was dying and this was the end of a long journey of hospitals, cancer wards and loneliness. Her daughter was all she had and the pain was overwhelming. Peter told her he was a pastor and that he wanted her to know that Jesus was waiting for her daughter. Jennie, hearing her father, just shook her head in disbelief. Peter then started to preach about how it was time to accept the Lord and repent before the Devil took her daughter. The old woman started to cry and rant in a foreign tongue that Peter couldn't decipher. Finally, when the noise became a problem; a nurse came in and told Peter to stop preaching.

"But you don't understand, she needs to accept Jesus before her daughter's soul is stolen by the Great Deceiver."

The nurse became furious, telling him that the woman was from Checkoslovakia and spoke little English.

"That's no matter with Jesus." Peter said. "Jesus made the language."

Then the old woman held up a Star of David necklace that she wore. Suddenly it was clear that she was Jewish. Peter's evangelical rant suddenly subsided and he sat back down.

Jennie couldn't take it anymore, and walked over to Peter. "You just couldn't leave it alone, could you? You're supposed to be here for Mom, not your blasted Jesus!"

Peter felt terrible. What was the matter with him? He got up and left the room. Walking around the cafeteria, he sat down with a cup of coffee. As he sat there thinking, a couple of nuns came over to him.

"You're the one on the cover aren't you?"

The nun showed Peter the latest issue of Christianity Today. There he was on the cover standing in front of Temple Christian church. The headline read; *Is this, the new voice of God?* Peter smiled and told them that it was him. He signed their magazine, then went back to drinking his coffee. He had forgotten about the magazine article coming out. He should have felt elated at the publicity, but right now he couldn't feel anything. All he could think about was Ann. His mind soared back in time to when he and Ann first met in the seminary cafeteria. He could hear her once again asking if he wanted more rice with his fried chicken. The memory was a tonic. He wanted no more reality, no more church and responsibility, no more of anything—just Ann. All he wanted was Ann. He closed his eyes and dreamed of being back in time with her. Once again they were talking, and walking and having picnics together. Once again they were holding each other, laughing, kissing, and loving each other. Glimpses of their wedding; the people, the cake, all of it flooding back over him. He saw himself standing at the altar when the preacher asked him if he took Ann Parks to be his lawfully wedded wife. Peter stood there mute as if in a trance. Suddenly his best man tapped him on the shoulder, shaking him awake. He opened his eyes and said;

"I do, with all my heart."

"You do what, Dad?"

Jennie stood there looking at Peter.

"What?"

"Dad, mom's out of surgery. You'd better come."

Peter and Jennie hurried to the post-op room where Ann was sleeping. The nurse came in and told them that Ann was still recovering from the anesthesia and would probably be awake in about an hour. When Peter asked how the surgery went, the nurse told him they were lucky. They only had to remove one breast. Peter walked over to Ann and took her hand, but she wasn't responsive. Jennie just stood there with tears running down her face. Peter hugged her and then said;

"Jesus has blessed her. We should pray."

Jennie reared back, looking in her father's face. She shook her head and left the room. Peter was totally confused. What in the world had he done now?

Chapter Eleven
When The Bible Isn't Enough

Ann awoke to a room full of flowers, but neither Peter nor Jennie was there. The nurse came in and asked her how she was feeling. She said she didn't know yet, but she was in a lot of pain. The nurse told her that was normal after losing a breast, and that she'd still have feeling in the breast even though it wasn't there; that it was common in amputees. Then the nurse showed Ann the Christianity Today magazine.

"I thought this might cheer you up, with your husband being on the cover and all."

Ann told her to take it away. When the nurse left, Ann lifted her gown and looked at her chest. It was a mass of bandages, but it was clear that her breast was gone. She closed her eyes, as tears streamed down her face. After a while she drifted off to sleep.

When Ann opened her eyes, Dr. Palatine, Peter and Jennie were standing at the foot of her bed.

"How do you feel, Ann?" said Palatine.

"Terrific. How would you feel if someone cut your chest off?"

Palatine asked if she felt phantom pain or sensations in the breast that was removed. She said she did. He explained that during mastectomy, small nerves are cut between the breast tissue and the skin. This process, as well as the spontaneous firing of electrical signals from the ends of the cut or injured nerves, causes phantom sensations. Palatine explained that the phantom sensations may go away or not, but that stress had a lot to do with it. Ann looked at Peter and said;

"That's no problem is it Peter? We have no stress, do we?" After she said it, Ann turned her head away from Peter and faced the window.

Peter smiled a sheepish grin and left the room with Dr. Palatine to talk about Ann's recovery. As soon as Peter was gone, Jennie came over and hugged Ann.

"Mom; please don't die."

"Die? Who said I'm going to die?"

Jennie started to cry. "No one, but I just couldn't..."

Ann hugged her and reassured her that she would be just fine.

Peter told Dr. Palatine that he was at a loss in dealing with Ann. "I know the one thing I can do to help her, and that is to keep my big mouth shut."

Palatine asked Peter what he meant by that, and Peter told him that no matter what he said, it was the wrong thing. "Every word I say only aggravates the situation. I think my wife and daughter hate me, doctor."

"You're that minister on the cover of that magazine, aren't you?"

"Yes," said Peter, "but I certainly have been a failure with them."

Palatine thought for a moment; then recommended Peter have a talk with Father Raymond, the hospital chaplain. Peter said he'd think about it. When they finished, Peter came into Ann's room. Jennie looked at her father and then wiped her face and left.

"Where are you going, Jennie?"

"I'm going home. See you tomorrow, Mom."

Peter and Ann talked for about an hour. Peter tried everything he could think of to get close to Ann, but there seemed to be a great chasm between them and a sadness in her eyes that he hadn't seen before. As he left her room, he decided to find Father Raymond. The chaplain's office was on the main floor next to the chapel. Peter knocked, but no one answered. Then he looked across the hall and saw a priest talking to a young couple. Peter watched from a distance, so he couldn't hear what was being said, but it was obvious that the priest was good at his job. After about twenty minutes, the couple left. The woman wiped the tears from her face as she passed. Peter approached the priest.

"Are you Father Raymond?"

"Yes"

"My name is Peter Andrews. Dr. Palatine suggested that I talk to you about my wife."

Raymond looked at him for the longest time, saying nothing; then his face lit up. "You're the guy on the cover of Christianity Today. I read the article, most interesting."

Peter followed Father Raymond into his office.

"Please sit down. It's not much; not like your office at Temple Christian. It was in the magazine." He showed Peter the picture of his office in the magazine. "It must be nice to have an office like that".

Peter sighed. "I can't seem to get away from that magazine today."

"Well, you're a celebrity now," said Raymond.

"I certainly don't feel like a celebrity. Look, Father Raymond, I need your help. I've been a very successful minister, trained to comfort my people with the Lord's help, but I'm a failure with my own family. I can't seem to help my wife at all. She just went through surgery for breast cancer and lost her breast. My teenage daughter won't speak to me anymore. I just don't know what to do. My life seems to be falling apart. Everything I say just makes things worse."

"What are you saying?"

"Well, I've quoted scripture, but it doesn't seem to help. It only inflames them."

Father Raymond got out his pipe, filled it with tobacco, lit it and then leaning back in his chair, sighed. "Look, Reverend Andrews…"

"Please call me Peter."

The priest smiled and continued. "Peter, then. When I came here to be a chaplain, I carried my Bible with me everywhere I went. I'd come into someone's room and the first thing I did was to quote some inane scripture. Patients were pleasant, but cold and unresponsive. I thought just reciting scripture and using the Lord's name would fix it. Like you, everything I said just made things worse. I didn't get it. I didn't understand what they needed from me. I was self-righteous and very judgmental. It wasn't until an old man, a Mr. Zara, yes, that was his name, God bless him, threw the Bible in my face and told me to get out."

"Oh my god, what was he an atheist?" said Peter.

Raymond laughed. "No. This old man was the Supreme Patriarch of Antioch and all the East, Supreme Head of the Universal Syriac Orthodox Church, and a direct descendent in the line of Saint Peter."

Peter sat there in shock. "And he threw the Bible at you? Why?"

Father Raymond smiled. "Because I deserved it; quoting scripture was just hiding behind the Bible. It was easy to rattle off memorized Biblical passages and be done with it. The real challenge for me was to be present with the person, to hold their hand, to listen and have empathy with the pain that they felt."

When Peter questioned him about being a Christian and saving their souls, Father Raymond laughed.

"Peter, there is no need to save a soul that's not lost. Salvation is like climbing a mountain. There are many paths to the top. Christ's message was one of compassion, not judgment. Our task is to do what He would have done. Read your Bible, Peter, He didn't judge people unless they were hypocrites. I think there are more hypocrites in the Christian church than in all the other faiths combined."

Father Raymond took another puff on his pipe and smiled. "We talk about being our brother's keeper, but we condemn him if he doesn't believe what we believe, dress like we dress, love like we love, and pray like we pray. We Christians are quick to cast out and slow to embrace. Peter, your first challenge in being a minister is to be a human being. Your spirituality and your connection with the Christ will grow the more human you are." Peter struggled to understand. Father Raymond put his hand on Peter's shoulder.

"I think your wife needs a husband and a friend, not a minister right now. And I think your daughter needs a compassionate father and not a judge. Remember, as pastors, we must tend our flocks and that means we serve them, protect them, understand them and above all—love them—without conditions. In short, Peter, your job in your family is to make sure that your wife and daughter don't feel like they are alone. Love them, don't minister to them. That's your first ministry. All the rest doesn't matter."

Peter thought long and hard about what he had heard. Part of him knew that he heard the truth, but another part of him railed against anyone interfering with his divine mission. He stood up and stepped away from Father Raymond.

"I'm sorry, Father. I can't be what I'm not. I am called by God to preach and save souls. The rest doesn't matter."

Father Raymond shook his head in frustration. "I feel sorry for you, Peter. Some day someone will come along to tell you this again. I hope by then you haven't lost everything and are ready to listen."

With that, Peter left the hospital. He didn't go back to see Ann. He put his feelings aside. He was good at that. The only thing that was important now, was God's work. He went to the church to prepare his sermon for Sunday, but felt alone.

Her mother's surgery and father's attitude had left Jennie feeling like she was also alone, even though Rod was a big help—he was the one person she felt she could talk to. The next day, Peter and Jennie brought Ann home from the hospital. She was still in pain, but each day it subsided a bit. In addition to feeling abandoned by God, Ann also had to deal with the feeling that her own body had turned against her and attacked her; that cancer cells manufactured by her body were attacking her other cells. It was a strange feeling. She had spent her whole life taking care of herself and priding herself in looking good and now she just didn't care how she looked.

For Jennie, her mother's illness was a gateway to more drinking, drugs and time with Rod. She rarely went to church anymore and didn't care what people thought or said. She also didn't care that she was the minister's daughter. Her relationship with her father had deteriorated since he slapped her. He could never bring himself to apologize to Jennie and she felt like she could never trust him again. Peter continued to work day and night at the church, finding any reason he could to not be at home.

Two weeks after the surgery, a Federal Express delivery was waiting for Peter when he got home. He called out to see if anyone was home but the house was empty and dark. Turning on the lights he saw a note on the table that told him that Ann and Jennie were out shopping and wouldn't be home until after ten o'clock. Peter took the Federal Express envelope into the library to have a drink of Scotch while he opened it. The envelope contained a letter from Time magazine.

Peter's eyes lit up as he read that Time wanted to put him on the cover and would be sending a crew to film him in his Sunday service in three weeks. It was signed John T. Elson, Religion Editor and Assistant Managing Editor. Peter couldn't believe his luck. Just nine months ago he was a nobody in the Christian movement, now he was definitely going to be famous—first the Christianity Today cover, now Time's cover. This would launch his bid into politics. He felt on top of the world! The first thing he did was to call Jeremiah.

Jennie and Ann sat down in a quiet restaurant next to the shopping mall. They had shopped for several hours until they got hungry. Sitting there in the restaurant, Ann asked Jennie if something was bothering her.

"You mean something beyond the usual crap from Dad? Well, I've kind of been hesitant to bring it up, Mom, with you being sick and all…"

"Go ahead Jennie, what's going on with you?"

Jennie took a long drink of water, then looking around to make sure no one from the church was close by, she sighed. "Mom, I haven't been feeling well lately. I've been throwing up."

"Have you seen a doctor?"

"I don't need to see a doctor. I know what's wrong."

"Well, what is it? God, I hope it's not…"

"Mom. I'm pregnant."

There was total silence between them, as the waiter came over to get the orders. After he left, Ann took hold of Jennie's hand.

"I'm here for you Jennie. Is it…?"

Jennie nodded. "It's Rod's."

They ate their dinner in silence, rarely looking up. Finally Ann asked Jennie;

"Have you prayed?"

Jennie laughed. "It's a little late for that, mom".

Ann shot back; "It's never too late to pray."

"Maybe I should pray for Dad cuz he's gonna freak out when I tell him."

Suddenly the moment changed as they both looked at each other. "Jennie, you can't tell your father; not right now. If you do, it'll ruin him."

"So what? Who cares anyway?"

"Look, I know things have been rough for all of us, but he's still your father and he deserves respect".

"So when does he start earning my respect? "It's a little hard after the way he treated us."

"Jennie, your father has been under a lot of stress. I never realized how difficult ministry would be or how much it would cost us all. We've got to give this some time. You won't start showing until your fourth month."

"I don't know if I can just keep it a secret. Rod and I have talked about maybe getting married, but if we don't work out, I could always have an abortion."

Ann looked up at Jennie with genuine fear in her eyes. "Jeremiah! Oh my god, he'll never allow this to happen. Whatever you do, Jennie, if you decide to have an abortion, you have to leave. You'll have to get as far away from Temple Christian as you can."

"Why? What's so terrible about Jeremiah? I mean, he's creepy, but that's all, isn't it?"

"No, Jennie, that's not all. There's something very malevolent about Jeremiah, something so sinister and evil that he will never allow your baby whether it's living or dead to interfere with his plans."

"Mom, you're freaking me out."

"Sorry, I guess I just got carried away. Everything will be all right, you'll see. I'll make sure of that. Whatever you decide, I'll stand by you. Now let's get out of here."

Ann and Jennie hugged each other as they left the restaurant. They were closer at this moment than they had ever been before. They would see this through together, whether Peter was part of it or not.

Chapter Twelve
Jennie, My Jennie

The following days seemed to tumble one after another. While Ann struggled with her recovery from the surgery, Jennie had her own issues to deal with. Peter was rarely available now as the day approached when Time magazine would arrive. This was all complicated by the news that Time Warner's CNN would be covering Peter's sermon and planned to interview him live for a special they were planning called: 'The New Face of Christianity'.

When Jennie talked to Rod about their plans for the baby, he was distracted and not really sure about whether they should keep the baby or abort it. Jennie told him that she just couldn't go through with an abortion and that if she did, it would destroy her father. Rod told her he didn't care what the abortion did to her family, just so long as it was what the two of them wanted and the church didn't find out. They talked about adoption, but once again Rod told her that the church would never go along with it.

Their relationship was slowly starting to crumble. Jennie felt alone and confused. She tried to talk to Ann, but her mother seemed distant and depressed, and she certainly couldn't talk to her father. Peter had to be kept out of it. She turned to the only friend she that she could never do without—booze. The house was stocked with all kinds of liquor and no one seemed to notice that she was drunk every night after dinner. She was sinking into a hole of despair and there didn't seem to be a way out.

When she and Rod had a fight one night, she was crushed when he said terrible things about her and the baby. Her world was crashing in on her and the darkness seemed to get thicker each night.

Ann knew that Jennie was in trouble. She was aware of the drinking and although she was worried about Jennie's depression and feelings of loneliness; she just didn't feel like she had the energy to help her. Despite Dr. Palatine's assurance that it was normal, Ann couldn't shake the feeling that the daily pain she felt was indicative of more physical problems. She also felt a foreboding about her life and her family. The more Peter excelled in his ministry, the blacker her mood became.

This was especially true when she found out that Jeremiah's last name was Faust. All of her gut feelings about him were now validated. Suddenly, Ann's inertia disappeared. She had to find a way of warning Peter. Convinced now that they had all made a pact with the Devil, she called the church to try and reach Peter. This was the last day before the media's blitzkrieg on Sunday. When the receptionist finally answered the phone, Ann was told that Peter was somewhere in the building but no one seemed to know just where he was.

Ann slammed the phone down and immediately got in her car. Jennie came running out of the house in tears.

"Mom, please, I need to talk to you. Don't go, please."

"Sorry, Jennie, I can't talk to you now. You'll have to solve your problems your own way."

Jennie was crushed. The only person who could have helped her has now abandoned her. As Ann's car left, Jennie turned slowly and walked into the house. She methodically went from one room to another, drinking whatever liquor she could find. Drawers were thrown open and contents scattered through out the house. Finally, she opened a drawer in Peter's upstairs office and found what she was looking for. There it was—a 38 caliber revolver. Peter had purchased it for Ann when he worked late at the church. Jennie opened the cylinder and checked—it was fully loaded. She wiped her face, took another drink, got in her car and left.

As Ann pulled into the church parking lot, she noticed all the media vehicles from CNN. There were more than a hundred members of the television crew roaming about, carrying cables, setting up cameras and control units. Ann made her way through the chaos to Peter's office. Finding it empty, she talked to his secretary.

"I think he's in the basement, Ann. He said he wanted to find an old video tape of one of Dr. Remington's old sermons."

Ann made her way down the stairs and into the basement, which was the size of a small football field. There were hundreds of storage rooms of furniture and records. It took her over an hour to find Peter. She heard him curse as he slammed his finger in a door. Finally she saw him at the end of the hallway.

"Peter… it's Ann."

"Ann, what are you doing here?"

"I had to see you. I have this dreadful feeling that something bad is going to happen, and I wanted to warn you before tomorrow."

Peter smiled a condescending smile. "Remember Caesar when his wife had dreams? 'A coward dies many times before his death. The valiant never taste of death but once.'"

"Yes, Peter, I remember the quote, and I also remember what happened to Caesar."

"You're being a bit melodramatic, aren't you?"

"Look, Peter, I'm genuinely worried about you and Jennie. She's been drinking a lot lately."

"What's wrong with Jennie?" asked Peter.

"That's for her to tell you."

"I haven't got time now, Ann. I've got to find a Remington sermon for my talk tomorrow."

"Well, let me help. What are you looking for?"

"A room. There's a room down here someplace that has lots of video tapes in it."

Peter and Ann continued to look for the secret room. Finally Ann spotted a black curtain hanging from a doorway. When she opened the curtains, she discovered a door to another room. Peter came over and found that the master key, given to him by his secretary, opened the door. Once inside, they found hundreds of video tapes, video consoles, editing equipment and various boxes of cables and wires. As they looked through the tapes, they found several old Remington video tapes of his sermons. Peter instantly popped them into the console and started reviewing the sermons, while Ann looked around the room.

Just as Peter was about to finish reviewing the tape, Ann found a storage cabinet with more tapes in them. As she looked closely at the labels, she found their names written on them.

"Peter, I didn't know they video-taped your sermons."

"They didn't, he said. The system went down shortly after we arrived and it's being repaired."

"Well, what are all these tapes doing here with our names on them?" Now Peter was interested.

"What tapes?"

Peter took one down that was labeled "Peter and Ann Andrews (PRIVATE)". He inserted the tape into the player. They stood there with their mouths open in shock. Here they were; in bed making love; the two of them naked on video tape.

"Oh my god! "Peter! Did you know about this?"

"Hell no, but I'm going to find out."

By the time they got back upstairs, everyone was gone except some of the video crews from CNN and the security guard at the gate. They both went back to his office. They had to do some thinking.

"What are you going to do, Peter?"

"The broadcast is tomorrow. I'm staying here tonight," Peter said. "After my sermon, I will confront Jeremiah and then we'll take these tapes to the police. This is against the law."

"Peter, you realize that the publicity will kill you. Your career will be finished."

"I don't care," he said, "I've had it. Right now I'm not worried about the press."

"But what about me, Peter, it will ruin me and Jennie as well. If they have naked video tapes of you and me, don't you think they have tapes of our daughter as well?"

"Those bastards; I'll kill them!"

"Look, I have an idea. Let me take the tapes home with me and I'll hide them someplace in the house. After your sermon tomorrow; after the publicity and press, we'll meet with Jeremiah and the Board of Trustees."

Peter thought long and hard about it. "All right, that's our plan. You take the tapes. We'll make them pay, one way or another."

Ann kissed him and left. Peter spent the rest of the night preparing his sermon. He had changed his mind now. He was going to rock the church with everything he had wanted to say right from the start. This was judgment day, and he was going to bring the wrath of God down upon them. The next morning came too early for Peter. He shaved, showered and dressed for church. This was going to be a day to remember. As the morning went on, he grew more and more angry as he thought about last night and the video tapes that they'd found. He'd left instructions that he wasn't to be disturbed by anyone except family that day. He didn't want to see Jeremiah or anyone else connected to the church—not until after it was all over. Then he would confront them. Ann planned to sit in the balcony where she always sat. She had the tapes with her in a canvas bag. As Peter looked into the mirror, he thought about his whole life and the strange journey that he'd taken. He thought about the mysterious voice. '*Be at peace. All things work according to my plan for you.*' It all seemed like a giant cosmic joke. How could God do this to them? He had given his whole life over to preaching the Gospel, only to be destroyed now.

Peter opened his closet and took out a white linen suit. This was to be a special garment for a life-changing day. After he finished dressing, he got on his knees and prayed for help. Then he began reading his Bible.

Ann made her way into the church to her place of honor. There were thousands more in attendance that day. Everyone was thrilled at the media attention. Jeremiah was busy talking with CNN and the Time magazine writers and photographers. The plan was to go live on CNN for the sermon; then Time would conduct their interview in Peter's office. Photographers were setting up shots around the sanctuary and taping various dignitaries from the city. The mayor was there with his entourage, along with several dozen police officers and city councilmen. Jeremiah was in his element. This was to be the day that Temple Christian would finally gain national prominence. No one knew, but he planned to announce the creation of the Peter Andrews Senate Exploratory Committee during the press conference.

Jennie walked through the crowds unnoticed in her jacket and dark glasses. She wanted to be invisible, and that day she was. As she walked down the long corridor towards Peter's office, a security guard stopped her.

"I'm Jennifer Andrews. My father is expecting me."

The guard motioned her past. That was easy, she thought. Her mind was clear now. She knew what she must do. She knocked on the door and Peter responded;

"Who is it?"

"Jennie," she said.

"Come in."

Jennie walked in and found Peter reading the Bible. As she looked around to make sure he was alone, he never even looked up at her.

"I... ah... wanted to wish you good luck... and tell you I'm pregnant."

It was a thunderbolt that struck Peter in his very soul. All of the rage that he felt toward Jeremiah and the church was now standing before him in his own flesh. Like a demon possessed, he rose up and screamed.

"You Jezebel! You whore! How dare you come in here and contaminate this day with your debauchery. God will strike you down, girl! God will cast you down into the pit! He has no mercy for the harlot, and I have no mercy for you either! Get down on your knees and ask God to forgive you of your wickedness, trollop! Cast out the defiler, great Lord!"

Jennie was crushed. She burst into tears, begging him to forgive her. She threw herself on the floor and grabbed Peter around the legs and sobbed, but he felt nothing but contempt for her. Like an avenging angel, he brushed her to the floor with his foot. He stood over her with his Bible, reading one damning verse after another. Jennie screamed and reached for her purse. Opening it, she pulled out the gun. With all her might, she tore the Bible out of his hands.

"You damn me?" she screamed. "Then I damn you!"

Pointing the gun at her father, she hesitated. For that moment, neither of them moved or said anything. Then she turned the gun on herself and pulled the trigger. As the bullet exploded into her head, her blood splattered the room, covering Peter. Jennie collapsed to the floor.

Standing over her, Peter said nothing. In shock, a fog seemed to cover his eyes. As if nothing had happened, he slowly turned and picked up his Bible; not noticing that it too was covered with blood. At that moment, he could hear the choir beginning their opening hymns. As he had done so many times before, he methodically opened his private door to the basement, and descended the steps into the lift area to be taken up to the church platform. Still in shock, and covered with Jennie's blood, the platform lifted him like Lazarus from the dead.

The choir was just finishing their Hallelujah chorus when Peter ascended into the air. The crowd automatically stood up and cheered, screaming and praising God. Then one by one as the audience focused on Peter, the cheers and applause started to fade. As they recognized the blood on Peter they started to murmur. Most thought it was all a theatrical effect for this special day, but suddenly a woman close to the platform screamed.

"It's blood! He's covered in blood!" Then several more started to scream. Others just stood there in shock. CNN and the entire crew scrambled to get close-ups of Peter's face and body. The gruesome image filled the television monitors. Peter then raised his arms and shouted out to the congregation.

"Behold, you worship a false God!" He looked behind him to the large stained glass image of Christ on the cross. "This is not Jesus! He is not here! You have been lied to and manipulated. You have been controlled. You moan and grovel and give your money, not to God, but to them." Peter pointed to the balcony where Jeremiah and the Board of Trustees normally sat. They have used you. They have used God. You look for the antichrist?? I tell you that he is there."

A woman stood up and screamed out to Peter.

"Save us, Peter!"

"I can't save you. I can't save myself. I am condemned. I have killed. Thou shalt not kill, sayeth the Lord, and I have killed my own daughter. Jennie! My Jennie!" Peter screamed out and fell forward off the platform. Ann stood up in the balcony and screamed.

"Peter!"

With that, hundreds of people rushed over to Peter, while several in the balcony called out for a doctor to help Ann. Peter lay on the stage floor with his eyes wide open, his body twitching on the floor. Pandemonium erupted in the sanctuary, as police and paramedics fought the crowds to get in.

While all this was happening, Jeremiah and a news crew were on their way to Peter's office to set up the interview. Isolated in the staff section of the office complex, they were unaware of what had happened. Jeremiah was almost giddy with excitement and what he had accomplished. This was his big day and he was determined to make it count. "We'll do the interview in Peter's office. You know, he's a very devoted family man, with a lovely wife and daughter." As they opened the door, they stood there in shock looking at Jennie's body and a room covered in blood.

Both Peter and Ann were taken to the hospital, while the coroner was summoned to pick up Jennie's body. The police were everywhere, as the news crews salivated over the scandalous story. It would make the evening news in Chicago, New York, Atlanta and around the world. People streamed out of the church in shock. It was all destroyed. Jeremiah sat alone in Peter's office. His world had collapsed that day as well.

Peter was treated for shock and a broken arm at St. Anthony's Hospital. After three weeks, he was taken to Northside Sanitarium for an extensive battery of psychological tests. The doctors decide to commit him for an undetermined length of time for observation.

As for Ann, she was treated for exhaustion and shock and released the next day from the emergency room. The doctors tried to get her to stay, but she was determined to leave and see her daughter, who had been taken the county morgue for an autopsy. After that, she moved out of the church parsonage and disappeared.

About two months after Peter's commitment, a woman in a long dark coat with a scarf over her head walked into the institution. She walked slowly and stopped several times to cough and catch her breath. When she finally reached the reception desk she looked around and then coughed again.

"Are you all right, lady?" asked a nurse

"Yes. Is there a Peter Andrews here?"

"Yes, we have a patient by that name, but I'm afraid you can't see him right now. He's in isolation."

"That's all right; I wouldn't want him to see me like this anyway."

"I'm afraid his doctor, Dr. Gaskin is also unavailable. Would you like to wait for him to return?"

"No, I, ah… have this cold, you see, and I just want you to give Dr. Gaskin something. This bag; it was a present from my daughter. I'm Peter's wife. You just give this to him and tell him that if Peter ever gets well, to give it to him. Peter will know what it all means."

"Are you sure you don't want to wait?"

"No, no time now, got to go. This cold, you see."

The nurse took the paper bag and watched the woman leave. She could tell that the strange woman was very ill and wondered if she would ever come back.

Chapter Thirteen
To Be Born Again

All of the memories of Jennie's death faded as Peter opened his eyes once again. He didn't know how long he had been lying by Ann's grave. The sun was gone now beneath the cold, grey Chicago sky, and it was starting to get dark. Peter slowly got up, picked up his suitcase and walked off the hill. He never looked back; it was just too much to bear.

The days that followed were filled with more pain and uncertainty. He went back to look at Temple Christian from a distance. Now he was just a shell of the man that was once proclaimed as the new voice of Christianity. Bearded, worn and ragged; he stood in an alley across the street from what was once his church. He watched the cars and people coming and going and after an hour or so, he turned and walked away. That life was behind him now. What lay ahead was the unknown. His mind was filled with nothing but uncertainty. What should he do? Where should he go? There was no one to ask. Ann was gone. Jennie was gone. He couldn't ask a God that he no longer believed in. He was alone now and just wanted some peace.

He walked around the city, like a derelict on the make. He slept in cheap hotels and ate whatever blue plate specials he could find at cafes and diners. He had some money on him; just enough to get along so he didn't have to beg.

It was on a Saturday that he saw her. He stood there on the street outside the Ventura Travel Agency on Third Avenue. Looking in the window he couldn't pull himself away. There she was, Ann, his wife, or someone who looked like her staring at him from a travel poster. "Come home, come home to history". It said. Looking at the woman, he was transfixed by the resemblance to his wife. What was it about her? What compelled him? Then he saw it; around her neck was a necklace. It was the same cross that Jennie had given him. Was it a coincidence? Was she trying to tell him something? At the bottom of the poster the woman said, 'I found myself in Turkey.'

Peter walked inside. The shop was very small. Only enough room for a single desk and a table of brochures. A dark-haired woman of Middle Eastern decent sat behind the desk talking in a foreign language that Peter didn't understand. When she hung up the phone he inquired about the woman in the poster. No, she had no idea who the woman in the poster was or any information about the cross around her neck. He then asked about the location in the poster—the Roman columns and white terraced pools in the background. The woman told him that it was Pamukkale, Turkey, and that the pools were therapeutic healing pools. She also told him that the ruins were the remnants of an ancient Roman town called Hierapolis. Peter left the travel agent and walked toward a park about two blocks away.

Sitting on a bench he couldn't get it out of his mind. For the next three weeks, he walked back to the shop and just stood in front of the poster staring at the woman, the pools, the cross and the message. 'I found myself in Turkey.' The words burned themselves in his mind, until he couldn't sleep.

In his dreams he saw his body in the steaming pools of Pamukkale. He could feel the healing waters cleansing his mind of his guilt and rage. His days held only emptiness. He had to do something. He was sick of his own idleness. He looked in his suitcase and found an envelope. Inside the envelope were his financial records, checkbook and credit cards. He had forgotten that he still had some funds left. He knew what he must do.

The next day he walked into the Michigan Avenue National Bank and enquired about his money. Most of his credit cards had been closed by the church, but he did have one old Mastercard left that was good. He also had $10,000.00 in his checking account. They tried to talk him out of it, but he closed his account and left with the cash. Walking with more purpose than he'd had in months, he went back to the travel agency. He needed to get away for a long time and now he knew where to go.

When he finally went back into the travel agency again, the woman said she wondered how long it would take for him to finally come back. He looked at brochures for the area and they discussed travel options. He told her he wasn't interested in a cruise and a plane was out of the question. If there's one thing he wanted, it was to disappear. He didn't want to run into anyone who knew him or had seen the press about him. That he didn't tell her. When he asked if there was any other mode of travel, something that wasn't so public, the woman showed him a picture of the Andrea Valencia, a Greek freighter that shipped out of New Orleans. When Peter asked her how many passengers were allowed on board and how long the voyage, he was told that the Andrea Valencia only took on seven passengers and the trip would take about six weeks, depending on cargo and shipping schedules. At $2,500, it was a bargain. Much to the woman's surprise, Peter paid her in cash. As he was leaving, she stopped him. "You know, I almost called the police when you kept coming back to my window every day. You're not running away from them, are you"?

Peter smiled and said, "No, just running away".

The Andrea Valencia was scheduled to leave New Orleans in three days—just enough time for Peter to take the train from Chicago. The trip to New Orleans would give him time to think and relax. His mind longed for the peace of loneliness and the absence of humanity.

That Sunday night, he boarded the City of New Orleans for the 19-hour train trip from Chicago to New Orleans. He purchased a one-way ticket on the sleeping car, hoping to get some sleep and solitude. The City of New Orleans was a gleaming step both into the past and the future. All decked out in art deco chrome and wood, it was an impressive improvement from years gone by. The movement of the train was a welcome vibration from the harsh reality of Chicago's cold grey skies and bundled vagabonds. As he traveled, Peter watched the soiled buildings and vacant lots disappear into the evening fog.

After dinner, he sat in the dining car nursing a couple of beers until he felt sleep coming on. Staggering back to his compartment, he wasn't sure whether he was drunk or just stumbling from the train's movement. Sleep would be the dark cloud that would let him rest his mind. There was nothing like a train to put you to sleep. He'd always been able to sleep in a moving car, even when insomnia haunted him in his bed at night.

The following morning, the train pulled into the station and Peter unloaded his suitcase and went to get a cup of coffee. He still had a full day before boarding the Andrea Valencia, so he checked his finances before setting out to buy some clothes and toiletries that his travel agent told him to get. As he walked the streets, he could see the dry docks and the loading of the many different freighters, cruise ships and barges from the Mississippi. As he walked toward the city, he passed a newsstand. He hadn't seen a newspaper in weeks, so he stopped.

There wasn't much happening in the world that he cared about, but something on the top magazine rack caught his eye. There he was, on the cover of Religion Today. The caption was *Have You Seen This Man?* Thank God he looked nothing like he did when that picture was taken. His beard would hide him, but his name was a problem; Peter Andrews. Some one was bound to catch on if he gave his name.

He pulled out his passport and looked at it. Suddenly he remembered that it had been the church's policy to only put the first initial on all his documents, so as not to attract too much attention when he traveled. P. Andrews; that could stand for Paul or Peter. He pulled out Jennifer's cross that hung around his neck. What was it she called it? Yes, that was it; Saint Philip's Cross. He would be known by Philip Andrews while he traveled. With a sigh of relief he felt comfortable walking in complete anonymity.

Peter's first task was to do some shopping for jeans and other shirts and casual clothes for the voyage. After a few stops at the shops at Canal Place, he wanted to taste New Orleans restaurant fare. After asking a few strangers in the French Quarter, he decided on the Port of Call restaurant at Dauphine and Esplanade. It was just what he was looking for. According to the locals, the Port of Call was established in 1963 as a steakhouse. It started as a quiet, small neighborhood restaurant open only at night, but then grew into a popular destination for locals and tourists alike. A seafarer's dream, it looked like every port of call dive seen in film noir movies of the 1940s.

It took Peter several minutes to adjust to the dark atmosphere. This was perfect; no one would ever find him here. He could sit there and imagine Bogey and Bacall at the table in the corner. He looked at the menu and felt somewhat adventurous.

"I'll take a burger and fries and something to drink."

When the waiter asked how much courage he had, Peter looked perplexed.

"What do you mean?"

The waiter told him that he could recommend two drinks: the Windjammer – a blend of several tropical juices and two different kinds of rum—or if he was game, the Neptune's Monsoon.

"What's in it?" Peter asked.

The waiter only smiled and said that it was an old recipe used frequently as a last request by pirates condemned to walk the plank. Peter laughed and told him to bring it on, and that he could take it.

When Peter finished his lunch, he started to get up and immediately fell to the floor. His head was spinning and as he staggered to get up, the waiter told him he'd better not drive. Peter told him he was walking, or at least stumbling. All of a sudden he felt a gut-wrenching fear that he'd never get to the ship unless he had help.

"Look, I've got to get to the Andrea Valencia freighter. She's docked at Berth #2 and I've got to get my boarding pass and get checked in by 5:00 today."

The waiter hesitated to help him, but changed his mind when Peter showed him a fifty dollar bill and told him it was urgent. With that he passed out.

Back in Chicago, Wendy walked down Michigan Avenue toward the subway station. She was excited to be starting her new job at WIND Radio. It had been a difficult transition from school and the Northside Sanitarium. She had a lot to think about and wrapped herself tightly in her wool coat. Yes, it was spring in Chicago, but it would be another month before she would really feel warm. As she waited for the crosswalk light to change, she felt someone tap her on the shoulder. She turned around but there was no one there. She continued to look around but there was no one or nothing even close to her. It was probably my imagination she thought and turned back towards the street. That's when she saw it. A magazine had fallen off a rack at the newsstand. She reached down to pick it up. As she walked over to give it to the newspaper vendor, she turned it over and gasped. On the cover of Religion Today was a picture of Peter Andrews. The caption read, *Have you seen this man?* Wendy reached into her purse and pulled out the three dollars for the magazine. She didn't look inside, but quickly put it in her purse.

Although her day was filled with meetings, research and long periods of writing copy for the news department, she couldn't get Peter's face out of her mind. At noon, she turned down an invitation of her new co-workers for lunch at the Bistro, saying she had some personal business to attend to. Grabbing a quick sandwich from a vending machine, she sat down in the Atrium to eat and read. The magazine article was old. No new information about the whereabouts of the Golden-haired Evangelist that stunned a nation and then disappeared. Thank God they didn't know about his commitment at Northside. Thank God they didn't mention what happened to his daughter; only that her death and his wife's death had sent him into hiding.

She questioned herself. Thank God for this and thank God for that? Certainly God had everything to do with this tragedy, but it was nothing to be grateful for. Wendy stopped in the restroom to freshen up her make-up. She looked at her face and remembered how he had looked at her. She felt something for him and she was sure he also had been touched by her. Although they never spoke of their feelings or the depth of their relationship, they both knew that one day, perhaps many years from now, they would find each other again. She took the magazine back to her desk and put it in a shoe box in her desk with the rest of the photos and mementos of her days at Northside with Peter.

A deafening banging sound woke Peter the next morning. Groggy and confused, he looked around at what seemed to be a ship's cabin. He felt like he'd been shanghaied and dreaded meeting what he was certain would be his Captain Bligh before the crew threw him overboard. His mind was confused. Half conscious and half awake, he slowly walked over to the port hole. As he stood there watching the giant cranes loading crates and containers into the hold, he sighed in relief. Yes, he had made it aboard the Andrea Valencia. He didn't remember anything from the time he took that first swallow of that damned drink; the Neptune's Monsoon. As a wave of nausea hit him, he headed to the bathroom, vowing never to drink again. Peter took a drink of water and sat at the desk in his cabin. A booklet under the telephone caught his eye. It was a written history of the ship.

The Andrea Valencia was purchased by the Greek government in 1990. Originally called the SS John W. Brown, it was one of the last Liberty ships from World War II. FDR named them Liberty Ships for the first ship in the Lend-Lease program for England, The Patrick Henry.

She was still a handsome lady and still had her stern-mounted 4-inch deck gun. Although it hadn't been used in years, it could come in handy to ward off pirates.

As Peter opened the door of his cabin, he was brushed by a tall lanky sailor. Peter tried to say hello, but the man was moving so fast that all he got in response was some sort of growl in a language he didn't recognize. As Peter continued to walk down the corridor, he passed the Chief Engineer's cabin. He looked inside but no one was there. What he did see was several bottles of liquor and a collection of photos of a woman and little girl. This was very unusual, as he had heard that most men who served on freighters could never keep a wife and children and so remained single. In looking around there must have been over a hundred pictures on the wall. Peter wondered why the Chief Engineer had spent so long at sea if he had a loving family at home. There must be some other reason why any man would spend so many months at sea away from a wife and child.

Peter made his way to the main Officer's Mess. It was a nicely furnished dining room with coffee pots and sweet rolls all laid out for the crew and passengers. Grabbing a cup of coffee and a roll, Peter sat down just as Chief Cook came in to check the cabinets. A rather stout black man who looked like he had no trouble sampling what he cooked, he nodded hello.

"Good morning. Checking the stores, I see."

The Cook turned and shook Peter's hand. "I'm Pasquel, the Chief Cook. You got any trouble with the food here, you talk to me, not the Captain."

"Understood," said Peter.

It was obvious that the cook was sensitive about his cooking and didn't want any trouble with the passengers. Just as Peter was finishing his coffee, a middle-aged woman came in to get a drink of water. She introduced herself as Mrs. Waldham from Staffordshire, England. Peter invited her to join him for a cup of coffee and asked her if she was traveling alone. She said she should have been with her husband, but he had died of a heart attack. She went on to say that it had been his dream to take a freighter around the world, but he died a week after he purchased the tickets. Peter offered his condolences, saying he would be happy to accompany her on the trip as long as he was aboard, since he was also traveling alone. She said she was very grateful for his kindness. Peter poured her another cup of coffee.

"I'm curious. What was your husband's line of work?"

"He was a minister," she said.

Peter quickly wanted to change the subject, but couldn't. "He had a large congregation in Staffordshire. It's a very old church."

"You know, I have the strangest feeling that I've seen you somewhere before. Have you been to England?"

Now Peter felt compelled to move on. As they moved out of the Officer's Mess and onto the upper deck, it was good to see the crew loading the containers and crates. The sun finally broke through the clouds and Peter felt a new day was starting for him. The ship was getting ready for an adventure and he was hopefully riding the wave to a new life.

Chapter Fourteen
To The Sea And Beyond

The Southern sky burned with flames of burnt orange as the sun set over the water. The boilers belched steam and smoke as the Andrea Valencia rattled and vibrated. Finally the lines were cast off and she slowly pulled away from the dock. The tugs pushed her forward as the old ship waded out of the Port of New Orleans.

Peter felt the ocean breeze whip his face as the ship's engines picked up speed. Finally the city started to fade into the night sky, and the cold wind forced Peter to go inside. Peter made his way toward the main hallway below the bridge, then down the steps towards the Officer's Mess. As he walked into the dining room, he was introduced by Mrs. Waldham to the other passengers. Robert Allen was a young writer from New Jersey who was working on a novel. His brother, Jason Allen, had recently lost his wife to cancer. He was a high school history teacher who was on sabbatical. He told Peter that rather than sit around the house, he decided to go on the cruise to get away from small town attitudes. And then there was Miss Wilson, an 80 year old poet who had been published in numerous magazines. She was working on a collected works book. She had to get special clearance by a doctor before they would let her go as there was no physician on board. They were all very pleasant if somewhat dry and stand-offish. Peter was also introduced to Charlie, the Chief Engineer; Robare, the Chief Steward; and Patrick, the Steward's Assistant, who busied himself by serving everyone water and coffee. Although some of the passengers didn't hesitate and started to eat; all of the crew waited until the Captain came into the room.

Captain Lysander was an imposing man; over six feet tall with fiery red hair and full beard. If his figure didn't command respect, his deep voice could make the dishes vibrate. Just as the passengers began to reach for the food, Captain Lysander bowed his head and said a prayer to bless the food and bless the voyage with calm winds and tranquil seas. With that, everyone dug in. The food was plentiful and basic. After dinner, the passengers retired to the Pilot's Deck Bar for drinks. Although there had been new restrictions on the crew drinking after the Exxon Valdez disaster, the Captain still allowed an occasional lapse for appropriate situations. Everyone was more than genial and friendly after a few days of travel.

Peter enjoyed the warm tropical breezes that flowed south of the Florida Keys as the ship made its way around the infamous Bermuda Triangle. At night the passengers' conversations turned to discussing the Triangle or what the crew referred to as the "Port of Missing Ships" and the "Hoodo Sea". Since no one knew what caused all the mysterious disappearances, there was plenty of conjecture and speculation. Some thought they might be aliens or some other paranormal phenomena from Atlantis. Captain Lysander, overhearing the conversation, said the sea was a mysterious place and that anything can happen when the waters turn black. He went on to tell them that Christopher Columbus had seen strange animals and dancing lights in the area. When the passengers asked if the ship were going to go through the Triangle, he said the ship would avoid the area because the insurance was more expensive to pass through those waters. After he left, Charlie, the Chief Engineer, said that Lysander's father had gone down on one of the freighters that disappeared in 1948. When Peter asked which ship, Charlie told them it was the Samkey. Charlie lit his pipe with a great flourish, then blowing smoke rings around his head, he began his tale.

"On January 24th, 1948, the S.S. Samkey, with a crew of 43, left London for Cuba, having taken on board 1,500 tons of small stones and sand. On January 29th, the freighter Innesmoor reported sighting the Samkey steaming on her course without any sign of trouble. On the 31st she radioed that all was well and that there was a strong southwest wind. That was the last message received from her. No trace of her was ever found by the search vessels. It is possible that she was struck by heavy seas which caused the stones to shift, until she finally rolled over and sank.

"Is that what you think, Charlie?" asked Peter.

"I think something very strange happened. That ship was overwhelmed by something that was so sudden in its onslaught and so dire in its effect that no signal of any kind was made from her and she just vanished from sight. Who knows, maybe some night, like tonight without a moon, the ghost ship Samkey might be seen with her ghostly crew. But you must not talk about her around the captain as his father was the captain of the Samkey."

Everyone sat there in absolute silence. Suddenly everyone except Charlie and Peter got up and ran outside to the lower decks to look for the ghost ship, Samkey. Peter looked at Charlie and smiled. Charlie's eyes squinted and he slowly got up and left the room. At that point Lysander came into the room.

"Where'd everybody go?"

"They've all gone out on deck, captain." said Peter

Lysander laughed. "Old Charlie been telling you the Samkey story, eh?"

"Yes, captain. Sorry to hear about your father."

Once again Lysander smiled. "He told you my father died on the Samkey, didn't he? My father is a retired baker in Rome, and he's in excellent health."

This time Peter laughed.

"So much for sea stories," Lysander said.

Over the next few weeks, Peter got to know the Allen brothers. Robert was working on a novel about the sea, but Jason just wanted to be left alone in his grief. There was something about writing that interested Peter. He had never before thought about writing anything, but something inside him was telling him he would someday write his story. At this point, he knew he wasn't ready, but maybe someday his life would mean something positive to someone. Maybe there was a lesson to be learned.

The days were long as the Andrea Valencia made its way north towards Spain and the Mediterranean. Peter spent most of his time in his room at night and on the deck by the pool when the wind wasn't too strong. About two weeks out, Captain Lysander came by for a swim. Peter was busy reading a book about European history and hardly noticed Lysander standing over him. As Peter looked up, something shiny sparkled in the sun. Moving his head to get a good look, he saw that Lysander had an identical cross around his neck.

"You wear the cross of St. Philip," said Lysander.

"Yes, it was a gift from my daughter."

"It must be painful to lose a daughter that way."

"What are you talking about?"

"I know. I know who you are, Peter Andrews."

Peter's turned his head away and looked around to see if anyone had heard Lysander's remarks. He had been careful not to tell anyone who he really was, and had been careful to use Philip as his first name since he boarded the ship.

"How did you know?"

Lysander walked over toward the main cabin way entry door. "Follow me."

Peter sighed and followed him into the Captain's cabin. Peter was apprehensive as he looked around. The cabin was simple, but well appointed in red leather and dark mahogany. Lysander walked over to his desk and grabbed a magazine. He tossed it to Peter. It was the Religion Today magazine that Peter had seen before he boarded the ship.

"I should have known that someone would catch on." said Peter.

Lysander picked out a pipe and began smoking.

"So, where are you bound, my friend?"

Peter walked around the cabin and stopped to look at a wall map. He pointed to Turkey.

"I'm going there and don't ask me why because I don't know. I saw a poster that said something about coming home to Turkey. I guess I'm just running away."

"You're in good company. Most of us sailors are running away from something. We run from women, families, and even life itself. Life at sea can be very healing, at least for a while. There's something very freeing about the sea. When the land disappears, all you can see is the sea and sky. You forget about the land and all of its responsibilities and memories."

"Sounds lonely—I long for the isolation of the sea." said Peter.

As Peter sat down, Lysander took out a cross from around his neck. "You see, I too wear the cross of Philip. It was given to me many years ago when I first became a Captain. I wear it to bring me luck."

Peter looked again at the magazine.

"Does everyone know?"

"It's almost impossible to keep secrets aboard a ship."

"I suppose it was foolish to think I could hide by taking another name."

"You know Peter; I believe that there has to be a reason for me to be here. Sometimes I can't see the reason, but eventually it comes to me. I'm not talking about my job as captain. I'm talking about some other reason."

"I don't know what you're talking about."

"I'm talking about the fact that you're on this ship. So there's gotta be a reason beyond your running away. You're a minister, or at least you used to be a minister. So maybe God put you here for a reason."

"God gave up on me, or I gave up on God a long time ago."

"That may be Peter, but you think about it just the same."

With that, Peter left the captain's cabin and went back to his room. He had a lot of thinking to do. Why was he here? Was he really just running away or was he running to something. Ever since Jennifer's suicide, his life just wasn't worth living. If only he'd been there for Ann. She died alone. Peter lay on the bed staring at the ceiling until sleep took him. The days dragged on at sea. When you've lost your life compass, the sun and sea and stars are cold and heartless. He thought a lot about what Captain Lysander said about God having some purpose for him here. He didn't know if that was true or not, but now he wasn't going to let anything get in the way of his escape from his past, not even God.

About a week later, Jason Allen sat down next to Peter in the Pilot's Deck Bar. After some small talk about the weather and the ship's course, Jason and Peter got around to talking about the one thing they had in common—the death of their wives. Unlike Peter, who felt guilty about his wife's death, Jason did everything he could to save his wife. Peter asked Jason how he handled his wife's illness.

"I remember when Helen got the news. The doctor called me and told me to have her call him as soon as possible. Well, of course I panicked. Helen was furious with him for talking to me first."

"That's when you found out?"

"We went down to the oncologist's office. I remember wondering why all these women were there without their husbands. I couldn't imagine Helen going through this thing alone."

Peter walked over to the bar and poured himself a cup of coffee.

"Jason, I think some men have a lot of trouble dealing with things they can't control. You know women are more courageous than men. They can handle catastrophic events that are out of control. But men… if they can't do something to solve the problem, they feel…"

"Impotent. Yes, I know. I felt that way. Helen was depressed and scared. Hell, we both were, but she accepted her powerlessness as time went on. She prayed, but I couldn't. I didn't even know where to begin. How could I ask a God to heal her, when I didn't even believe in a God, any God."

"What did you do?" asked Peter.

"What you would never expect. I got on the Internet and found dozens of prayer groups and prayer chains and asked them, no matter what their religion, to pray for Helen."

"So there you were, an atheist, reaching out all over the world to ask for prayers?"

"The reality was, I would have asked the Pope for prayers, if I had half a chance, because I wasn't in my head. I was in my heart and it was breaking. How was it for you?

"I had all the tools, Jason—ministry, the Bible, religious education, counseling—all the tools and yet I failed miserably. I let Ann down. I was so inflated with my own ego and self importance that I had no room or time or compassion left for my wife. The hardest thing, for both my wife and me, was that if you're a dedicated born-again Christian who does all the right things and believes with all their hearts that God blesses you… to then be struck down by that same God."

"It's not supposed to happen to good Christians, is it Peter."

"No. That's not what we're taught. Our God supposedly blesses the righteous and punishes the wicked, however I've come to believe that God punishes everyone, no matter what you believe."

"You used to be a minister. What happened?"

"It's a long story. This God thing… it destroyed my wife, my child, and it almost killed me. I can tell you that for me it was a seductive poison that promised me the heights of fame and fortune, but then…"

"Peter, I know a little bit of the Bible; this sounds like the story of the Devil's temptation of Christ where he promised him the kingdoms of the world if Jesus would bow down to him."

"You are very perceptive, my friend. Perhaps you're right. Perhaps

I was tempted and was destroyed by my choices."

They spent the rest of the day together talking about life and religion and the world. Jason talked about the intense bigotry and hate of his wife's family and how they told her that God had cursed her with cancer because she had left the church and married an unbeliever. He also related how much torment her family caused for his wife.

"Her last days could have been filled with peace and acceptance, but instead were filled with terror that she was going to Hell. I don't understand that kind of hate, Peter. Do you?"

"I have witnessed a great deal of pain and suffering, and much of it caused by well-meaning Christians."

"Christians… Helen's family was real religious; evangelicals, you might call them. You know the type—died in the wool, blood of Jesus stuff. Anyway, when my wife married me, they couldn't deal with the fact that I wasn't religious. At first, I just got the cold shoulder, but eventually when I told them that I didn't believe in their God, all hell broke loose. It all created a lot of tension in our marriage. My wife was torn apart. She left them and their church. She just got fed up with all the bigotry and judgment. Anyone who didn't believe exactly the way they thought was going to hell, no matter how good they were."

"Jason, look these people are idiots. I'm no Christian and no one should ever believe anything I say about this subject, but I know that this is exactly why people want nothing to do with religion and especially Christianity."

"Well all I know is that I'm an atheist."

"Jason, that makes two of us."

Peter had found a friend—a soulmate bound together by grief and a mutual contempt for all things religious.

About two weeks later, Charlie cornered Peter near the pool. He told Peter that he needed some advice. When Peter told him he was the wrong person to ask for any kind of help, Charlie said he didn't know who else to turn to and really needed some help with his relationship. Peter agreed to meet him that night in Charlie's room.

"Please understand, Charlie; I'm no longer a minister, so I don't know how much help I'll be."

"That's all right. I read the article in that magazine, so I know what you mean, but you also know a lot about people and God and stuff."

"Okay, what's the matter, and what are you looking for from me?"

"I got this problem. I'm married and got a little girl. They live in Barcelona, but I haven't seen them in eight months. I hate it that we're apart, but every time me and my wife get together, I get crazy."

"What do you mean… crazy?"

"It's like something inside me takes over and I get real controlling. I won't listen to my wife. I become a bully to my daughter. I'm crazy jealous and torn apart inside. It's gotten so bad that I had to move out. Maybe it's from my father. He was this way too. He came from a culture that my mother used to say hated women."

"I don't know what to tell you, Charlie. I neglected my wife when she got cancer. I pushed my own daughter aside because of my insane judgments against them. I used the Bible and my own twisted religious thinking to drive them away. Now they're dead and it's my fault."

"I feel like there's something broken inside me, like something's missing," said Charlie

"Charlie, I think there's something missing in all of us, especially men. Look, I don't know how I can help you. I'm just as lost as you are. I could tell you to pray, but I'm not sure that would do you any good. I could tell you to read the Bible, but mankind has used it for thousands of years as a tool against women like your wife and mine."

"So what should I do? I'm going to see my wife and kid next month, and I don't want to be the same way I used to be. I can't do this again. I've got to find someone who can help me."

"I can only give you one piece of advice. When you see your wife, see her as you first saw her, when you fell in love. Be grateful for her while you have her. Don't be like me, and waste the time you have with her. She may be gone tomorrow and then what have you got?"

Charlie nodded and told Peter he was grateful for his words. As Peter left, he didn't know whether he had been any help or not. All he knew is that Charlie's dilemma was not so different than his own. The only difference was that Charlie's family was still alive. He had one more chance to make things right. Ann and Jennifer were gone. There was no chance to change things; to make things right again. It was too late to see them, to talk to them, to tell them he was sorry for everything.

Peter walked the deck that night alone. He looked up at the stars and drifting clouds. There was a cold nothingness in the air. He remembered how he felt when he was back at the sanitarium, looking out the window at the cold gray sky and falling leaves. His mind told him to be honest with himself, to get it out, and so he did—to the sky and clouds and stars.

"God? If you are still there or were ever there, I need something. I don't know what or who, but my life needs some kind of direction. I can't undo what I have done. It would do me no good to repent. So, if you are, give me something, a branch to hang on to, before I drop."

As the wind whipped around Peter, he heard a high-pitched screech, then he saw the tip of the wing of a white bird from the corner of his eye. A feather floated down and landed on his shoulder. He grabbed it and looked up. The bird was nowhere to be found. His mind dismissed the incident. It probably just nested in the hold while they were in port and finally got loose. He took the feather and put it into his pocket.

Peter walked back inside the Officer's Mess to get a cup of coffee. Pasquel was there cleaning up. As Peter sat down, the feather fell out of his pocket. Looking up at the cook, he felt the urge to explain.

"The strangest thing happened. A seagull flew by me while I was on the deck and dropped a feather on me."

"There are no birds this far out." said Pasquel.

"Yes, I know. I wonder what it means."

Pasquel looked at the feather. "This is no seagull feather. It belongs to a dove. In my country it's a sign of peace. It means you are on the right path."

With that, Pasquel left the room. Peter twirled the feather in his fingers and for the first time in his life, he felt he was part of something mysterious. Only time and events would tell.

Chapter Fifteen
The First Messenger

Miss Rosalind Wilson was a site to behold. The moment she made her entrance onto the Andrea Valencia, she caused a stir. Dressed in a light blue sari and 80 years old, her demeanor and energy put many a younger sailor to shame. Over the next two weeks, Peter came to know her. She had been married to a British officer assigned to protect Lord Mountbatten, the last Viceroy of India. During World War II, she started studying with Mahatma Gandhi. When India won its independence from Great Britain in 1947, she moved into the ashram and became one of Gandhi's favored students.

Peter was fascinated by Miss Wilson. The more they talked, the more layers of an incredible life came to light. Sharing a cup of coffee in the Officer's Mess the next morning, Peter had to delve into her background once again.

"So tell me Miss Wilson, what was it like to study with Gandhi?"

"Well, when I moved into the ashram, it was the most beloved time of my life. We were all so excited to finally see independence. It was a marvelous and dangerous time. You see, there was a great movement toward partition. Gandhi never wanted to see India and Pakistan separate, but the politicians convinced him that without it, there would be civil war."

"It happened anyway, didn't it?"

"More than a million died in the following months. It broke his heart, Peter. A year after independence, Gandhi was assassinated by a Hindu who thought he had sold out to the Muslims."

“It seems that the world never learns its lessons, does it.”

“Every great religious teacher has given us basically the same message for thousands of years. We follow them and proclaim them as great teachers, rabbis, or gurus and then we kill them and build shrines to them as gods, but we never really understand and embrace their message.”

“Are you talking about Christ, Miss Wilson?”

“No, I’m talking about Jesus.”

“I don’t understand. Aren’t they the same?”

“No. One is the man, the other is the enlightenment.”

Noticing that Peter was totally confused by what she said, Miss Wilson got up and left. Peter watched her leave and started to ask her to explain, but changed his mind. It was obvious that he had some thinking to do. The rest of the day, Peter spent the time alone with his thoughts. When the other passengers and crew tried to talk to him, he just shook his head and walked away.

His mind drifted back to a conversation that he had with Jeremiah. He was adamant that Peter refer to the Lord as Jesus, not God or Christ. What was it about that name? What was the difference? If people identified with Jesus, what or where did it lead them? Peter thought about the word Christ. From his studies he knew that the word came from the Greek word Khristos, which meant ‘the anointed one’.

Over and over he thought about what effect it would have to connect with Christ rather than Jesus. He thought about the way so many people had become obsessed with Jesus the God, and not Jesus the Christ. If Jesus was the anointed then maybe, just maybe… did he dare think it? He had to talk to Miss Wilson. He had to find out. After dinner that night he cornered her on the deck watching the stars.

“Hello, Peter,” she said, or should I say Philip?”

Peter smiled. “My attempt at keeping my identiy a secret.”

“There are no secrets, Peter. Everything comes to light, sooner or later.”

“I’m beginning to understand that. Miss Wilson, there’s something I have to ask you. You said that there was a difference between Jesus the man and Christ the enlightened.”

“It’s a wonderful night, isn’t it?” she said

“I’ve been thinking about the difference, and when I think about the way people seem to connect with the word Jesus; it’s different than when they connect with the word Christ. I think that there is a human connection with Jesus, as someone you can feel and identify with—a human to human link."

"Peter, Jesus is the person whom we call the Son of God. No one can hope to really be like him because we think of him as divine, like God. You know, of course, that Jesus always referred to himself as the Son of Man. He kept turning his Apostles away from thinking of him as divine. Remember, 'These things you will do and greater.' If we only connect with Jesus the man, whether human or divine, how can we hope to achieve the great things that he predicted?"

"Yes, but if we connect with the Christ the anointed, then the enlightenment that we seek might be possible."

"Enlightenment can come to any and all, if they choose. That is the message of all faiths. Our connection to the divine is direct. The Kingdom of Heaven is within."

"Oh my god, that was Jesus' message. The anointing is universal. It can come to us all. No wonder Jeremiah was so adamant about using the word Jesus. You can't control people if they are powerful, but you can control them if they feel unworthy, guilty, sinful and disconnected from the divine."

"Peter, you can't control enlightenment. It is as individual as your fingerprints. When we experience God, it is unique to us. It can't be described or controlled. Like the wind; we can't see it or where it comes from or where it is going. We can only feel it in the here and now. Enlightenment is only available in this moment. This is eternity. This is the kingdom, Peter, right here in this space where time does not exist."

"And what of Jesus?"

"Jesus came here like other great teachers, to show us the way. Religion has focused on him as a personality. They've built their cathedrals and temples to honor him and in doing so, they have ignored his message. Christianity long ago discarded his message to be inclusive and serve humanity. Instead they created a God to praise. They gathered wealth and power, went to war, killed and destroyed people by the millions—all in the name of winning souls for Christ, whom they had the gall to call The Prince of Peace."

"This puts a whole new light on my work in the church."

"Peter, I've studied with Gandhi, the Dali Lama, and more gurus than I can count. So much of what we've been taught about Jesus, his disciples and the early days of what we have come to call Christianity, is distorted and false. If you want to understand Jesus the man, study his language, his people and his customs. Then you will understand what he was really saying."

"You mean Aramaic?"

"Yes, the language of Jesus and his people."

For the next three weeks, Peter began to study Aramaic, thanks to several books in Miss Wilson's collection. Everyone started to wonder if he was ill as he rarely left his cabin for hours during the day. It was a wonderful time. He hadn't felt like a student in years. He read the George Lamsa Aramaic translation of the New Testament with a new fervor that he thought was dead inside him. Gradually, he began to realize that all that he had been taught in the seminary was either incomplete or totally misguided. The whole scope of the man Jesus and his ministry was turned upside down. For once Peter saw the real message that Jesus had taught. All of his anger and rage at God was suddenly gone. He saw the real meaning of the Gospels and why their message had been changed or hidden for thousands of years.

In the early morning hours, Peter strolled along the deck gazing at the stars and thinking. His life had taken on a new depth of meaning. His whole identity as a minister was no longer important. For the first time he saw himself as just a human being, devoid of all the trappings of religion. Now he felt an inner sense of peace that seemed to follow him day and night. His only regret was that Ann wasn't there to share it with him. If only she were alive to understand this new feeling.

The next week, Miss Wilson was on deck talking to Jason about the ship. When Peter approached, he told her that he and Jason shared a common bond of grief with both of their wives, having died of cancer.

"Cancer is a terrible disease." she said, "It doesn't have to be, but for so many of us, we seem determined to create it."

"What do you mean?" said Peter.

"You must understand that in many cases our disease is created by our thoughts. We are all powerful and creative beings. Whatever we think we create. It's not to say that those with cancer consciously think that they want cancer, but their destructive thoughts, together with their feelings of unworthiness and the lifestyle they lead, create the disease."

Both Jason and Peter were confused and shocked. Before they could react, Miss Wilson stepped forward to explain.

"Cancer is a disease that is caused by deep resentment held for a long time until it literally eats away at the body."

"But my wife Ann was a saint, Miss Wilson. I can't imagine what resentment she might have had."

"Peter, generally something happens in childhood that destroys the sense of trust. The experience is never forgotten. If this was true for your wife, then she lived her life with a great deal of self pity. Because of her belief system, she may have had a feeling of hopelessness and helplessness. She may have blamed herself or others for her misfortune and lived her life with great disappointment."

Peter was stunned. Everything she said struck him like a knife.

"I have to tell you that my wife was sexually abused as a child by her father. She told the truth and he was arrested. She always blamed herself, even though it wasn't her fault. She felt she was called to ministry, but the church wouldn't allow it because she was a woman. I think she was resentful that I was accepted as a minister, but she could never be."

Miss Wilson put her arms around him and hugged him.

"My god, it's no wonder she developed cancer—so much pain; so much heartache. I've come to believe that in our minds we are all victims of victims."

"So, what's the answer, Miss Wilson?" said Jason.

"There is only one answer, my friends. Forgiveness."

Both Jason and Peter answered at the same time. "Forgiveness?"

"Yes; we must learn to forgive ourselves, our family, our friends, our parents, our children, and even our God. That is the road to healing, but unfortunately very few take it."

As Peter and Jason sunk to the deck chairs; they looked at each other, trying to comprehend the words they'd heard. Miss Wilson patted them both on the shoulder and then left the deck. Jason sighed and opened up.

"I just realized that my wife felt so much resentment at being judged by her family. She never felt worthy. No matter what she did, she could never please them. In the end, when she needed them most, they turned on her. I think she thought God turned his back on her as well."

Jason's eyes welled up with tears. He wiped them with his handkerchief and then composed himself a moment.

"I tried to be there for her; to comfort her, but it was like I couldn't get through. Something from her childhood took hold of her and she seemed to revert to this little girl trying so hard to please Mommy and Daddy. In the end, all she got in return was judgment. I hated them for that. You know, her family refused to come to the funeral unless their own preacher could cast out the Devil during the service."

Peter was shocked. He had seen how devastating Christians could be in their self-righteous judgment before, but never like this, and not with so much cruelty.

"What did you tell them?"

"I told them, 'I'd like to tell you all to go to hell, but I'm sure you're already there.'"

Peter laughed. Jason looked startled; then he too laughed. It was a much needed moment of light-heartedness for them both. It was good to laugh again.

* * *

The ship now entered the Mediterranean and the waters leveled out to calmer days and nights. Peter felt more complete than he had felt in a long time. Everyone on board had grown very close and felt like family. It was good to feel connected again. Captain Lysander noticed the change in Peter and asked him to come to his cabin for another chat.

"What did you want to see me about, Captain?"

"Come in Peter, come in. It's been several weeks since we talked and I thought we might just renew our conversation. How are you enjoying the voyage?"

"I've really found a good deal of peace since we last spoke. I'm grateful for the whole experience."

"Good. Then you found your way, Peter?"

"Well, I'm not sure I've found *my* way, but at least I don't feel like I'm running away any more. I don't know exactly where I'm going, or what's ahead for me, but I feel more peaceful about the journey now."

"Good. We'll be making a couple of stops in a few days. We'll unload and take on new shipments in Rome and then it's on to Piraeus in

Greece and then to Kusadasi in Turkey. Is that still your destination?"

"Yes, Captain. How long will our stops be?"

Lysander opened his shipping log book to check on the cargo arrangements.

"In Rome, we should be there for two, maybe three days, depending on the stevadors. The last time we dropped anchor, they were on strike and it took us a week to finish with our cargo. In Piraeus, maybe half a day at most; it's a huge port and they have lots of dock workers to handle the cargo."

"And in Kusadasi?"

"Well, let's see, perhaps six or seven hours if we're lucky. I expect you should be at your destination by the end of next week at the latest. By the way, Peter, before you leave us and just in case I get too busy and forget, I wanted to give you the name of someone that I think you need to meet."

Lysander handed Peter a piece of paper and a newspaper clipping with a photograph in it. Peter read the paper.

"Sister Alissa Galatas. The address here is in Pamukkale. Who is she?"

"She is a good friend and very wise teacher. I really don't know if she's still alive, but when I knew her several years ago, she was in her 90s."

"You say she's a good teacher?"

"Yes, she knows things about early Christian history that no one to my knowledge knows. She may be able to give you an insight as to where you need to go next. The newspaper article and picture will at least show you what she looks like, even if you can't read Turkish. By the way, there's a book in the ship's library that will help you with a few words and phrases in Turkish. You'll need it when we dock in Kusadasi."

"Thank you Captain. You've been a good friend."

"Arkadas. That's *friend* in Turkish."

Peter spent the next several days studying Turkish. He managed to learn a few phrases and some words, but gave up on the entire language as it was beyond him. The following Wednesday, the ship's horn and whistle blasted away at 5:00 AM. The other ships and tugs in the harbor responded with a blaring symphony of discordant sounds. Peter jumped out of bed and staggered to the porthole in his cabin. There must have been a hundred ships of all sizes and flags surrounding the Andrea Valencia.

"Rome; we must be in Rome."

As he made his way to the Officer's Mess, the other passengers were wandering about, looking in all directions to see the approaching port. The ship pulled into Civitavecchia to begin docking procedures. After breakfast, Miss Wilson asked him if he'd ever seen Rome before. He told her this would be his first time, so she suggested that they see the eternal city together. He thought it was a wonderful idea, since she had been to Rome many times. They both bought tickets for the one-hour bus ride to the city. It was a beautiful day and for once he felt like a tourist. The Captain gave each passenger who planned to return a docking pass and time table. It was Wednesday morning and the ship was due to leave port on Saturday at 10:00 AM. Lysander told them all to not be late because the ship waits for no man. He had three days to enjoy himself.

Chapter Sixteen
The Empire Of The Church

Miss Wilson suggested that they stay at the Concordia Hotel on Via di Capo le Case in the heart of the old city. She knew the owner and had stayed there many years ago. Peter exchanged his dollars for euros and they registered. They had rooms next to each other overlooking the Spanish Steps and Trevi Fountain. It was a lovely hotel and very reasonable. For lunch they ventured to the rooftop to take advantage of the garden café. Overlooking all of Rome, they could see St. Peter's Basilica in the distance. As they sat there drinking a cup of coffee, Peter closed his eyes and again thought of Ann.

"What are you thinking Peter?

"Oh, I was just thinking about my wife, Ann. She would have loved being here."

"You know it's practically a sin to be in Rome and not *be* in Rome?

"I get the message. Be here now?"

"Precisely. Now what looks good on the menu?"

"I don't know. I'm just so happy to be here. You decide."

When the waitress came over to take their orders, he was struck with how much she looked like Wendy. He hadn't thought of her in months. There was something about Wendy, but what was it? Their time together in the sanitarium felt like a thousand years ago. Being here in Rome made him question his memories. Did it really happen? Was he ever a minister with a wife and child? Did he ever go crazy? With that thought, he felt the cold metal of the cross around his neck—Jennie's cross. He felt it with his fingers, feeling the gold symbol. Yes, it was all real. And in that instant he felt a slight moment of remorse for all the mistakes he'd made.

"May I take your order, ma'am? the waitress asked.

"Yes, we'll have a selection of your finest cheeses, fruit, and breads—oh and a nice salad with your special Mediterranean dressing."

"Sounds great," said Peter

"Ten years ago I stayed here and this was all I could afford. Now that I'm rich, it's all I still want. You'd think my palate would have become more sophisticated, but I'm afraid I'm a victim of habit."

Peter remembered what Wilson had said—that we were all victims of victims. He thought about it and made a decision. Maybe he had been a victim of victims and certainly he had made many mistakes in his life, but today was a new day and he was not going to be a victim any more. That part of his life was past. Not forgotten, but for once, he felt its power over him start to weaken.

"I have to tell you Miss Wilson that at first glance, I love Rome. Its colorful monuments, and temples and happy people are a delightful change from the cold, gray skies of Chicago."

"Of course, it wasn't always like this. I think it was Augustus Caesar who said, "I found Rome brick, I left it marble.'"

After lunch they walked around the plaza in front of the Spanish Steps and threw coins into the Trevi Fountain. They decided to tour Rome in a horse-drawn carriage, and the first stop was the Colosseum. They started at the Colle Oppio adjacent to the Roman baths; then walked through the Colosseum's arena.

"It's amazing," said Peter, "that so many Christians remained faithful despite all of the persecution and torture. I don't know if I could have withstood it and died for my faith."

"Well, you must understand that most Christians believed that Christ's second coming was going to happen in their own lifetime. I'm sure many of them felt like he would intercede at the last minute and stop their agony and death."

"You know, this place reminds me of the Jesus Temple. It was huge and built like this, of course on a smaller scale, but it was just as impressive. The fellow who was behind it all had an organization called the Jesus Factory; a sort of manufacturing enterprise with just one product, Jesus. He had over a thousand churches, each one sending him 10% of their income."

"It sounds ghastly, Peter. What was the point of it all?"

"It was all about power, political power that is, and greed. Everything was done to control the people. Make them afraid; manipulate them so that they all felt like victims. Of course, they weren't really victims, but being persecuted was good for the cash flow."

"It all sounds so similar, doesn't it, Peter? Rome was the ruler and terror of the world. Eventually the little band of followers called Christians conquered the Roman Empire. The horror of it all, however, was that they traded one empire for another one called Christianity."

"It was an empire, wasn't it?"

"Yes, it still is. The great challenge for all of us, as Christians, is that in order to save Christianity, we must go back to the simple message of love and forgiveness that Jesus taught.

As Peter looked around at the most beautiful city in the world, he had to stop and remind himself that it was a monument to an empire built on brutality and power.

"It's just amazing to me, that an ordinary carpenter from Nazareth with a few followers could topple the Roman Empire."

"That's where you're wrong, Peter. Jesus was a man like you and me, but he was anything but ordinary. He never would have wanted this. His mission was so simple, so pure, and yet all of this; the cathedrals, the basilicas, the Vatican, the huge mega churches in your country, and the 38,000 different denominations, are all a testament to the confusion and corruption that is the Christian religion."

"I'm sure, Miss Wilson, "He would take one look at all this and turn his back on what was created in his name."

"So true, so true."

After all the tours and walking, it was time for a leisurely dinner back at the Concordia Hotel. Miss Wilson said she was too tired to join him on the rooftop, so she had her dinner in her room. Peter had to admit that she was looking a little pale lately, but he wasn't going to allow himself to worry about anything. As he sat there sipping his evening glass of wine, he looked out at the fiery, orange ball of a sun setting on the Italian rooftops. He was here, in a place he never thought he'd see, and he was grateful to be alive.

The next day, Miss Wilson felt better and joined Peter in touring several of the cathedrals, along with Castle Saint Angelo and the Pantheon. As the carriage turned the corner, the Pantheon came into view. As they walked through the mammoth temple Miss Wilson gave him a historical reference.

"The Pantheon, Peter, was dedicated to the gods by the General Agrippa, who helped defeat Marc Antony in the battle of Actium."

"I saw a statue of the Virgin Mary. Is it now dedicated to her?"

"Yes, many temples and monuments that were built to honor pagan gods were later turned into monuments honoring the saints. This was an attempt to get the pagan worshipers to embrace the Christian faith. Many of the ancient temples and churches named for the Virgin Mary were originally dedicated to the Goddess."

"There seems to be a lot of interest in the idea of the Goddess."

"Yes, it's a yearning for women to identify with a female god."

Their last stop was Saint Peter's Basilica and the Vatican museums. As they walked through the galleries and gift shops, Peter browsed through a large book of Michelangelo's works. When he came to the Creation of Man in the Sistine Chapel, he called Miss Wilson over.

"Look at this. There, you see God stretching out his hand to Adam. His other arm is around a woman. Who is that?"

"That's Sofia, the Goddess and divine feminine nature of God. As I said before, early Christians venerated Sofia as the Goddess. Today she has other names, like Mother Nature."

"This is so fascinating. No one in the seminary ever talked about this."

"There is so much about the history of women that you and other men don't know. We are here in Saint Peter's Basilica. Peter, like many of the disciples, was married. Their wives accompanied them on their journeys. Some say that the disciple on Jesus' right in the Last Supper, was Mary Magdalene."

"I wonder what Simon Peter would think of all this?" asked Peter

"You know Rome had many Gods, but Judaism had only one; and it was a God so remote and unreachable that you couldn't even say his name. Then Jesus came along with a message that the Kingdom of God was at hand and within. To him, God was close and personal. In fact, he called him Abba, which means father, in Aramaic."

"Miss Wilson, I wonder why Christianity needed intercessors between us and God? First there was just God and man spoke to God directly. Then Jesus came along and the church told us that we could only get to God through Jesus. Then, when that wasn't enough distance, we had the Virgin Mary. She became the intercessor between us and Jesus."

"Yes, and then there were the saints which were the intercessors between man and Jesus and Mary. Finally, you had priests who became the intercessors between the people and God and Mary and the saints. Confusing, isn't it?"

"Very, all of these layers between human beings and the creator."

Peter shook his head. It didn't feel right. That night after their tour of the Vatican and the cathedrals, they both sat on the rooftop café to continue their conversation. When the waiter brought over the latest English newspaper; the headlines were all about new allegations of priests sexually abusing children in Ireland and Germany.

"What a tragedy;" he said.

"It's all part of the problem that the church and much of Christianity has had with women. For centuries they have been second class Christians."

"That's what Ann said."

"Your wife?"

"Yes, she said those very words. I know the fact that she was denied ordination, simply because she was a woman, had something to do with her death. I just feel it."

"Your mind and heart have opened."

"Miss Wilson, the more I look around, the more I feel that Christianity has gone astray.

The next day, Miss Wilson said she didn't feel well and wanted to stay in her room and rest. Peter spent much of morning looking at art museums and after lunch he strolled though the many bookstores looking for unusual books about church history and the Gnostic Gospels. One bookstore specialized in biblical history and alternative versions of the Bible. To his delight, he found an entire series of books on the Gnostics and the Aramaic language. He purchased several books by Rocco Errico; that looked to be commentaries on the Eastern Pashita texts.

He decided that it was time for him to be about his own journey. The next morning, they checked out of the hotel and took the bus back to his ship. After a rather disappointing dinner onboard ship, he went back to his cabin to read. It wasn't long before he fell asleep. That night he had the first of many dreams that would mark his journey.

Peter was vaguely aware of himself in a valley. He looked around and could see that he was standing in a rocky gorge. He heard the sound of rocks being crushed and walked over to a ragged man who was crushing them with a large hammer. When Peter approached, the man stopped and turned around. The man was old and weathered. His beard and hair were wild and covered with dust.

"Who are you?" Peter asked.

The man did not speak, but turned around and continued to crush the rocks with each blow. Once again, Peter asked the question,"Who are you, and why are you crushing those rocks?"

The man finally turned around and faced Peter. "I am the rock."

The man turned around again and started breaking the rocks with his hammer. Finally the old man sat down and collapsed. Peter rushed over to him to try and help him. At that point, the man handed the hammer to Peter. "It belongs to you now."

Peter reached down to take the hammer, but he was filled with a terrifying dread. As he hesitated, the old man gasped and died. Peter tried to pick him up, but the old man's body vanished into dust. Peter looked down at the pile of dust and saw something shiny. He picked it up. It was a cross, the same emblem that Jennie had given him. He looked back down at the hammer and a light flashed before his eyes. At that point Peter woke up in a sweat. He wandered around his cabin. It was four o'clock in the morning. He grabbed his robe and went out on the deck. The sky was filled with clouds, but every once in a while he could see the stars breaking through.

Peter sat in a deck chair and threw a blanket over his legs. What did it mean? Who was that man, and why did he give Peter the hammer, and why did he feel so frightened to pick it up? Night after night, Peter had the same dream and each night at four o'clock in the morning, and woke up in a cold sweat. This went on for four nights. Finally Peter was determined that he was going to find out what would happen if he picked up the hammer. As he went to sleep, he told himself that he would not be afraid.

As before, he dreamed the same dream. At that same moment when the old man handed Peter the hammer and said that it belonged to him now, Peter took hold of the hammer and raised it high over his head. With all his might, he brought it down smashing a huge rock into small stones. As this happened, a flash of light knocked him over. When he looked up, he saw four huge stone pillars before him. He stood up and slowly walked through the four pillars. When he reached the other side, he saw that he was in a Roman amphitheatre. He walked down the steps into the center of the arena. Looking up, he saw twelve stone statues circling the arena. The statues were arranged with six statues on each side of a large stone arch in the center. As Peter looked at the statues, they all seemed to be pointing toward the arch as though they wanted him to go through it. Once again, he felt an uncontrollable fear. As soon as he was conscious of his fear, he woke up.

He laid there on his bed, breathing heavily. What was going on? What was the meaning of all this? The next night, he had trouble going to sleep; perhaps it was because the ship hit some heavy waters and listed fore and aft all through the night. Finally he got to sleep about two o'clock. Once again, he found himself standing before the arch. This time he felt that he had to go through the arch and walked slowly forward. Ahead of him a brilliant light grew stronger with each step. He felt compelled to press on into the light. Was this the end of life tunnel that people talked of during a near death experience? Was he going to die? He pressed on into the light and in the warm light he felt enveloped by an ethereal love. His mind soared with a clarity of purpose that he had never felt before.

Suddenly he was aware of a divine presence ahead of him. He walked forward slowly. From a distance, he heard a rushing sound like a stream or waterfall. Within the sound of rushing waters, he heard a voice. The light ahead of him began to change, swirling until it looked as though it formed the shape of a woman. Then the voice became clear. It was the voice of a woman. He shook when the voice spoke.

"All of Christianity was born in the imagination of woman."

Peter was stunned. He immediately woke up, but heard another voice. This time it was the voice of the old man.

"Prepare yourself for the Apostle of the Apostles."

Suddenly he was awake. He got up and sat at the foot of his bed. Over and over his mind heard the warning, prepare yourself for the

Apostle of the Apostles. Who was this Apostle of the Apostles and what in the world should he do to prepare himself? He couldn't stay in his room any longer. He had to get out, get some fresh air and think this thing through. Since the ship was bearing into the wind, the air was too cold, so instead he went to the Officer's Mess to get a cup of coffee. He was surprised to see Miss Wilson sitting at a table doing a crossword puzzle.

"Good morning, Miss Wilson. Can't sleep?"

"Hello Peter. I rarely sleep through the night anymore. So much to do and so little time now."

Peter winced. He caught her meaning. After all, she was eighty and apparently she thought that her time was running out.

"How did you like Rome, Peter?"

"I really enjoyed my time there. It is such a beautiful city. A couple of days is just not enough time. I could have spent two days in the Vatican alone."

"Yes, the first time I went to Rome I spent three weeks and barely scratched the surface of seeing all the ancient wonders of the city. Tell me, what was your favorite part?"

"I guess the place that touched me the deepest was Saint Peter's tomb. Maybe it was because my name is Peter or that I used to be a minister, but whatever the reason, I felt that all the grandeur and marble in the Vatican and in Rome was…"

"Far removed from the simple lives and messages of Jesus and his disciples?"

"I can't help but think there's something wrong here, maybe not just here, but with all of Christianity. Tell me, what do you know of the Apostle of the Apostles."

"Where did you hear this?"

"I've been having dreams and every night when I wake up, I hear a voice that tells me, 'Prepare yourself for the Apostle of the Apostles.' Any idea what it means?"

Suddenly, there was a strange look in her eyes. Her face turned white and she had the death mask. Her voice was hollow and flat, as if something or someone was speaking through her. "I haven't much time. Listen carefully. Write this down in your mind. Each person has a soul. From the ancient Hawaiians we come to know the Huna. That soul has three parts or souls. Unihipili, or the lower soul, is the animal nature. It is the home to our emotions—like love, fear, anger, jealousy and hate. This is where violence is created. Uhane, or the second soul, is the middle part or intellect. It is the home of all logic and reasoning. Order and balance reside here. When mankind is reasonable and just, it is the middle soul that is in control."

Peter sat there stunned. The words seemed so strange and foreign. He reached over and grabbed a pencil and some paper to try and copy down what she said.

"I have little time left and I must finish this."

"All right, Miss Wilson, I'm listening."

"But there is another part of the soul, the Aumakua, or higher soul. This is the residence of the divine. It is from here that mankind communicates with God. It is also from here that we communicate and have union with all other higher souls. This is the activity of prayer. This is the essence of the Oneness that we feel when we are in touch with the source of all goodness. This is the seat of the Christ the Anointing. Jesus was able to create miracles, because he acted from his higher soul. Remember, he said, 'These things you will do and greater.' This higher soul exists beyond the limitations of the physical body. It will not interfere with our day to day lives, unless our lower souls ask for help. This is what is meant when we say that the intellect cannot understand and know God. This blending of the three souls into one soul, when it is in perfect harmony, is both masculine and feminine; the androgynous self. As God is spirit, God is both masculine and feminine in nature, so are we.

When a soul is in trouble, when tragedy strikes and we dwell in what we the call the 'dark night of the soul,' then the lower soul, at the instruction of the intellect, the middle soul, calls upon the higher soul for spiritual guidance. You must understand that the intellect cannot contact the divine. That is why we cannot intellectually know God. We cannot put the experience of the divine connection into our thoughts and words. We can only feel spirit. Christ told us that the Kingdom was within; but understand that the Kingdom can only be the individual's experience of the soul. That's why there are so many religions. We experience God and then try to put that into words. The moment we try to understand it and communicate it or use it for our own purpose, we have lost our divine connection."

Once again Peter had no words. He sat there just looking at her, writing as fast as he could—one page, two pages, and more.

"You will go to Turkey, Peter, to Heiropolis. There you will meet your next messenger. There you will meet the Apostle of the Apostles. There are 'Messengers' and there are 'Guides'. The Guides help you find your way along your path. They prepare you to meet the Messengers. The Messengers are sent from the Divine. They bring a unique message of love and peace and comfort. Prepare yourself, my friend. Be at peace. All things work according to God's plan for you. You are the one, Peter. You are the one they've been waiting for."

"Miss Wilson, what on earth are you talking about?

Just as suddenly, her color returned and her eyes lit up and her voice was back to normal.

"What?"

"You said I am the one, that I'm the one they've been waiting for. Who are they, and what do you mean by I am the one?"

"I haven't the foggiest idea what you're talking about."

"Look, I wrote all of this down. I couldn't get all of it, but you talked about the ancient Hawaiians and the Huna, and the three parts of the soul, but see here…"

Peter looked down at the paper on which he had eagerly copied her words, but all of the words looked like a jumble; some kind of foreign or ancient language."

"Wait, what the heck is this? I don't remember writing this. I can't even read it."

Miss Wilson looked at the paper. That's Aramaic; you've written in Aramaic, the language of Jesus."

"That's crazy! I can't write Aramaic."

"Look, Peter, it's very late and I'm very tired. We'll talk again."

With that, Miss Wilson gathered her things and left the room for her cabin. Peter had no words. He sat there taking it all in. Her words penetrated his mind and heart and no matter what his intellect told him that no matter how crazy it all sounded, something inside him said that he was listening to a great soul—a Mahatma, as the Hindus would have called her.

Peter spent the rest of the night trying to decipher what he'd written. His mind was so tired. He thought about the three souls—the lower, middle and higher soul. He understood that the middle soul was the intellect and the higher soul was the divine connection, but the lower soul? He couldn't quite understand. Then out of the confusion of his own mind, it hit him.

At Temple Christian, Jeremiah wanted him to stay away from the intellect and concentrate on the emotion. He even told Peter to say Jesus at least thirty times because it made a connection with the people, a connection that translated into dollars. All of a sudden it made sense. If a minister could keep his congregation in their emotions—fear, love, anger, etc.—then when the plate was passed, their intellects would not be making a decision about how much they could afford to give. Out of their emotions, they would open their wallets and give, whether they could afford it or not. It was no wonder that Jeremiah's churches were doing so well. He had to admit it. Jeremiah was diabolical and twisted, but a genius.

That night he slept soundly. There were no dreams and no haunting memories to plague him.

The next morning, the noise of last minute loading of cargo woke him up. They had docked in Piraeus, Greece. The normal noise and excitement of docking in a new city and port was noticeably absent. Peter saw a small boat dock next to the ship, with several doctors along with four men with a stretcher.

"Is someone sick?" asked Peter.

Captain Lysander seemed preoccupied and didn't look up as he said, "Miss Wilson passed away this morning. We're making arrangements to have her body taken to a morgue in Athens."

The news hit Peter to his core. Just a few hours earlier, they had talked of souls and Christ and the spirit of God.

"She said something last night, or this morning, about the fact that she didn't have much time left. I think she knew it was coming."

"I've seen many a seaman," said Lysander, "who knew he was about to cross the bar. There's a look in their eyes; it's the look of oncoming death."

"Yes, I've seen it. What was it? She said something about finishing... How did she die, Captain?"

Lysander lit his pipe and took a long, grand sigh.

"Heart attack, I imagine, although we won't know for sure until we get the coroner's report. Oh by the way… she left a note saying that you were to have all her books, that you would know how to use them."

"Did she say anything else? Anything at all?"

"Apparently she saw Jason Allen early this morning around five o'clock. He told me that she told him that his wife never died and that neither would he. Does that mean anything to you?"

"Yes, I know what she meant." said Peter.

"She was a great lady," Lysander said.

Peter poured himself a cup of coffee and sat down.

"She still is."

The morning gave way to the noisy conversation of the ship's crew loading cargo. The harbor was bustling with ships and craft of all sizes. Peter couldn't quite identify his feelings. He should have felt sad, but there was an enormous sense of peace that came over him. He had come so far from that little church on Chicago's North Side. He thought of Ann and Jennie, Wendy and Doctor Gaskin. How could he be here now, in Greece, when just a few months ago he was confined to a mental institution contemplating suicide?

He walked out on the deck to watch the stevedores do their thing, handling the cargo. The seagulls were swooping and diving to get what ever morsels they could find on the ships and in the water. It was a beautiful day, and he was grateful for Miss Wilson and all that she had taught him. He would miss her, but then his mind quickly reminded him that they would meet again in many guises and many forms.

Chapter Seventeen
The Second Messenger

Peter spent the time in port reading and writing. He had tried to keep a journal ever since he boarded the ship; getting down his thoughts, fears, and hopes for the future. Miss Wilson's personal traveling library was extensive; containing the Gnostic Gospels of Thomas and Philip and Mary. There were at least a dozen different translations of the Bible, including Hebrew, Aramaic, Greek, and Latin. He thought back to Dr. Carlisle at the seminary. Peter had been so impressed with his octagon library. Now he could actually read these kinds of books. They no longer had to be hidden.

The voyage from Piraeus to Kusadasi was the last leg of his journey. His mind returned over and over to the poster he saw in the travel agency. *Come home to History, Come home to Turkey.* Peter spent the day on the deck watching for the approaching port. At night he schooled himself on the history of Turkey and the Christian church. More than any other place, it was the birthplace of Christian doctrine. It was the land of Troy and the Trojan war, the birthplace of the Trinity and the Councils of Nicea and Constantinople. It was also the birthplace of Homer, Paul of Tarsis, and where John, Bartholomew, Philip and Mary Magdalene preached, and where Mary, the mother of Jesus died. When hundreds of thousands of Jews fled the inquisition, the Ottoman Empire welcomed them to practice their religion in peace. It was a marvelous land and Peter felt, for the first time, that he was indeed going home.

A few days later, the Andrea Valencia's horn broke the morning light. Peter jumped out of bed, dressed and ran up to the bridge. There it was, Kusadasi; the new Turkish name for the ancient port of Ephesus, where

Paul preached. The sparkling water was luminescent and as bright as any port in the Aegean, and the Mediterranean sun felt especially warm on his skin. After he packed his belongings, he headed to the officer's mess for breakfast. Everyone was there and he took his time saying his goodbyes. Jason wished him well and said that although he still didn't believe in God, he would pray for him anyway. Peter hugged him and told him it didn't matter whether he believed or not, and that his prayer was appreciated.

He had one more stop to make before he disembarked. Making his way through the main corridor, he knocked on the Captain's door.

"Come in," said Captain Lysander.

Peter stepped through the threshold and just stood there looking at Lysander smoking his pipe.

"Well here we are, Peter. Are you all packed and ready?"

"Yes; I wanted to thank you for your words and friendship."

"You have traveled far."

"I have the feeling that my journey is almost at an end. There is so much I need to learn, Captain. I've said my farewells to all the passengers and crew, that is, all but one."

"Yes, I know. We will all miss her. How long do you plan to stay?"

"I don't know. I know that I must go to Pamukkale and Hierapolis. Beyond that, I am at the beck and call of the wind."

"Now, you're beginning to sound like a sailor. We'll be back here next year and you can check our schedule with the port authority. If you are not captured by bandits or dead and would like to travel once again with us, we would love to have you."

"Thank you, Captain."

"Friend?" said Lysander.

Peter smiled and shook his hand;"Arkadas"

Peter made his way off the ship and walked toward the port promenade and the main shopping district of Kusadasi. He browsed through the many colorful shops and found a place to store most of his belongings and books. He purchased a backpack and a good pair of walking shoes, as he planned to tour Kusadasi and Ephesus by foot and then eventually walk the hundred miles to Pamukkale and Hierapolis. As he walked he talked to the people. Although he didn't know much Turkish, he managed a few words and many shopkeepers could speak English. He found the people to be more than friendly and eager to talk to an American.

This was Turkey; the land of Christian doctrine where in Antioch the disciples first came to be known as Christians. He stopped in a shop window and caught a glimpse of himself in a mirror. He hadn't bothered about his appearance in a long time and it showed. His hair was now long and his full beard hadn't been trimmed in weeks. As he looked at his face he had to laugh. If he had been wearing a long robe and sandals, he could have been mistaken for a modern version of Jesus himself.

He visited all the historic sites: the Temple of Artemis, the Basilica of St. John, and last but not least, the last home of Mary, the mother of Jesus. As he walked through the rooms of the old stone house, he found himself lighting a candle to her in the anteroom and then he said a prayer to her. He had never been a Catholic and certainly never felt the adoration that Catholics felt, but there was something about this place that touched him. For the first time he thought of his own mother. They had never been that close and she never really understood him or his view of the world, but she had always been supportive and for that he was grateful.

He finished his prayers and walked out of the house where he found a fountain called The Water of Mary. This was supposed to be blessed waters for healing. He took a drink and noticed that it tasted salty. He sat under a tree outside the old stone house and thought of Ann. He wished she could have shared this with him. She wanted so to be a minister, but the prejudice of the times held her and many women captive to priests and ministers and the highest powers of the clergy. Peter thought of Mary and what her life must have been like. Looking at the old stone house, it was obvious she wasn't rich. It was ironic how lowly her life was on this earth and how high her station had become with so many millions.

Peter couldn't help but wonder what she thought of Jesus and his ministry. Did she approve? Was she lonely? Did she even understand what her son was trying to do with his life. She must have been devastated when they killed him. How the life must have gone out of her eyes when he died. He wondered about Ann, too. Once Jennie died, and he was committed, he never saw her again. She was a good mother. What a tragedy that her only child killed herself. He felt guilty and said another prayer. This time he prayed to Ann, asking her forgiveness for Jennie's death. After sitting in the garden for a while, he seemed to gather himself to begin again. He had a journey to finish.

He left the grotto and found his way to the road toward Pamukkale. After walking several hours in the dusty heat, he came to the small town of Selcuk. It was here that the ruins of the temple of Artemis were found. The temple, now just a few stones and a lone column, had been one of the seven wonders of the ancient world. How ironic to see what always becomes of man's monoliths of faith. Just as he had seen in Rome, nothing lasts forever even if it is blessed by the Gods.

Peter spent that night at the Urkmez Hotel in Celcuk. It was an inexpensive and charming place for a short rest. The next day, he decided to visit the Isa Bey Mosque; one of the oldest mosques in Turkey. Built in 1375 during the Ottomon Empire from the stones from the Temple of Artemis and the remains of the old city, Ephesus, it was now only a shadow of its old glory. As Peter walked the ancient grounds, he saw an old man sitting in the garden. As Peter approached, he realized that the man was having a last bit of lunch.

"Good day," said Peter.

"Peace be with you, friend."

"Arkadas," said Peter.

"You know our language?"

Peter laughed. "Only a few words."

"If you only know one word in any language, it is good to know the word 'friend.'"

"Yes. Beautiful day, isn't it?" said Peter

"God blesses us with good weather."

"Tell me, are you connected with the mosque?"

"You might say so. For forty years, I was a professor here. Now, I am retired. They have younger men to say the prayers and lead the flock. Are you a believer?"

"No."

"Not a Muslim?"

"No."

The old man looked up at Peter's face.

"You're not a Jew."

"I, ah… used to be a Christian."

"Used to be?"

"Yes, I don't believe anymore."

"Ah, an intellectual."

Peter laughed and sat down next to the old man. "No, just an unbeliever."

"So young not to believe. Tell me, this god who you don't believe in, what is he like?"

Peter couldn't help but laugh a little. "Well, let's see. He's a god of judgment, of condemnation, of hate and violence. He's a god that separates men from each other and demands great temples to praise Him instead of feeding the poor."

"Such a god. No wonder you don't believe. If I had a god like that, I wouldn't believe in him either."

"As a leader of your faith, you must have a strong belief in God."

"It is not as simple as you think, my young friend. I have been many things in my life. I have been an atheist, agnostic, Christian, Jew, Hindu, and a Buddhist. I have studied at many universities and ashrams all over the world. As a young man, I used to believe that the more knowledge I had, the more religious I would be and the closer my connection to the divine. But knowledge and books and degrees—I have twelve of them and even beliefs have little to do with it."

"I don't understand." said Peter.

"It doesn't matter. Tell me, what do you do?"

"What do I do? Let's see—I used to be a minister, a Christian minister."

"A priest?"

"No, Protestant."

"So, what were you protesting?"

"Everything."

"And now... who are you now?"

"Right now, I'm not doing anything."

"I didn't ask what you do, but who you are."

Peter thought for a moment. "I don't know who I am now. I used to know. My life used to be clear, but now I guess I'm in some kind of fog. All I know is... No, I don't think I know anything now. Maybe I never did. All I know is that I'm through with religion.

"There is an old saying. *'God gave human beings the truth, then the devil came along and said, we'll organize it and call it religion.'"*

"You don't believe in religion?"

"I believe in the experience of God. Whenever we try to explain how we feel when God touches us on the shoulder, we invariably mess it up. When I was young, I would ask the question of my students, do you believe in God? And they would always say yes. Then, I would then ask them why."

"Why? Why did you ask them that?" asked Peter.

"Because they would always tell me they believed because they were taught to believe. Their father, mother, or someone told them about God and they just came to accept it. Then I would ask them again—why? Why would you accept someone else's experience of God? It may be right or wrong, you don't know. Then I would tell them to go. Get out, and find your own experience of God."

Peter took a long pause and looked at the old man again. "I think that's what I'm doing."

"Good. You know Jesus is said to have made the statement; 'Where two or more are gathered, there I am in the midst of them.'"

"Yes, Matthew:18:20," said Peter

"He did not say… where two or more Christians are gathered. My God is a god who welcomes everyone, no matter who they are—but I can see that you are troubled."

The old man put his hand on Peter's shoulder and with great caring like a grandfather;

"What is it you want from me?"

"I'm lost. I don't know who I am anymore."

"When you are what you do… When you don't, you aren't."

Peter repeated the words over and over again. They were simple words but so very profound.

"You are on a journey, my young friend. I have lived a long life and can tell you only this. Be at peace. Remember who you really are. Be the change you wish to see in the world. Share your story and make a difference. The world is in desperate need of enlightenment. I pray you are the one to bring it."

Peter rose up and took the old man's hands in his and kissed them. Then he thanked him; turned and walked to the center of the courtyard. Just then, he thought of something he wanted to ask him, so he quickly turned around, but the man was gone. He thought it was strange. He couldn't have moved so quickly, being so old. Peter searched the grounds, but the old man was no where to be found. He saw a young Muslim cleric walking in the outer courtyard and stopped him.

"Excuse me; I'm looking for an old gentleman. He must have been in his 90s, white beard, white coat, black pants, sandals. Have you seen him?"

"You must be talking about Father Aziz. He was a very beloved professor at the school. I was one of his students."

"Well, I must find him. Where is he?"

"You won't find him here. He hasn't been here for two years."

"That's impossible. He must be wandering around here someplace. I was just talking to him. He was there, on that bench eating his lunch."

"That's where he always came each day to eat his lunch."

"Look, just tell me where he is!"

Peter started to frantically run around the courtyard, opening doors and peering into leaded glass windows. The cleric, by now was more than a little disturbed, and was just about to call one of the local guards, when he yelled out, "You won't find him here. Father Aziz died two years ago. His grave is out back in the cemetery."

The blood ran out of Peter's face. He ran outside to the cemetery. After several minutes, he finally found the grave marked by an ornate tombstone. Most of it was written in Turkish, but Peter did make out the old man's name and the dates: Born, Istanbul, 1900 - Died, Celcuk, 2010. That would have made the old man one hundred and ten years old. There were some words under his name. 'O bir farklilik yapti' Peter saw the young cleric standing off to the side of the cemetery watching him with several guards close by. Peter motioned the cleric to come closer to the grave. The cleric warily walked over, followed by the two guards.

"Please, I'm very sorry, but if you would… What does that mean?" asked Peter

The cleric looked down at the tombstone and then said;

"It's Turkish… It says, 'Make a difference.'

Peter was stunned. He turned and walked out of the mosque, not saying a word. The cleric shook his head as he watched him go.

"Crazy American!"

Once outside, Peter found a stone to sit on by the edge of the road.

He knew he had met another messenger. He took out his notepad and although his hand was shaking, he tried to remember every word the old man had told him, and write it down. When he finished, he got up dusted himself off and walked down the road.

His mind probed the question that he had never asked himself—who was he? What was he? If he wasn't a minister, what was he? If he wasn't a Christian, what was he? As he walked further towards the hills, he felt like Moses must have felt when he was cast out of Egypt by Pharaoh. He had been Prince of Egypt and now he was a beggar in the desert. Peter told himself that he too had been cast out, but not by a king or potentate, but by himself. He had brought all this on himself. There was no one to blame, not even Jeremiah. He merely offered the thirty pieces of silver. It was Peter who took them with both eyes open.

He was alone and empty. He now knew that everything he had accomplished was nothing. No matter how much money he made, how important he had become, it was all just dust, like the dust on the road in front of him. He had been everything, and now… he was nothing. He was a nothing in search of something or someone, but who or what it was, was somewhere ahead of him.

Although he was impatient to get on with it, another voice inside him told him that this was not the Turkish way. This was an ancient and patient land where things happened slowly. He reminded himself of this again and again as he walked.

Chapter Eighteen
The Third Messenger

The road to Pamukkale was long and dusty. The wind from the west was fierce and made it difficult for Peter to walk. After about two hours, he found a cave by the side of a hill. The cave was filled with markings of graffiti and local teenage statements of love and adoration, but as Peter went further back he found ancient carvings of early Christians. Embedded into the rock were the fish, the cross, and at the farthest corner of the cave ceiling, he found the ancient cross of Philip. There it was, a cross surrounded by two squares and encircled with a ring. In all of his study, he had never come across the symbol until Jennie gave it to him on his ordination—and now in Turkey. It seemed to be a sign urging him to go on. He thought again about the cross that Jennie had given him and the one around Lysander's neck. What was it about this symbol that had become so important? As he sat down in the cool cavern, he pulled out a crust of bread and ate. Smiling, he grabbed hold of the cross around his neck. Closing his eyes, he sensed a feeling of completion growing inside him.

After resting about an hour in the coolness of the cave, he sensed that it was getting late. Walking out into the bright Turkish sunlight, he smelled the air. It was sweet; not like Chicago or New Orleans. He turned around to see if there were any other travelers on the road, but found it empty. He adjusted his bag and started to walk the road again.

The sun was setting as he made his way into Pamukkale, this place they called the Cotton Castle in Turkish. It was a beautiful village that contained hot springs and travertines, terraces of carbonate minerals left by flowing waters. The ruined city of Hierapolis was nearby and was a Mecca to tourists seeking their own connection with the ancient past. How different this was to his years in Chicago where history was a blink of an eye compared to the thousands of years of history all around him. He spent an hour or two just wandering around the small town looking at the shops and stopping to examine the many ruins that lay by the side of the road. This area was covered with hundreds of small and large blocks of stone and crumbled columns from Hierapolis. It was here that Philip spent his last days preaching with Bartholomew; John and his sister, Mariamne, later to be called Mary of Magdela; and where Philip met his martyrdom.

Peter decided to stay in a small hotel to conserve his funds, so he stopped at the Kervansaray. It was lovely and typical of the hotels in the area. This one, however, had a rooftop restaurant and ever since Rome, Peter had grown fond of watching the sun go down from the rooftop. That night he nursed his wine while gazing at the colored lights on the surrounding ruins and travertines.

The next morning he asked the hotel owners if they knew Sister Alissa Galatas. They were not familiar with her, so he set about walking through the town from shop to shop asking if anyone knew her. Around ten o'clock, he felt hungry and saw an old woman selling bread.

"Kahvalti?" she said.

Peter knew just enough Turkish to know that kahvalti meant breakfast. "Yes, kahvalti, breakfast, what have you got to eat?"

"Simit"

Simit was a twisted circular bread ring flavored with sesame seeds. Peter paid her and took the simit. As he was getting out the money to pay her, he pulled the newspaper clipping of Sister Galatas out of his pocket, and he showed it to the old woman. She studied it for a long time and then finally she nodded her head like she knew the sister. Hoping she knew English, he took a chance.

"Do you know her?" said Peter.

The woman shook her head, as if she didn't understand English. He knew he had to find the words in Turkish. Stuttering a bit to find the words in his mind, he said, "Ah, where is she?, No… Ah, where soot she?

She nodded and smiled. "Sen onu biliyor musun?

"Where soot she?"

The old woman backed up like she wasn't sure she could trust him.

"Arkadas... friend," said Peter, pointing to the picture of the sister in the paper.

She smiled again then took him to the corner. Pointing north, she said "Aziz Philip Cleopatra git."

This time Peter smiled. He took out his English to Turkish guidebook and looked up the words. If he understood her properly, she told him to go to the Cleopatra Pool and take the road north one mile to the cross of Saint Philip. He walked toward the many therapeutic pools and spas that dotted the landscape around Pamukkale and Hierapolis. Once he found the Cleopatra pool, he followed the road north. It took about an hour to reach the area where the cross should have been visible, but no matter where he looked, he couldn't see it. Finally he saw an overgrown path that led into the forest. He followed it for about a mile, when he came to a clearing. In the distance, he saw a large, Roman column on a hill. He walked toward the column and there, down the other side of the hill, was a grove of trees with a stone wall surrounding a very old cottage. In the yard by the gate was the cross of Saint Philip. It was the same symbol he wore around his neck and had seen in the cave. Once again the cross was leading him on. He walked down the hill toward the cottage. There was a wooden pole at the gate with an old bell and cord hanging from it. This was obviously some sort of device to announce a visitor, so he pulled the cord, ringing the bell. After a moment, a young woman came to the door. She looked to be a servant girl, all dressed in black.

"Yes. What do you want?"

Peter was amazed that she spoke English. "I am here to see Sister Alissa Galatas. Captain Lysander sent me. He said they were friends."

"Just a moment, I'll see if she'll see you."

Peter paced back and forth. His mind filled with doubts; what if she wouldn't see him, he thought. He's come so far, only to be turned away. Then he saw the woman in the doorway motioning him in. Peter sighed in relief as he and walked up the stone steps into the cottage. The rooms were small and dark. The walls were covered with crosses, crucifixes, statues of various saints and an altar to the Virgin Mary. Peter was ushered into a room at the rear of the cottage. A very old woman all dressed in black sat in a rocking chair. He stretched forth his hand to introduce himself, but was stopped short by the young woman who told him that the sister was blind.

"Arkadas, Captain Lysander," said Peter.

"You are a friend of the captain? As you can see I speak English, but I cannot see, at least with my eyes. What is your name?"

"Peter. Peter Andrews"

The old woman gasped and started to shake. She asked for water and the young woman immediately poured her a glass.

"I'm sorry, Sister, if that was a shock."

Gathering herself she waved off his concern. "I am ready now. You are Peter and your coming has been foretold. For years I have been waiting for you, waiting for you to be ready. Now you are here. I have many things to tell you before you continue on your journey. I am very old, as you can see."

The young servant girl interrupted her. "She's one hundred and ten years old."

"Sh-sh… too much to say. Not enough time for that. I will tell you what I can, what they want me to say until the end. Then there will be no more."

"I am so grateful for your time, Sister."

"Time is short. Listen well. I have been a nun for sixty years. I have served my Lord well, but now it is time for you to be given the message. For many years I studied the scriptures and the religions of the world. I was a teacher and writer of many books. When I was young, I wanted desperately to be a priest, which of course was impossible. I should have known then that the church would never allow me to wear the mantle of Christ, but being a stubborn girl I insisted."

"My wife also wanted to preach the Gospel, but she too was denied."

"Your wife, where is she? Is she with you?"

"She died—of cancer."

"Then she is with you."

"Yes, I believe that, at least some of the time."

"You must have faith. Life is hard when God is denied. I became a scholar with a mind of my own. I served in many missions, including Calcutta, and Burma, and then I was sent to Salvador. That is where I met Monsignor Oscar Romero. I worked with him and the poor for several years. I was with him on the day he was assassinated."

"I have heard of him but don't know much about him or why he was killed," said Peter.

The old woman paused and wiped a tear from her eye. "He was a wonderful man, a saint. The people's Archbishop, they called him. But what many didn't know is that he was an orthodox pious bookworm, just like me. Perhaps that is why we understood each other so well. No one thought he would become the leader that would shake the very stones of the government, but when his assistant Father Grande was killed, something inside of the Archbishop changed."

"What changed? asked Peter.

"I think he caught a glimpse of the real message of the Carpenter. He stood up. He stood up for the poor. They were killing the peasants by the thousands each week. Bodies piled up in the sewers and rivers and garbage dumps. He challenged the government and the army to stop the killing. He condemned them for abusing the people. He even told the soldiers to disobey their officers and do the will of God. That's why they killed him."

"I don't understand, Sister, what does this have to do with me?"

"I tell you this because he has come to me in my dreams and told me of your coming. You are the one who will speak for us. The church; the church must stand for the people. Please understand me. When I say the church, I'm not just referring to the church of Rome, but the entire Christian church as a whole. We Christians claim that we believe in Jesus but we have forgotten his message. There is no need for cathedrals and large churches of glass and gold when the poor are in such need. The church has lost its way. We no longer fight for justice and the poor, instead we fight for power and privilege, for influence and political power. If the church is to survive, it is the people who must change it. Not from the top, but from the bottom."

"I don't understand why you are telling me this. I am no longer a minister, and I'm certainly not an important prelate of the church. Who do you think I am? I have no power to change anything."

"Who do you think you are?"

"I'm a nobody."

"Peter, our Lord built his church on nobodies. Do you think these men, the disciples, were men of power and influence or men of great wealth? Why do you think he chose these men to follow him?"

"I don't think I really know now. I used to spew out some trite scripture that I learned at seminary about faith and leadership and strength of character, but I have come to question what I've been taught."

"Question everything, my son. Therein lies the wisdom of God."

"So, why am I here?"

"You are here because you agreed to be here. Before this time, you and all of us agreed to bring a new message into the world; a message of compassion and union with the true spirit of God."

"Sister, I'm confused. You say I agreed to be here, but I've never been to Turkey before, never met you or Captain Lysander and don't even know why I'm here right now, let alone sometime in my past."

"Peter, before we are born, we agree to come here to learn the lessons that have eluded us in past lives. All those who share our journey are part of our solution. If we don't learn the lessons in this life, then we will just come back and be 'born again'."

Peter felt like a huge brick had been dropped on him. The whole concept of re-incarnation had been thrown out of the church years ago. His mind fought this with all his might.

"Sister, with all due respect, I don't believe in re-incarnation. If it were true, there would be no need for Jesus to have died for our sins."

The old woman smiled and laughed. Peter was totally shaken and confused, and she was delighted at his dilemma.

"I can see you are very troubled. Enough for today, come back tomorrow and we shall talk again. Before you go, take this book with you and read it, my friend."

Peter looked at the book. It was *Reincarnation in Christianity: a New Vision of the Role of Rebirth in Christian Thought by Geddes MacGregor.* As he walked out of the cottage, he felt like he'd stepped into another dimension. His mind was reeling with conflicting thoughts of what he'd been taught and what he really believed. Right now, he didn't know what to believe. God, he wished Ann was here so he could talk to her. She would know what to say. She always had a clarity of wisdom that could cut through all the church dogma and find the obvious truth. But what was the truth? Did anything really make sense now?

That night, Peter walked the streets of Pamukkale and waded in the Antique Pool, an ancient spring filled with broken ruins of Hierapolis.

As he sat there enjoying the warm healing waters, he closed his eyes and tried to understand what the sister had told him. It was true that re-incarnation was commonly believed in the early years of the church, but the church had condemned it. He had to find out.

After he got back to his room, he spent the whole night reading the book that the sister had given him. As he read the chapters on church history, he could see that reincarnation was a common belief of the people at that time of Jesus and there were over 200 instances in the Bible that spoke of reincarnation and the eternal nature of the soul that existed before and after the physical body. Peter read of the condemnation of Origin, one of the great spiritual leaders and thinkers of the early church, because of his writings about the eternal soul that exists both before and after death. Origin's teachings had been declared heresy by the Council of Nicea.

After reading for several hours, Peter had to get away and think. He walked the streets, stopping at a bar and then a shop and then another café for a cup of coffee. Each encounter with a patron, or shop owner or passerby, caused him to question whether this or that person had been born again. Some people seemed to have an appearance of being from another time and place. Some looked Turkish; some looked Greek; and some looked like they had just stepped out of the ancient city of Hieropolis. As he sat on a bench outside a park, he remembered something, an old memory of when he sat on the steps of a large building. It was during a break in a lecture at the seminary. He sat there teaching other students who encircled him on the steps. As he spoke, suddenly in a flash he saw himself dressed in a white toga as were all of the students around him. Peter was aware that he was either in ancient Greece or Rome. It only lasted a moment, but he remembered thinking that in that instant, he knew he had lived before.

Later that night, as he laid in his bed trying to go to sleep, he thought back about his life; his early days as a child, a teenager, a young man, a student, a minister, a husband, a father, and a mental case. He had to laugh at his life and wondered if he knew Ann in a previous life. Their relationship seemed so easy, like they had known each other before. As he drifted off to sleep, his one comforting thought was that maybe if he knew Ann before in a past life, he would know her again in a future life. And what about Jennie? Where and when did she come from? Sister Alissa had said that all of the souls that we encounter are part of our journey and had all agreed to help us face the lessons we needed to learn in this life. She also said that if we didn't learn those lessons, we would have to come back and do it all over again. That's something he just couldn't face, not tonight. And with that he fell asleep.

The next day he once again rang the bell outside the cottage, and once again he was ushered into Sister Alissa's presence.

"You look tired, my son."

"I didn't sleep well."

"You read the book, I see."

"I read the book. I'm not sure of it yet, but then I'm not sure of anything."

"That's good. Like Moses, you are raw metal now and ready for the Master's hand."

"Perhaps."

"God is speaking to you, Peter. You must let him in. He has much to show you and you have much to do."

"I try to listen."

"Then listen now. Jesus, the carpenter, our Lord, had two great missions. He had first to dismantle the laws and customs that kept people separate from each other and from God. His first mission was Compassion. He welcomed all, no matter who they were, or what they had done. His ministry was a ministry of outcasts and the unclean, the forgotten and the poor. That's why it was so dangerous. He had unlimited patience for the sinner, but none for the hypocrite. He had to push the powers of his day to uncover the lies and greed. He demanded that they change, not from the outside in, but from the inside out. His Gospel was embraced and supported not only by a few disciples, but by influential women who not only believed in him and followed him, but also supported him with their gold and silver. They did this because they understood his teachings of compassion. He brought hope and comfort to the powerless and that was why he was dangerous. That is why they killed him and that is why they killed Archbishop Romero."

"What of his second mission, you said Jesus had two."

"The second mission was of the spirit, but that is not mine to teach. You will be given that by the Apostle of the Apostles."

"Who is that?"

"You are to go to the Garden of the Apostles. You will find it near the Saint Philippe Martyrion. This is the place where the Apostle Philip was crucified. Go now, my son and may God bless you on your journey. Be at peace, all things work according to God's plan for you."

Peter took her hands and kissed them. There was a sweet smell of lavender about her. He slowly walked out of the stone cottage and up the hill toward the familiar Roman column. As he turned to wave goodbye, the cottage was gone. It was as if it had never been there. He should have been shocked, but somehow he expected it.

Chapter Nineteen
The Garden Of The Apostles

Peter stood before the entrance to what was once an ancient Roman arena. The stone walls long since crumbled to just a few blocks scattered around a circular overgrown garden. There was nothing about it that looked inviting or remotely interesting, even to the most ardent tourist. What was she thinking sending him here? What was he thinking standing here after a two hour walk from town? It was all so bizarre. Obviously she wanted him to enter the garden, but for what purpose?

He looked up at the darkening sky. Storm's coming, he thought. Maybe this wasn't such a good idea. Wait; what was he afraid of, getting wet? He had to have courage. He'd come too far to turn back now.

"I've got to finish this." As Peter stepped through what was once a gateway or opening, something started to happen. A lavender mist gathered at the base of the crumbled walls and as the mist rose, each block became more visible as it was added to the wall. He watched with amazement as the garden started to come to life. Plants that had long been dead started to grow before his eyes. Flowers bloomed and twisted their vines around ancient columns and began their regeneration into a new vibrant plant. Each of the twelve columns grew before his eyes until it reached eight feet in height. On top of each column a statue started to appear. The statues became more visible with each second until each became whole. Twelve carved men atop twelve columns all fashioned in white marble. Peter stepped closer to each column and saw a name carved in relief.

The first to appear was the Apostle Philip, then one by one each of the apostle's names appeared: Andrew, Bartholomew, John the Beloved, Thaddaeus, Thomas, Matthew, James the Less, James the Brother of John, Simon the Zealot, Judas Iscariot, and Simon called Peter. The statues were arranged six on each side of a ten foot center column that was empty. This center column bore only the name, Apostle of the Apostles.

Everything glowed with a magical light that was both electric and warm. The entire garden's energy had changed from decay to luminous life. Peter touched the leaves and flowers around him and each touch gave him a charge of electrical energy that was visible. After a few minutes the entire garden was alive and new again. The sky over the garden started to change as well. The dark and foreboding storm clouds broke into a beautiful blue window over the garden. The sun streamed through the opening as if Heaven was blessing this holy place. Peter's senses were overwhelmed with beauty and awe. His body started to shake and he broke into a sweat. His brain started to throb with sharp pains moving through his hands and feet. Then everything went dark and he fell to his knees and collapsed. Like Saul on the road to Damascus, Peter felt his mind and body lifted up into a new awareness. He heard the sound of rushing waters and a familiar voice gradually penetrated his mind.

"Be at peace. All things work according to my plan for you."

The voice and the vibration of the garden released so much energy that Peter felt numb and his mind drifted into a dream state—barely conscious of his body, but somehow aware of the birth of a new reality. He must have laid there for some time because when he opened his eyes, he felt that there was another presence in the garden. He struggled to get up and look around. Peter's eyes focused on a being of light that stood far off in the garden. At first Peter thought his mind was deceptive, but then he was overcome by fear and panic. Was this the Christ? As Peter grew closer, he could see that the being was a man with dark, curly hair and flashing blue eyes. As fear overtook Peter he started to tremble. Who was this being, and what did it want? Again, Peter heard the rushing water.

"Be at peace, Peter, you are not in the presence of the Master."

"Who are you?"

"I am Philip; the one they called The Greek. I am from Bethsaida, the city of Andrew and Peter. I lived in Galilee and brought Bartholomew to the Master. I was with him during the feeding of the five thousand and at the last supper. I came here to Heliopolis with John, Bartholomew, and Mariamne. I bring you good tidings from the twelve and blessings from our Master."

"Jesus?"

"His name was Yeshua ben Joseph or as you would call him today, Joshua son of Joseph."

"Yeshua… The Bible says there is so much evil in the world."

"Purify your own heart, Peter, and the world will become pure. You must understand that there is much in your Bible that is not accurate. This has led to much confusion and tragedy. Many have died because they could not bear the word as it has come down through the ages."

"I have always been taught that every word in the Bible is the word of God and that the Bible is infallible, but it doesn't surprise me now that we got his name wrong or that the Bible has many errors. I've learned that much of what I was taught in the seminary was wrong."

"Put not your faith in words, Peter. Put your faith in what your eyes behold and your heart feels, for that is truth unaltered. When you experience the divine, like this moment, you will feel absolute and unconditional love like you have never felt before. As our Master said when he healed the infirmed and blind, go and tell no one. Why would he tell the healed to not speak of the miracle of their healing?"

"I don't know." said Peter.

"Because our Master knew that words would only confuse and lead others astray. Each of us must experience God personally. Believe in this only. Believe not what others tell you of their experiences with the Divine. Trust that God speaks to all of us, each day in our own language and in our own thoughts and feelings. Understand this; go to Yeshua, or Jesus as you call him, to verify each of His teachings for yourself and to discover your true nature. You cannot really understand the Master until you understand his language, his customs, or his times."

"You speak of Aramaic?"

"This was the common language of his tribe."

"What am I? Why am I here, and what would you have of me?"

"You have been chosen, and you have chosen us. You wear the cross of Philip, my cross."

"My cross … tell me, if it's your cross, what does it mean?'

“The cross in the center is not a crucifix. It is an empty cross because it signifies the resurrection of our Lord. The first square around the cross signifies the four disciples that came to Heliopolis to spread the word; John, Bartholomew, Philip and Mariamne. The second square represents the great commission to spread the word to the four corners of the Earth.”

“And the circle?” asked Peter

“The circle represents the unifying presence of God and the power of the Apostle of the Apostles.”

“The Apostle of the Apostles; I keep hearing about that. Who or what is that?”

“When you are ready, it will be revealed. You have come a long way, Peter. Your life has been filled with great success and great tragedy. You have lingered in the dark night of the soul. To come out of the darkness you must follow the light.”

“I have failed at everything—my wife, my daughter, and my career. I have lost all hope in ever finding joy again.”

“Believe that your soul is eternal. It existed before the world and will exist after your present life is at an end. You have had many lives. Know that Ann and Jennifer were with you at the beginning and will be with you again.”

“That is comforting.”

“Each soul has things to accomplish, tasks to finish, goals to meet and past injustices to right. All those who are closest to you in this life, have agreed to bring these lessons that are needed in order for you to complete this life’s mission.”

“I don’t even know if I’m a Christian anymore.”

“You have been a Christian, a Jew, a Muslim, a Hindu and a Buddhist. You have been all things in all times and places. You have always been a searcher for truth, and that is good. All souls must experience all things—different faiths, rich and poor, young and old, lover and hater, sickness and health, black man, white man, male and female, child and invalid. It is all grist for the eternal mill. That is why it is so pointless to judge and condemn those who are different or believe that those who see God differently are lost. When we condemn others, we condemn ourselves. Each soul must understand that if is hasn’t already been all these things, then it will become all these things in due time.”

"But what of my ministry? I have failed God's calling. That mission is over."

"You failed because your mission was corrupt."

"No, I was corrupt, not my mission."

"Nothing is corrupt that is made by God. Your mission was made by men who were led by greed, ignorance and ambition, as is the church."

"You speak of my church?"

"I speak of the Christian Church universal. I speak of all Christianity and those who are in power within that body. Christianity has lost its way. It has become corrupted by power and greed. It has twisted the gentle words of the Master and used his message and his name to judge, condemn and ostracize those who are different and those of a different faith. The Master's teachings were filled with tolerance, love and compassion. His name has been used to conquer lands, armies, and people. The name of Jesus has been used to justify violence and hate and compel unbelievers to worship him or face torture and death. So much pain and destruction has been wrought by the use of his name, that it has become the 'Anti-Christ', that which is against his message. This is not his way. This is an anathema to Heaven. All that is against love is against God. All that is for love is for God."

"Are we wrong to believe that Jesus is the only way to God?"

"God is like the top of a mountain. There are many paths up the mountain, but some believe that because their vision is small, that their path is the only way. They cannot see what God sees. God is Love."

"If that is true, then how could a loving God condemn anyone?" asked Peter.

"No one is condemned by love. There are only two forces in the universe—love and fear. Any person, group, government or religion that uses fear to manipulate its people is not close to God. Everything that is good comes from love: compassion, understanding, faith, cooperation, joy, happiness, and peace. Everything that is not of God, comes from fear: hate, judgment, condemnation, exclusion, manipulation, criticism, worry, violence, war, torture, and death. Whatever unites us is of God. Whatever divides us is not of God. Be warned of those who use words to divide us. They think they have no accountability for what they say. Be aware your words have power—more power than you think. Every word you speak and every thought you think is bound to you and will eventually create your world. All will be held accountable for their words, thoughts and deeds. You cannot avoid it. What you sow, you shall reap. If not now, believe that the day will come when you will see a reckoning."

"Are you saying that our thoughts and words create our world?"

"Yes; the Master taught us that we would do even greater works than he. We are all creators. We create each day with our thoughts, words and deeds. His message was one of empowerment. He came to show us another way to think, believe and act, and that if we understood him and followed him and changed our lives in his manner, then all power would be given to us as creators. As he said, *Have you not heard that you are gods?*"

"And what have we created? A world of violence, hatred, poverty and war." said Peter.

"Peter, if you do not like what you have created—change it. Understand that you must start from the inside with your thoughts, then your words, and then your deeds. It is then that your world will change. The Master said, *If you love me, live by the principles which I have taught you, for Love cannot rebel, but seeks total unity and perfect peace.* That is why you have been chosen by the Master and by the twelve to bring a new unity to the faithful and those who weep for peace among the faiths.

"For too many years, the world has seen the results of the corruption of the name Jesus. They have forgotten his message or denied his mission in order to conquer and destroy. They would rather believe in Jesus, than what Jesus taught. This is not what he intended. This is not why he came. As he turned over the money lenders in the temple, he would today turn over the pulpits of the hypocrites who cast out and condemn in his name, all the while filling their coffers with gold. As he condemned the Pharisees and Sadducees for their greed, hypocrisy, and manipulation of the people, so today he would also condemn those who claim to speak for him while preaching hate and bigotry."

Peter's mind raced. He trembled inside for fear of what might be asked of him.

"Are you talking about?"

"I speak of the anointing. Jesus the man became Jesus the Christ, the Anointed. Most favored of God. None of us can become Yeshua ben Joseph, but all of us can receive the anointing, the Christ, for the Kingdom of God is within you, Peter, and all humankind. All carry the divine spark that radiates the love of the Most High. As the Master was the Son of God, so then are all of us sons and daughters of God. All are most favored. All are divine."

"How can we know that this is true? Mankind's actions are anything but divine."

"Deep inside you, in your own soul you will find that connection with the eternal. You will have to separate yourself from the world and its noise, but understand that this connection is as strong today as when you were born. As the Master said, *unless you are like little children, you cannot enter the kingdom.* As children, we are pure and innocent. We know nothing of hate and bigotry and judgment. We accept others without fear and mistrust. We see in them the divine spark that burns brightly inside of us. It is only after the world enfolds us that we forget who we really are. We are not humans who are having a spiritual experience; we are spiritual beings who are having a human experience. This is what Yeshua was teaching us, and this is what you are to teach—for on this day, the mantle has been given. Do not be afraid, Peter. You have heard my voice many times. *Be at peace, your path is given. All things work according to my plan for you.* Remember?"

"Yes, I remember."

"Peter, kneel down."

Peter's heart raced as he knelt before the apostle. He could feel the warm touch of Philip's hands upon his head. As Philip spoke, Peter felt a radiant cloak of absolute love descend upon him.

"Peter, blessed are you among all that seek understanding and the Christ. You are to receive, this day, a new commission. As the Master said; *All authority has been given to Me in heaven and on earth. Go therefore and make disciples of all the nations, ... I am with you always, even to the end of the age.* Now, we give to you this mission to bring into the world a new message of understanding and acceptance, of compassion and absolute love. To begin a new reformation of what the world calls Christianity. Be known not as a Christian, for that has become corrupt, but rather say that you are a follower of the Christ. Speak the truth to all who would listen. Speak not of sin and judgment, but of love. Let others see Jesus in you in the way you speak and act. Welcome all, believers and unbelievers, for all are on the path, whether they know it or not. Unto you I give the essence of power, the power to speak the word, to not falter with fear, but to know deep in your heart and mind that God is within you and you walk the path of the Christ. Know also that all of the powers of the twelve will be given you in due time. Go now and ponder what you have been given."

Peter was so weak in bone and sinew that he could hardly speak.

"I don't know what to do now. Please don't abandon me!"

"You are not alone. There are many who attend you from the other side. Come again. More will be given you. Prepare yourself for the Apostle of the Apostles."

The next morning, Peter awoke in the garden. It was no longer radiant and splendid, but was covered with weeds and brush and dust. He wondered if he had been dreaming. It was all so unreal now—the garden, the columns, the statues, the plants and flowers and the Apostle. Was this a hallucination?

The two-hour walk back to town seemed to take days. Peter felt as if time had stopped and that he was not completely in his body. Everything around him—the road, ancient ruins, cars and people passing—looked like they were all moving in slow motion. He started to remember something about how people reacted when they had spiritual experiences and visions. His mind told him that no, he wasn't crazy and that it was normal to be having the sensation of an out of body experience. It was bizarre, but not painful. For that he was grateful.

When he got back to the hotel, the manager told him he had been worried and that if he didn't come back today, he would have called the police. Peter reassured him that he was all right and not to worry. That afternoon, he sat on the rooftop restaurant in a daze. He forced himself to eat, but he wasn't really hungry. He was thirsty, however, and drank ten glasses of water. If water represented spirit, then he understood why he was thirsty, as his spirit was weak. After while, he lay down in his room and slept. He dreamed about his childhood when his parents took him into an Eastern Orthodox Church. One look at the menacing icons terrorized him and taught him to fear God. His screaming forced his mother to take him out to the car. This was his first encounter with the Christian God and his evil looking Apostles. For many years, he would have nothing to do with either.

Chapter Twenty
The Twelve Powers

Peter stood outside the Garden of the Apostles reflecting on what he'd seen and felt. His dream of childhood terrors in an Eastern Orthodox Church had compelled him to visit a church on the edge of town that morning. Now, he stood here trying to understand why, given the way he felt about the church, he should be chosen.

He closed his eyes, took a deep breath, and stepped through the garden opening. Once again the garden came alive and once again the figures atop the columns appeared. When he opened his eyes, the Apostle Philip stood before him.

"Once again, Peter, you have come here to understand what your mission is and to receive the Twelve Powers. The Twelve Powers, each given by one of the Apostles, represent the twelve faculties of God. These are the fundamental aspects of your Divine nature, but they are as yet undeveloped. Yesterday I spoke to you about the essence of Power."

POWER:

"What is power, and how should I use it?" asked Peter.

"Power is the faculty that enables us to have authority over our own emotions, inspirations, and thoughts. Our greatest creative power is generated when we seek not man's power, but God's power. This power is accessed when we go within. Use your words carefully, for they are the generators of this power. Whatever word follows the I AM sanctifies who and what you are. The I AM calls upon the creative power of the Universe to manifest into your reality what you desire."

"This gives new meaning to God's answer when Moses asked him who he was." said Peter.

"Yes, God is the Great I AM."

As the Apostle spoke the words I AM, Peter felt a thickening in his tongue and was now aware of another presence beside him. He felt hands placed upon his head.

STRENGTH:

"I am Andrew, Peter, Apostle of our Lord the Christ."

"You are the brother of Cephas, are you not?" said Peter.

"Yes, When I knew in my heart that Yeshua ben Joseph was the Messiah, it was then that I brought Cephas to our Master. Peter, I bring you the quality of strength. Not of brute force, but of the gentle strength of character that will be required of you. Strength is the faculty of steadfastness, dependability, stability, and a high capacity to endure. It is more than physical; it is a depth of spiritual awareness, courage and confidence. The Master spoke of turning the other cheek. This is nonresistance, and it is the highest form of inner strength. Know that you can do all things through the Christ that strengthens you."

When the Apostle Andrew had said this, Peter felt a tingling sensation in the small of his back.

"I must ask. What are the sensations that I feel in my body?" asked Peter.

"You are feeling the Divine source of the powers that are given. Each power generates from a part of the body. This is creation, Peter." said Philip.

Peter was once again aware of another presence.

WISDOM:

"Peter, blessed are you. I am James, son of Zebedee and brother to John. Like my brother and Cephas, we were fishermen. For the Messiah, we became fishers of men. I was present with the Master at Gethsemane when they took him to be crucified. Be not sad of heart for our Master lives even now, as do we all."

"Then the resurrection was true?" asked Peter.

"Doubt it not. We are all eternal. The opposite of death is not life.

The opposite of death is birth. Life has no opposite, because it is. Peter, I bring you the power of Wisdom. Wisdom and Judgment are the creative forces with which we appraise, evaluate, and discern our decisions. You will need wisdom each day to separate the world's chaos from your true spiritual nature, which is peace. Remember that knowledge comes and goes, but wisdom lingers."

At this point, Peter felt a sharp pain in the center of his chest right at the solar plexus.

"You feel pain there, Peter, because you are weak."

"Wisdom, yes, I know." said Peter.

WILL:

"Peter, you have much to do and much to learn. I am the Apostle Matthew. I was a tax collector and not favored among the people. I gave up much to follow the Master. You will also have to give up much to follow him. I bring you the dominant spiritual attribute of Will."

"I have followed my own will, much to my own destruction and the destruction of those I loved most in the world," said Peter.

"As the Master said in the Garden of Gethsemane; *Not my will, but thy will be done.* You too will have to make God's will the master of your own life. Understand that your will is the decision making, directing and choosing faculty of the mind. Your ability to discern whether to say yes or no to the world's offers will determine your spiritual growth. Remember that we are often the closest to the Creator when we are in the depths of failure, for it is then that we stop listening to our own counsel and follow the still small voice of the most high. It is there when our will is crushed that God's voice is understood. Remember also that God sees everything and is not limited in vision as we are. Allow your divine nature to connect with God in your decision making. Before you decide, stop, breathe, and listen for the message from the divine."

"Yes; not my will anymore, but God's will in my life."

As he said that, Peter felt a throbbing in his head that made him stagger. Over and over his thoughts screamed out—not my will—not my will—not my will—your will—your will!

UNDERSTANDING:

"Be warned, Peter, not to trust your own mind and thoughts when your own will tells you that your perception is all. I am Thomas, so called the doubting Apostle. I had to see and touch before I would believe. Our Master appeared to me and then I believed. I bring you the power to understand the creative nature of the Universe and gain spiritual intelligence. The world says, I will believe it when I see it. But I tell you this great law of creation: You will see it when you believe it. Your thoughts, passions, and strong faith, together with your willingness to act, will bring your creation into reality. When you pray, believe it will be so, and then do what is necessary for God to move in your life. So often, you have prayed and then sat passively waiting for God to act, but God waits for you to act. When you do, then God will act."

"I prayed for guidance, but I see now why God waited for me to act." said Peter.

"All that has occurred is because of your willingness to act, to venture out and come here to Hierapolis. You have learned, and that is why you were chosen. Blessed are those who are willing to be led, even when they know not the path that God provides."

For the first time, Peter felt a sensation in his body that was not painful. The right side of his forehead had a warm glow like sunshine. He knew that it was good.

RENUNCIATION:

"You are here Peter, because you were willing to separate yourself from your old beliefs. This is the power of Renunciation that I bring you. I am Thaddaeus, also called Jude and Saint Jude by some. Renunciation and Elimination is the power to release false beliefs and those that are in impediment to your spiritual growth. Many have clung to childhood beliefs about God and our Lord that are not true, but their love of these simple stories and fables give them comfort in an ever changing world. It takes courage to be willing to release ourselves from these beliefs. As Paul has said: *When I was a child, I spake as a child, I understood as a child, I thought as a child: but when I became a man, I put away childish things.* Be not afraid to change your beliefs and embrace the unknown. Be not afraid to not only separate yourself from old beliefs, but also from those who cling to these old beliefs. You are not alone in your search for truth. God is always your companion on the path, and once you have opened truth's door, you cannot close it and cling once again to old lies and delusions. Surrender to God's will and know that you are on the path of spiritual enlightenment."

Peter felt a tingling sensation in his lower abdomen and spine and knew that there were still remnants of old fundamentalist thinking that he had to abandon.

LOVE:

"Be not afraid, my friend, to abandon that and those who do not love you. I am John, called the beloved of our Master. I stood at the foot of the cross and watched him die and watched over his mother, Mary. I tell you that the unending love of God brings life for the Master and for all of us. I bring you the quality of Love, not carnal love or selfish love, but unconditional love. This is God's love for all mankind, and it is the harmonizing and unifying force of the mind. Understand that unconditional love accepts what we cannot change and thereby allows it to pass away. Most do not understand God's love and are quick to judge others as not being worthy of divine compassion and acceptance. Remember that the Master said, *The rain falls on the just and the unjust alike.* God blesses all, whether they believe or not, whether they are good or bad, whether they are rich or poor, black or white, male and female. All humanity and living things are held in the gentle embrace of a loving God. Do not attach yourself to those who believe in judgment, for God is love, and love—I speak of spiritual love—does not judge. All that love are of God. All that judge are of fear and have shut themselves off from that divine loving parent."

Peter felt a radiating power of warmth and tenderness like he had never felt before. This was God's love and as it swept over him, he felt all of his worries and cares disappear.

IMAGINATION:

"The power of your mind is a great comfort to you, Peter. Be free of fear to release your creative powers. I am Bartholomew the Apostle. Philip brought me to the Master and when I saw him, I knew that he was to be the one called Messiah. I traveled with Philip and John and Mariamne to Heliopolis to spread the word of hope. I bring you the power of Imagination, for this is the unlimited traveler of the mind. Imagination is the part of the mind that is most God like. It is the creator of new ideas, that with the force of spirit and passion becomes real in this world. Be not afraid to let your spirit soar in your imagination, for God's great gift to mankind is the freedom to think and envision a better world. It is those who were fearless in their thinking that brought God's ideas into form. Believe in your own power to imagine. Believe in God's power to bring your dreams into reality, for this is creation."

Peter's mind took him back to when he was a child; how he loved to pretend he was flying. He had a wonderful imagination when he was young, but gradually as he grew older and wiser, he left it behind. Now he would have to find it again.

LAW AND ORDER:

"I speak to you now of law and order. I am James, called James the Less, because I was the younger brother of James, the brother of John. My life was devoted to the law, and the order that comes from the law. Understand now that I speak not of man's law, but of spiritual law, the law that governs the Universe. God creates the order and from that comes the law of spirit. Mankind has free will and it is spiritual law that this will shall never be taken away. Be aware that as a creator, you cannot break the laws of spirit. What you sow, you shall reap. This is a spiritual law. In the East, they call it Karma. Understand that in all things there must be balance. Live your life with all things in moderation and follow The Middle Path. This leads to enlightenment."

"What is the middle path?"

"To follow the middle path is to focus on the balanced view of life. I speak not of just a middle path between extremes, but a higher path of spiritual calmness. This is the way of peace and contentment. The middle path is free of attachments. Nothing in this world lasts forever. Every thing and every one will pass, given time. Love and love alone is eternal."

ZEAL:

Peter felt an uneasiness as Simon the Zealot approached.

"I bring you instruction on the power of Zeal, Peter. I am the Apostle Simon; a fighter in the spirit of the Maccabees. I exhort you to be not afraid to show your passion and zeal for God's word. This power will rise up in you to give force to your actions and focus to your words. Zeal will give you great intensity, but it will not give you temperance and wisdom. Only understanding and love will give you the patience and the calmness to resist the anger that may rise up in you. It is common for those who believe it is their mission to save souls, to speak the harmful words of division, judgment and condemnation. They think that fear will bring unbelievers to God's word. They are misguided and confuse their own will for that of God's will. Be warned that your zeal turn not into anger. If you are angry, ask yourself why you cannot accept the world as it is. Ask yourself if you feel compelled to bend others to your will because you are sure you are right. Ask yourself if you believe you are out of control, and blame your reactions on others. Know that you are angry by choice. Remember this, that if you see yourself become enraged over a minor thing; then understand that you have responded to an old wound that has never been healed. Heal yourself and come to peace with those who may have wronged you. Forgive them and forgive yourself. This is the way to contentment and compassion."

Peter felt a devastating pain at the back of his neck and immediately saw the face of Jeremiah. He knew that he had never even approached the idea of forgiving him for what he had done. Peter also knew that he must find a way to forgive Jeremiah one day. The sky grew dark and threatening. The garden suddenly felt strange. Peter looked around and saw a figure approach. He was not a being of light, like the other Apostles, but Peter felt no threat.

LIFE:

"I come before you to save you from myself. I am Judas Iscariot, thought to be the betrayer of our Lord. I bring you the power of Life and the understanding of a life well lived and not a life misspent."

"All Christianity has cursed you for what you did." said Peter.

"My name is shameful to me for what has been done, but I will tell you that I was never cursed by my Lord. I did not understand his way. I thought he would free himself and free us from Rome. The freedom he brought, I did not understand. His way is the way of freedom from our own oppression. We so often trade one oppressor for another, because we believe ourselves to be victims. In my mind, all I saw was a life that was condemned. Everything justified my belief that I was not worthy. This is what I have come to say, that whatever you believe in your mind, you will create to justify that belief. If you believe yourself to be a man cursed by all humanity, then every word and deed will curse you. If you believe yourself to be favored by God, then likewise your beliefs will create favor and goodness.

The creative life force flows from God through our senses. It is holy and pure. It fills us with love and desire and compassion. In its purest form it serves without thought of itself. In its most selfish form, it merely desires pleasure without any thought of service or tenderness. When this happens, its only purpose is the immediate gratification of the senses. When wisdom, understanding and judgment direct it, it moves in ways that enhance one's spiritual life. It becomes life-affirming and brings us closer to each other, resurrecting our spirits in loving union. When it is wasted, it divides us and leads to a deadening of the spirit. Live your life, Peter, as though each moment was precious. Be here in this moment, for that is where eternity is. Do not dwell in the past, for it is gone, or the future, for it will never be. Trust in God to provide and have faith. As it is said, *Give us this day our daily bread.* Be content with the needs of this day only, for you may not have tomorrow. I know now that my life with the Master was wasted in the corruption of my own mind, but that within my mind laid the seeds of salvation. For it is said; *As a man thinketh in his heart, so is he.* Think only good thoughts of yourself, Peter, and let your mind be transformed."

FAITH:

"Blessed are you, Peter, for God will send a new message through you into the world. I am Cephas and Simon called Peter, the rock and the first Pope by many. I bring you Faith. Faith is the assurance of things hoped for and the conviction of things unseen. Faith is our ability to perceive the reality of God's kingdom of good, despite evidence to the contrary. It is this faculty, that of expectation and definite assurance in the power, presence, and promises of the divine, that unifies us all. God is real, and the blessings of spirit enfolds us all, regardless of our beliefs.

I have seen much in the world that grieves me. Many have been tortured and killed under the banner of the Master's name and under the authority of my position as first among the Apostles. An empire has been built, not on the message of the Christ, but on the greed and grasping power of men. They have, in the name of God, killed the old, the young, and all those who would not bend to their will. I tell you now that much of what has been built in the name of Jesus and in my name has become corrupt. These men have acted out of fear. As you have been told, those that spread fear are not of God. The world cannot continue in this way, for it is destroying itself. Know this now, Peter, that this is about to change.

I call upon you, Peter Andrews, to redeem my name and speak truth to power. Be courageous and know that God speaks for you and through you. The Master has said that if you are able, all things are possible to him who has faith—that is, if you are able. You must be willing to take on the mantle of the Christ to lead his people.

"Among all of the twelve, there was one that was most divine. It was this one who shared the private counsels of the Master, and it was this one that he shared his highest teachings. This one has been hidden from you by the masters of the world for fear, and the message has been lost. It is now time for the world to hear the message and embrace the Apostle of the Apostles. Kneel down, my son."

Peter started to shake as he sank to his knees. He bowed his head and was aware of all of the Apostles encircling him. A bright beam of light came from each being and centered on him. Suddenly, there was an earthquake and the ground trembled. Lightning filled the sky and the winds blew, then as quickly as it appeared, the storm quieted and it was still. Once again he heard the sound of rushing waters and Simon Peter spoke.

"I, Simon Peter, on this day give you, Peter Andrews, the keys of the new kingdom. Know that Christ builds his new church on the rock, which is the Holy Spirit, the Divine Feminine Comforter, whose symbol is the dove. This same dove descended upon Yeshua ben Joseph, called

Jesus of Nazareth, when he was baptized by John the Baptizer. And God said, *This is my beloved son in whom I am well pleased.* This authority is given to you to preach a new Gospel, not of Jesus, but of the Christ, that all may know that they are loved, that the anointing is available to all who believe and are aware, and that all paths eventually lead to God."

Peter felt a withdrawing of the beings in the garden. As each one faded from site, he felt comforted by an overwhelming unconditional love. As he was about to get up, he heard the familiar voice of the Apostle Philip.

"Peter, you have been given the Twelve Powers, which are the aspects of God. You have been given the anointing of the Holy Spirit, the Divine Feminine, and the blessing of the Most High God. Go now, reflect upon what you have been given, for tomorrow you will be given the final message from the Apostle of the Apostles. Now follow the path of the Christ."

Chapter Twenty One
The Apostle Of The Apostles

Peter stood once again before the garden. His whole life had changed. He had gone from a rising young star in the evangelical movement, pastor of the one of the largest and most influential churches in the country, and well on his way to being a United States Senator and maybe one day president—to this. He was now a man who had lost everything; his wife, his daughter, his ministry, and his reputation. He had once lived in an elegant mansion with chauffer-driven limousines. Now he was an itinerant vagabond, homeless and friendless. He didn't know what was ahead of him or what was expected any more. With an overwhelming feeling of emptiness, he ventured forth into the void.

As he did, the garden began to change again, but this time the color of the mist traveled from lavender to pink. He could see a bright white light emanating from the center pedestal. A figure started to appear. As the being became visible, it lifted its arms and a pulsating beam encircled the garden until it joined itself into a white ring. The ring slowly rose up until it was high in the sky; at that point the being suddenly stood before Peter. He looked up and saw not the vision of a man, but that of a beautiful woman. Her radiance was so bright that it was hard to look at her. As she lowered her arms; the light inside her lessened and slowly he was able to see her as a real human being.

"Peter, you have been called to deliver a new message of the Christ."

"I am ready to receive it."

"I am Mariamne, also called Mary of Magdela and Mary Magdeline.

The other Apostles have referred to me as the Apostle of the Apostles, because I was most favored by my Lord. I have come to give you his words of counsel. This message has been hidden from the world's view by the pillars of the empire church for fear that the people would not understand. The church prelates wished to destroy the old religions of the Earth and convert the people to the new Christian religion. Many died in this effort. Now, it is time for the world to see the light of truth about God and Yeshua ben Joseph."

"What is that truth?"

"Let me first talk about Yeshua, who came to be called Jesus of Nazareth. There has been much written about him after he was crucified, but very little written while he lived. The Christian church has made him God. This would have been abhorrent to him."

"Was he the Son of God, and the Messiah?" asked Peter

"He was the Son of God, and he was the Messiah. But understand that we are children of God, sons and daughters all. He was a man. He ate when he was hungry, slept when he was tired, and laughed when he felt joy. He felt sorrow and anger, like any man. He came to bring us a message of hope and a challenge to see the world differently through his eyes. The freedom he brought was misunderstood by many. It was a freedom of the heart and mind. He believed in the goodness of the people and rebuked the hypocrites and forces that dominated them. Tell me Peter, who do you believe in?"

Not really understanding Mariamne, he recited the first thing that came to mind.

"I believe in one God, the Father, the Almighty, maker of Heaven and earth, of all that is, seen and unseen. I believe in one Lord, Jesus Christ, the only Son of God…"

"Peter, I asked you *who* you believed in, not what doctrine you have learned."

"I don't understand. I was only saying…"

"Do you really know what you are saying?"

"What do you mean?"

"The Nicene Creed was formulated at the First Ecumenical Council at Nicea. The Roman Emperor Constantine changed Christianity forever when he convened the first universal council of the church at Nicaea. The Council's purpose was to resolve a theological controversy over the nature of God and Christ. The results were the adoption of a universal statement of Christian faith known today as the Nicene Creed. It also changed the Christian movement and condemned all those who did not believe as they did. The church and empire became one and it is to this day. Many who would did not believe were excommunicated, tortured or killed as heretics."

"It's only words. Most Christians don't give them much thought."

"These words separated thousands from the community of Christ. Words continue to separate us from each other. There are many who call themselves Christians, who judge and condemn others who follow the Christ, but because they do not believe the creed; they are called non-believers. They are told that they are not real Christians. Some even say that they believe in the wrong Jesus, that one Jesus is true and the other is false."

"What nonsense. If this wasn't so absurd, it would be frightening." said Peter

"Many thousands have died because they refused to believe in words and man's written documents of faith. Some were persecuted because they believed that Jesus was a man. Some were persecuted because they refused to believe in the Trinity. Others were persecuted because they were Jews, like Yeshua. And others were persecuted just because they were women."

"I can't help but think of Ann, my wife. She wanted to be a minister, but the church wouldn't let her. I think that's part of what killed her. She felt called, but was denied."

"She was called, Peter. You both were, but she was denied because she was the way God made her. I was most favored by Yeshua, and after his death preached the Gospel of hope and love along with the other disciples. I was called directly by him, yet some would not listen to my words because I am created by God as woman."

"The church called you a prostitute."

"Such was the fear and ignorance of men in authority in the church. Lies were told, books were burned or hidden. Good men and women of faith were destroyed because they believed differently."

"Then if so much of what was written was lies, what should I believe?"

"Believe in his message of peace and justice for those who are oppressed. Follow his example. He is the example, not the exception.

Believe in the healing power of the Christ that dwells within you. Believe in the anointing of the Spirit. Believe in the all encompassing love of God, but put no faith in other's words."

"Should I not believe in the Bible?"

"Believe what you will of the book, but know that it was written by men for many reasons. God cannot be known by reading a book, but by your own experience with the divine. This I learned from Yeshua when we first met."

"Tell me about him."

"There was a light in him. You could see it in his eyes. When he looked at you, you knew nothing could be hidden from him. Your soul belonged to him and you were changed forever. So much is not known about him. What is in the scriptures is so far from who he really was. I will tell you that he had a wonderful laugh. He loved people, no matter their station or beliefs. There was a great compassion in him for the poorest among us. He felt very protective of them. I loved him very much."

"Mariamne, you sound as though you were very close to him."

"He was my husband. We were married at Cana."

"Oh my god!" said Peter.

"Why does this trouble you so?"

"Because Christianity will think this is heresy."

"It is time for the truth, and it is time for you to speak the truth to those who will listen. Understand that my name has been tarnished by the world and I have been diminished because I was his wife and companion and because I was given an understanding of his message. You must not be troubled about this. It was most common to be married in that day. Many of the disciples had wives, Peter among them. The women traveled with the disciples and some gave substance so that we could eat. Yeshua was called Rabbi, and it was required of Rabbis to be married."

"I don't know why it is such a shock to think of Jesus as being married, but it does make sense in so many ways. We've grown up with such hard and fast stories about Jesus that anything new seems to threaten our fantasies. Silly, isn't it?"

"This is the first part of my message to you. You must tell the truth about Yeshua. Tell of his love and compassion for all people. Tell of his treatment of men and children and women. This is most important for his message has been twisted and used to make men rich and make women prisoners in their own bodies."

"I know Ann would approve."

"The second part of my message concerns the very nature of God."

"My spirit is unsteady, but I guess I'm ready."

"God is spirit, Peter. God is not male or female. God is male *and* female. It is time for mankind to acknowledge and honor the Divine Feminine aspect of God."

"The feminine aspect of God, that's not in the Bible, is it." said Peter

"Hear the truth and understand from your own scriptures. It was written, *Let us make man in 'our' image, according to 'our' image, according to 'our' likeness...*"

"That's Genesis. Our image? Who is the *our*?" asked Peter

"It is also written; *Then the Lord God said, Behold, the man has become like one of 'us'* And also *'Come, let 'us' go down there and confuse their language, that they may not understand one another's speech.'* Also in the scriptures it is written, *Then I heard the voice of the Lord, saying; 'Whom shall I send, and who will go for 'us'? Then I said, 'Here am I. Send me!''*"

"I don't understand. Do you speak of another God? Another creator with God the Father?"

"Peter, I speak of the Divine Feminine. When the scriptures say, *Then I said, here am I. Send me!*—who did you think was talking?"

"I don't know. I've asked this question in seminary many times, but my professors never seemed to have an answer. I felt like they didn't know either."

"They knew, but they didn't think you should know. The answer to your question is the Divine Feminine, called Sofia, the Goddess. You know her as the Holy Spirit and the comforter that Christ said he would send to be with us for all times."

"This is more than I can handle!"

"When Yeshua was baptized by John the Baptizer and the heavens opened with a dove descending and the voice..."

"God said, *This is my beloved Son in whom I am well pleased,*" said Peter

"The dove—the sign of the Holy Spirit—is the ancient symbol of

Sofia. Peter, when I told you that God is spirit and that God is not male or female, but male *and* female, what did you think?"

"I don't know. I guess I've never thought about it much. I always just thought of God as Father. You know—an old man, like in Michelangelo's Sistine Chapel. God's always been male, I guess; at least that's what I was always taught. But if Ann were here, she would understand."

"What makes you think she isn't?"

"What?"

"Ann is eternal, just as you and I and all life. She is part of you, your better nature, just as Sofia, the Divine Feminine, is the better part of man's nature. She is the source of mankind's compassion, understanding and love."

"Everything in my being, my background, my belief system, wants to shout out that what you say is heresy and that all these are the lies of the Antichrist."

"For thousands of years, this was the thinking of men who were frightened of women's power. During the burning times, millions of women were tortured, hanged, beheaded and burned at the stake because churches, kingdoms, armies and the Inquisition called them heretics and witches. These gentle women who healed and comforted the sick and nurtured the dying were thought to be a threat to the power of men and their religious institutions."

"I had no idea. We were never taught this in seminary." said Peter

"Most Christians are unaware of their faith's violent history. Even today, women of all ages, races, and beliefs are brutalized, raped and killed, because of men's ignorance and fear. The world is filled with hate and violence, domination and greed. Ruled by fearful men, these countries, governments, churches and religions are corrupt with lies and fear. They have twisted the loving accepting message of God's prophets and visionaries in all religions, to keep women from the counsels of the powerful. It is no wonder that we have no peace. When you deny the feminine aspect of God, you destroy your soul. All of this is not just the signs of the times. It is a sign that the world is out of balance. The Divine Feminine has been hidden and caged for too long. It is time for the subjugation of women to stop and for mankind to honor womankind.

"I have long believed that mankind is going to Hell." said Peter

"For millions of girls, and women of all ages, this is Hell."

"It was for Ann and Jennie. I made life hell for them with my own arrogance and ambition. I was too caught up in my own importance. I had no time for them. All they wanted was to be happy and I…"

All of the dark memories of Peter's past broke over him. Like a wave that was about to swallow him and drive him deeper into his own hell, he broke down and sobbed. He wept for what seemed like an eternity. Finally Mariamne spoke, "Weep for them, Peter. Weep for all of the women of all ages that have suffered and died at the hands of ignorance and fear. Their suffering is over, but millions today still suffer and die. You cannot change the past, but you can change the future. This is why you are here and this is why you have been chosen."

"I am not worthy, Mary," said Peter

"I know, my brother, I know… But you *will* be worthy."

"What is mine to do?"

"Tell the truth, even when you are reviled. Many will come at you because you break their illusions. They will want to debate you about what they believe to be true. Remember, be not entangled in arguments about what is true or untrue or what did or did not happen. Tell them… Believe what you wish, but now tell me what it means."

Peter closed his hands over his face and breathed. He had heard and seen so much, and yet he still felt alone. As his hands slipped from his eyes, he saw a soft blue light appearing before him and a familiar voice.

"Peter, I am here with you," said Ann.

"Ann, oh God… I miss you so. I am so sorry, so very sorry."

"Be at peace my love. I am at peace. You have a great work to do and I will always be with you. Be not afraid, Peter. Tell your story. Tell our story. Christ and his disciples gave us The Way. You must have the courage to speak truth to power and give the world a new way."

"Ann… I..."

"Daddy?"

"Jennifer, is that you?"

"Yes, I am here, too."

"I love you, sweetie. I am so sorry. I was such a horrible fool. I was so filled with my own arrogance that I shut you and your mother out of my life. It was all my fault. I didn't understand. I didn't listen. I should have known."

"It's okay, now. I am at peace. That's what I wanted to tell you. I forgive you Daddy. I haven't forgiven myself yet, but I'm working on it. I guess I have a lot to learn.

"So do I, Jennie, so do I."

"Please, be patient and understanding. Don't judge people, especially if they're lost like me. There are many young girls like me that need someone to listen and understand our pain. I should have talked to you, but I just didn't think you'd understand."

Peter was overcome with emotions. Once again he started to cry. It was all so much. His heart was empty and full and breaking all at the same time.

"I love you, Daddy. Both Mom and I love you. Remember my cross, the one I gave you? It's a sign; a very important sign."

"What?"

Mariamne spoke once again, "Peter, the cross you wear around your neck, the cross of Saint Philip. You know the meaning of the cross and the two squares? They represent the four apostles who went to Hierapolis to preach the Gospel, and also the grand commission to take the Gospel to the four corners of the Earth."

"I remember."

"Now understand the meaning of the circle that encompasses the cross. It is the circle of protection. It is an ancient symbol of the Divine Feminine and the emblem of Sophia. This is to remind you that you are always protected by the unbroken circle of her love."

"Where am I to go and what am I to do now?"

"You are to go back from whence you came. Serve the poor and downtrodden again and wait. You will be given a sign when your ministry is to begin. Be patient and keep your own counsel of what has happened here. Now, my brother, kneel down for the final blessing."

Peter knelt down and immediately the wind picked up and a strange light gathered before him. It was so bright that he felt like his skin was on fire. He looked up and a being stood before him. Peter felt compelled to reach out and when he did, the being took his hands and held them. Peter closed his eyes as his fingers felt the holes in the being's wrists. He knew it was Jeshua ben Joseph. Peter heard the voice in Aramaic. Although he didn't know the ancient tongue, his mind understood the words.

"Our Father who is everywhere; let your name be set apart. Come your kingdom. Let your will be, as in the universe, also on earth. Provide us needful bread from day to day. And forgive us from our offenses, as we forgive our offenders. And do not let us enter into worldliness, but separate us from error. For belongs to you the kingdom, the power, and the song and the praise. From all ages throughout all ages; Amen"

Jesus took hold of Peter and embraced him. He felt the warm radiant heat of total love and acceptance. Peter looked up, but could not see his face.

"Use me—use me—use these hands," said Peter

Peter felt his hands get white hot. He looked down and sparks of electricity jumped between his fingers. Then this radiant heat traveled up his arms and enveloped his whole body. It felt as if he was being lifted up high into the sky. He was now certain that Jesus had given his blessing and all that had happened was true. He opened his eyes and Jesus, the Apostles, Ann, Jennie, and the garden were all gone. He sat there are the barren ground, stunned and unable to move. For the longest time he couldn't breathe, but he felt no panic, only love. His logical mind tried to convince him that it had all been a dream, but his heart told him it was all real. He had been changed—his body, his mind, his very soul was transformed. He felt as if he stood on the threshold of eternity. If he died in that moment, it would have been the greatest gift that God could ever give, but he did not die.

Chapter Twenty Two
The Mission

Peter spent the next six months traveling around Turkey, getting odd jobs in restaurants, shops and churches and doing handyman work. Before he returned home, he decided that he had to visit Istanbul. Once called Constantinople by the Emperor Constantine, it had throughout the centuries been the capital city of four empires: the Roman Empire, the Eastern Roman Byzantine Empire, the Latin Empire, and the Ottoman Empire.

There was only one place that he felt compelled to visit; the church of Haghia Sophia. He stood in the entry way and marveled at what he saw. The great Byzantine church stood atop the first hill of Constantinople. He listened to the tour guides explain how the church was named for an ancient martyr, Sofia, who witnessed the torture and death of her three daughters, rather than denounce her Christian faith. Haghia Sofia, which meant Holy Wisdom, was also part of the ancient Goddess worship that predated Christianity.

Throughout the centuries, Sophia stood for so much more. The very name meant the "source of wisdom". He thought back to Mariamne's words, that the world had hidden this compassionate feminine aspect of God. He remembered Michelangelo's painting of the Creation of Adam, in the Sistene Chapel. All of a sudden it dawned on him. Michelangelo had painted God the Father stretching out his arm to Adam, but his other arm held Sofia, the Divine Feminine Goddess. The story of the creation of man and woman had always been the story of the coming together of the male and female aspects of God. As children are created by the mother and father, so God's children are created by the same divine miracle. The world was in deep trouble and Peter had to get all of his thoughts down on paper. As he left Istanbul he knew he had a great deal to do, to prepare for his mission.

* * *

Back in Chicago, he stood on the sidewalk in front of the tiny clapboard church. It had been a Quaker meeting house until it was abandoned when the Quakers moved to the suburbs. Now it stood in a small vacant lot in one of the many forgotten urban areas of Chicago. Peter emptied the key from the small envelope, unlocked the padlock, and opened the door. This was to be his new church. Small as it was, the price was right.

Before he walked in, he looked around the neighborhood. He couldn't help but think how different this was from his last church. You could put 500 hundred of these little Quaker churches inside the main floor of the Jesus Temple, he thought. As he pulled the boards from the plain windows and opened the doors to air out the old meeting house, he couldn't help but laugh at his life and the journey that he'd been on. After sweeping out the place, he found some old black paint in the back hallway and painted a sign. What would he call it? While he thought, he painted the symbol of Saint Philip; the cross with two squares and a circle. Then it just became obvious—The Circle and the Cross Church. It would stand for the male and the female aspect of the Divine and the sacrifice and compassion that was required if there would be balance.

The weeks led to months in the little church. Peter fixed up the place and put a fresh coat of paint on the old boards. The benches needed repairing as well, and he did the best he could to make them sturdy. It was a small, simple church—only meant to hold about fifty to seventy-five people. Eventually, his reputation as a different kind of preacher got around the neighborhood. The visitors didn't quite know what to make of it—or him. Unlike other churches in the area, his sermons were absent the fire and brimstone, and he never brought up the subject of sin or judgment. It seems like all he ever talked about was love and taking care of the poor. In fact, the folks in the neighborhood called it the poor, little, love church. One day, a picture appeared in the local neighborhood newspaper about the church and with it a photo of the minister, Rev. P. Andrews.

Jimmy Sinclair was a photographer and part-time reporter for the Chicago Tribune. He walked into the main offices of the newspaper and asked Miss Stevens, the classified ads order taker, if Wendy Larsen had come in yet. He was told that she hadn't arrived, but if she wanted to hang on to her job, she'd better be on time. When Jimmy asked Stevens what she meant, she held up four fingers, "That's the number of days she's been out this month. One more absence and she'll get her pretty rear end canned."

Jimmy sat down and waited. About ten minutes later, Wendy came storming in all wet and disheveled.

"That damned taxi cab let me out right in front of a puddle and I was a direct hit for the cross town bus. Oh, hi Jimmy. Am I late, Miss Stevens?"

"You just made it, Wendy… with 30 seconds to spare."

"Thank God. What's up Jimmy?"

They both made their way back to her desk in the City Room. Her cubicle was a mess, like her apartment and her life. She'd never been able to get anything organized. Maybe that's why she didn't last at WIND Radio, too much organization or corporation or something. The real issue had to do with all the hate talk. She tried to listen, but just got more and more depressed at all the divisiveness and screaming. It just seemed like it was nothing but a place where angry white men could rant and rage about their changing world.

"Hey kiddo, I read this in the morning Gazette."

He handed her the newspaper and he sat down. She fumbled with the newspaper while she took her trench coat off. With one hand she drank her coffee and with the other hand she tried to eat the remaining part of a donut. She looked at the paper and couldn't find what Jimmy was talking about.

"There—right there—the article about the Love Church. Isn't that the guy you were talkin' about? You know—Andrews, the big-shot preacher who went nuts and killed his kid?"

Wendy read the article with rapt attention, squinting to try and make out the photo of the minister of the small church.

"No, Jimmy, he didn't kill his kid. She committed suicide, shot herself 'cause she got pregnant. It's hard to tell from this picture, but it could be him. I haven't seen him in years."

"He just disappeared, didn't he?" said Jimmy

"After he got out of Northside, his wife died. He was pretty broke up about it."

"Was he nuts?"

"No, but it was so strange. He'd been at the top of the world, you know—minister of that Jesus Temple. He's had it all, then lost it all. I haven't thought of him in so long."

"You had a thing for him, didn't you Miss Larsen?"

"Huh?"

"I mean, the way you talked about him it almost sounded like, you know, there was something between you two."

"Don't be silly. We were just friends."

The moment of reflection was smashed by the sound of the editor screaming for Jimmy to get over to the dog show for some pictures. Jimmy didn't stop to say goodbye, he just ran out, camera in tow. Wendy sat down at her desk and opened the drawer of her desk. Inside was a shoebox. She hesitated for a moment, then opened it. It was filled with photos of Peter and her, as well as copies of the magazine articles on Peter. As she looked down at the photos, she said, "Just friends… We were just friends."

The next day, Wendy called in and told the editor that she was working on a story and would check in that afternoon. It was a spring day in Chicago, and by all rights, it should have been warm, but not here, not in the "windy city". She made her way down South Racine Avenue to West Seventeenth Street. She parked across the street and ducked into a little coffee shop on the corner. As she sat down to drink her coffee, she watched the little church across the street. She played Russian roulette with her mind about whether she should go over and knock on the door or not. She didn't even know if he'd remember her or want to see her. So much had happened to her since Northside. Where did he go? What did he do with his life, and how did he end up here? Finally the coffee did a number on her and she had to go to the bathroom. Finding her way to the back of the shop, she opened the door and went in. The other customers turned and looked when they heard her exclaim, "Oh my god!" After a few minutes she came out of the restroom and was about to make her way back to her table when there he was, standing at the counter ordering a coffee to go. "Peter? Peter Andrews? Is that you?"

He turned around and seeing Wendy, he dropped his coffee on the floor. "Wendy, I, ah... Miss… I'm sorry about the coffee."

The waitress told him not to worry about it, that she would clean it up. They sat down at the table and just stared at each other for the longest time. Finally she broke the ice. "A beard? It looks good on you, Peter."

"The results of a sea voyage and a trip abroad. You look great, Wendy. I'm so glad to see you again."

"Me too, I saw an article in the Gazette about you."

They talked and talked and eventually they held hands and reminded each other that they were more than just friends. He took her over to the small church and showed her around, which didn't take more than five minutes.

"It's not much of a church, I'm afraid." said Peter

"A big change from the Jesus Temple, I guess."

"A big change." said Peter

"I never thought you'd get back into the preaching business. What changed?"

"What changed? I guess it's not what changed me, but who changed me. You had a hand in that, and Dr. Gaskin, but there were others. So, Wendy, tell me about yourself. What have you been up to? Did you get that job as a journalist?"

"Well, to tell you the truth, it wasn't as easy as I thought it would be."

"It never is, is it?"

"No, I guess not. I worked a radio station here in Chicago for a while. I did research and wrote copy. I occasionally had a news assignment, but most of the time I got coffee for the guys on top."

Peter nodded. He felt her disappointment. As Wendy talked on about life in AM radio, Peter's mind thought back to Ann and Wendy had in common. Like so many, Wendy had been held down and devalued. It was all part of the history of women and why he came back. It was what he was told had to change.

"So anyway," she said, "I just got fed up with all the hate and anger on the programs. I couldn't listen any more, and I figured if I couldn't listen to it, how could I work there. So I left. Now I'm at the Trib, at least I can be proud of what we do there."

"I glad, Wendy. You deserve to be successful."

"So, Peter, I'm curious. You said there were others who influenced you. I'd love to hear more."

"Well, let's see, where do I start? I guess the first person who really made an impact on me was Captain Lysander of the Andrea Valencia. That was a freighter that I caught in New Orleans, bound for Rome, Greece, Turkey, and beyond. He was a fascinating man, a true sailor and seaman. I was lost and very confused. He taught me that perhaps God wasn't finished with me yet and that maybe I had a purpose beyond my life as a minister."

"I know you were still in a lot of pain when you left Northside. I'm the one who put that letter from Ann in your Bible. I saw a man, I think it was Jeremiah, throw it in her grave at the funeral. I didn't give it to you right away. I thought it would be too painful. I'm sorry for that."

"Jeremiah. He's been behind so much of my pain. I think he may have had something to do with Ann's death. Someday, I have to face the fact that I have to forgive him and let him go, but I'm not there, not yet."

"You still miss her, don't you?"

"At times I think of her. Mostly I blame myself for not being there when she needed me. You know, I met this fellow on the ship. Jason Allen, like me, had lost his wife to cancer. Unlike me, he did everything he could to support his wife when she needed him most."

"Peter, we all handle things our own way."

"You know, Jason's in-laws turned on him and his wife and told them that the disease was God's curse. Can you believe it?"

"Yes, I can. Remember me? I got thrown out of my church, just for asking too many questions."

Peter laughed and so did Wendy. He reached out and held her hand and caressed it.

"Wendy, I've missed you."

"So, Peter… it's a shock, after all you've been through, to see you once again in ministry."

"I know, it's a shock to me too. I'm back, but I'm different—and so is my message. That's because of the wonderful Miss Wilson."

"Miss Wilson? Another young woman in your life?"

Peter laughed. She was a seasoned eighty year old world traveler and visionary."

"Oh," said Wendy. She felt a little embarrassed and just shook her head.

"Miss Wilson studied with the great Mahatma Gandhi. She taught me many things—among them the wisdom of the ancient Hawaiian Kahunas."

"What's that?"

"A very old group of wise healers with a very unique concept of the human soul."

"Sounds fascinating," This Miss Wilson… is she in Hawaii?"

"She died on the ship. I think they buried her in Athens; an appropriate final resting place for a great mind."

"I'm sorry. She sounds like she was a great lady."

"She still is. In Turkey I met Father Aziz, or at least I think I did. I'm not quite sure. He gave me a great gift."

"What was that?"

"He taught me to value the Experience of God and not the words that men write about God."

"I don't understand, Peter."

"I know. I'm not sure I do either. Then there was Sister Galatas, a strange messenger who talked of Monsignor Romero and of his compassion for the poor."

"I think I've heard about him. He was a South American priest, wasn't he? Didn't he get shot or something?"

"Yes. He was killed for standing up to the corrupt government. He spoke out against the abuse of the poor. When he told the soldiers to disregard their order to kill the people, they killed him."

"So she taught you about compassion?"

"Yes, compassion and reincarnation."

"Reincarnation? Isn't that against the Bible?"

"You know, Wendy, I've learned that reincarnation is in the Bible and was a strong belief of early Christians. The church took it out, most of it, and officially condemns it, but it's still there, if you look."

"Wow, you've really changed."

"I've discovered the real message of Jesus. It is so different from what we're teaching in churches today."

"That's why your message is different?"

"I have changed. I met… ah.. there was this garden called the Garden of the Apostles."

"Sounds so interesting; it would make a great story. Oops, journalist just came out, sorry."

"That's okay. I'm not ready to talk about all of that yet, but someday, when the time is right."

"Well Peter, so much has happened to you, to the both of us, but I'd like to come back and do what I can to help you here in this little church, if you'll let me."

"Well, I don't know, you see we have this huge staff of people and well they…"

Wendy frowned and then smiled as Peter broke down and laughed.

"The truth is, it's just me here and I'd love to have you help, but more than that, I'd love to have you back in my life again."

"That makes two of us, Reverend. Can I call you that, now?"

"No, just call me Peter."

"Okay, Peter it is."

They walked and held hands and hugged each other before she left. The drive back to the newspaper was all a blur to Wendy. He had come back, but he was different, very different.

The weeks passed with Wendy helping Peter out at his church. She washed windows, swept the aisles and gathered old song books each Sunday. She listened to his sermons, along with a huge congregation of ten or twelve regulars each week. He spoke of love and forgiveness and the value of a life of service. It was a simple message of pure Christianity, the way it must have been thousands of years ago when Jesus walked the Earth.

During the week, Peter and Wendy spent as much of their time together as possible. She was in love and knew that he felt something too, but so often she would see him with a far off look in his eyes, and wonder if he was thinking of Ann. She would ask him where his thoughts were, and he'd say Hierapolis. This was the garden that he mentioned, but never talked about. Of course she was curious. After all, deep down inside she was still a journalist. But she kept silent and didn't push it. Some day he would tell her what really happened to him in Turkey. He was her mystery and life was so much more interesting when you didn't know all the facts.

One Sunday, a young black girl came in the back of the church just as the service began. Wendy didn't notice her much as she would have blended into the neighborhood. She sat there and every once in a while she would dab at her eyes, like she'd been crying. Peter's sermon that day was on forgiveness, and he used the story of the prodigal son to talk about the problems that parents and children often have with each other. After the service, the young girl quickly left the building and ran down the street. Wendy walked out on the sidewalk to see if she could talk with her, but in a moment she disappeared around the corner.

After the service, she and Peter went out for dinner to a local café in the neighborhood. She told him about the young girl and that she seemed upset.

"I hope my sermon didn't upset her."

"I think she was already undone when she walked in. There's something about her, Peter. I don't know what it was, but she looked at me and we made eye contact. I smiled and there was just a trace of a smile. I think she'll be back, at least I hope so."

"So do I. We get so many young people, teenagers mostly, that seem so lost. I try to help them, but most of the time I think they've just shut themselves off from everyone, especially the clergy."

Two weeks later, Peter had a very disturbing dream. He saw himself in a concentration camp in Poland at the end of World War II. A very old man about to die, he clutched his canvas bag as a younger man tried to get him to hold on until the Americans liberated the camp. It was May 7th, 1945, one day before the 1st Infantry Unit of the American Army would liberate Zwodau, a subcamp of the Flossenburg concentration camp, the following day.

"Hang on, Jacob. The Americans are coming. You must not die now, my friend."

"I can't. I'm dying. I'm an old man. I've seen too much. You must do this one thing for me. In this bag—my story, my life—it must not die with me. Make sure they read it. They must know what happened here. I want them to know that this old Jew's life had meaning."

The younger man took the canvas bag and opened it. Inside were several hundred hand written pages. "I promise, Jacob. I will see that your story is told. God bless you, Jacob."

"You see, Samuel, even in this place we are blessed."

With that dying remark, there was a huge explosion and Peter immediately woke up drenched in sweat. The dream bothered him and it took him all morning to shake it off. More than he would know, the dream left its mark. The next day as Peter gave his opening prayer, he saw the same troubled, young girl from the week before. She sat in the back of the church. She was still upset and time and time again, she'd wipe her face and look down at the floor like she was ashamed. After the service, as she was about to leave, Wendy came over to her.

"Hello. I'm Wendy. I'm so glad you came back."

The girl said nothing as Peter made his way toward the two of them. Then the girls' coat fell open and it was clear she was pregnant. She motioned to her belly and said, "my father did this". Wendy cringed at the thought of the girl being raped by her father. The girl started to cry and shake. Peter opened his arms and held her for the longest time.

"You can stay here, if you want. I have a spare room in the back of the church. We'll take care of you, you and your baby." said Peter.

The girl smiled and kissed Peter's hands. As she bent over, a gold cross fell out of her sweater. Peter looked at it in amazement. It was the same cross that Jennie had given to him so long ago. It was the cross of Saint Philip. He looked down at the girl and lifted her face up to his and smiled. When she smiled, he saw Jennie's smile. His mind raced back to the day his daughter took her life. He had been so cruel, so judgmental and self-righteous. Wendy embraced the girl and stroked her thick, black hair.

"What's your name, child?" said Wendy

"Sophia," said the girl.

Suddenly, the color drained from Peter's face. His eyes grew big and he slowly stood straight up. He turned and walked to the back of the church into his office. Wendy was worried. She'd never seen this look in his face before. She told the girl to sit and wait. Rushing back to Peter's office, she found him standing over his desk.

He took out a key and held it in his hand. The sun streamed in from the window and as it hit the key his mind flashed backwards. In a fraction of a second he was back in Northside Sanitarium staring at the gleaming cross around Wendy's neck. Once again he was thrashing about on the floor cursing and screaming as he tore the pages from the Bible. He felt the pain in his mind and body as he lay tied to his bed in a straight jacket.

Then in an instant, he saw Ann, beautiful Ann smiling at him. He felt his arms about her and he was young again. Suddenly he saw himself kneeling in front of her grave and felt all the pain and guilt of her death. Staring at the cross on the tombstone he was once again propelled to standing outside the Jesus Temple, staring up at the giant cross that dwarfed all of Chicago's skyline. Once again he walked between the giant fountains of the Apostles and stood before the massive Jesus fountain drenched in blood. There standing before him was Jeremiah smiling and beckoning him to follow him into the vault of gold and political power waited.

He felt the wind in his hair and in another flash, he was back again on the Andrea Valencia, hanging over the rails staring at the moving ocean beneath him. Once again he heard Captain Lysander;

"...There's gotta be a reason beyond your running away. You're a minister, or at least you used to be a minister. So maybe God put you here for a reason."

As he stared at the ocean, he heard Miss Wilson's gentle voice guiding him to find the truth beyond what he had been taught. Once again he heard her say;

"You will go to Turkey, Peter, to Heiropolis. There you will meet your next messenger. There you will meet the Apostle of the Apostles. There are 'Messengers' and there are 'Guides'. The Guides help you find your way along your path. They prepare you to meet the Messengers. The Messengers are sent from the Divine. They bring a unique message of love and peace and comfort. Prepare yourself, my friend. Be at peace. All things work according to God's plan for you. You are the one, Peter. You are the one they've been waiting for."

The one they've been waiting for. Was this it? Was this finally God's plan. He saw the old withered face of Father Aziz smiling at him.

"You are on a journey, my young friend. I have lived a long life and can tell you only this. Be at peace. Remember who you really are. Be the change you wish to see in the world. Share your story and make a difference. The world is in desperate need of enlightenment. I pray you are the one to bring it."

Then in an instant, Peter stood once again in the Garden of the Apostles. Never before had he felt such fear and yet such peace. He knew instinctively what lay before him and that his destiny had been arranged long before this life. He started to tremble as he felt the weight of responsibility descend upon him. All that had happened both the good and the bad, the light and the dark had all been for a reason. He looked up, not hearing or seeing Wendy standing before him and heard the voice; that same voice that told him so long ago;

"Be at peace, all things work according to my plan for you."

Now the voice was different. It was a gentle voice, and Peter knew it was Mariamne, the Apostle of the Apostles, who now spoke in his mind.

"You are at a crossroads my brother. Before you lies a great challenge. To put Christ back in Christianity."

Ever since he was a boy, he had loved the hymn, 'Onward Christian Soldiers'. As he learned about all the violence that accompanied the song, he had put it aside. Now, once again he would be a soldier for Christ, and this battle would be for the very soul of Christianity itself. With a deep breath, he stopped and sighed. Looking down, he saw Wendy's face looking up at him. Her face was filled with confusion and fear.

"Peter, what in God's name happened to you? Are you all right?"

Taking a long moment to look around, he said; "Yes, I'm all right.

Slowly he opened his hand and took the key and unlocked a desk drawer. Inside the drawer was a wooden box. He took out the box and placed it on the desk.

"You asked me Wendy, about the Garden of the Apostles and what happened to me there." Wendy nodded.

Peter unlocked the box with a second key, he had kept hidden in a humidor. As he opened the lid, Wendy peered over his shoulder.

"It's time you knew, Wendy. It's time the whole world knew."

"What, Peter?" She asked.

Peter opened the box, as Wendy peered inside. There it was. The story; his story, truth to power, Ann had said. In the box was a stack of typewritten papers. On the top sheet were written the words; 'The Jesus Factory', by Peter Andrews.

Peter looked at Wendy, took a deep breath and grabbed her hand for support. They walked back inside the church and took Sophia's hand and they all walked outside. He looked at Sophia with her baby inside and thought of Jennie.

"Home?" Asked Sofia.

"Home" said Peter. Then he looked over at Wendy and thought of Ann. Wendy saw the sadness in his face and asked him;

"Are you thinking of Ann?"

Peter smiled and said; "Yes, I wish she was here."

Wendy squeezed his hand and said. "She is, Peter. She is."

Peter looked up and he was grateful for all of it. He took a deep breath and put his arm around Wendy. She smiled up at him and nodded. It was a beautiful day. The wind rustled through the trees and it felt good to be alive.

"Now it begins," he said.

THE END

Notes from the author:

…to balance the scales

To some who read this book, they might question my motivation and purpose. After all, what is a crime prevention expert and author of three books on rape prevention doing writing a religious book? In thinking about my life, I have also asked this question. I wrote my previous books because I felt there was a need for a different perspective. The motivation for this book is that and something more. I guess I am an anomaly in that most authors who have written rape prevention materials are either survivors, or scholars, or members of law enforcement. I am none of these. I am also not a women's rights activist, although I fervently believe in gender equality and women's empowerment. So, what's going on here?

If reincarnation is true, and I believe it is, then perhaps my soul's purpose comes from another life and another time. Does my life's mission and the motivation for all of my work come from another life when I was a monster, or does it come from a life when I was, like many women through history, a victim of suppression and violence? Who knows…

I do know that I believe that there is something inherently wrong in the world; the wars, the violence, the suppression of women and children, the disregard of our environment and total lack of respect for all forms of life, may one day destroy us. We have had thousands of years of the unquestioned reign of mankind without the kindness. We have seen the results of a world that has not only suppressed women, but also any reference to a more compassionate and feminine side of God. Much of this suppression was and is still sanctioned by the world's great religions, where women continue to be treated as second class Christians or worse. Is it time now for justice and a balance of the scales? I believe it is.

Many people today are starting to question the faith of their fathers; a faith in the child-like stories of male dominance and judgmental gods. They search for a more inclusive divinity that acknowledges that there are many paths to God. Many women today search for a new vision of that God, as Patricia Lynn Reilly put it; *A God That Looks Like Me*. This is the growing Goddess movement, which empowers women to be all they can be without fear. Some religions and institutions may call this heresy and dismiss this Goddess movement, but this search for a more compassionate God, is what I believe was at the heart of Jesus' message. This was the reality of the first century Christian movement, when differing views and beliefs about Jesus and his message were the norm.

This book is about that search in one man, and his discovery of the real meaning of the life and message of Jesus of Nazareth. Perhaps, the fear and chaos that we see in so many people today, are the signs that the world is in the midst of the birth pangs of a new God or Goddess. A God that is compassionate, loving, non-judgmental and accepting. I can only hope that this book encourages each reader to begin their own search for that unique experience of God, that experience we call enlightenment.

--- Scott Lindquist

To all my readers:
I would be grateful for your thoughts and/or reviews
about The Jesus Factory after you have read it.

You can send me an email at
SL.thejesusfactory@gmail.com.

About the Author…
Scott Lindquist, C.P.P., C.P.S.

Scott Lindquist is a certified Crime Prevention Practitioner and rape prevention expert. He is certified through the Florida State Attorney General's Office and through the Georgia Crime Prevention Association as a Crime Prevention Specialist in rape prevention. He is a graduate of the Florida Crime Prevention Training Institute. Lindquist has presented his crime prevention seminars to hundred and thousands of people in universities as well as corporations and government agencies. As a writer and expert in rape prevention, he has been featured in numerous international magazines, including Cosmopolitan (both in the U.S. and U.K.) She Caribbean, and B, an Australian magazine. His books on rape prevention have been lauded by police departments, rape treatment centers and colleges around the world. He has also been interviewed on hundreds of TV and radio stations worldwide. He has made it his life's work to work towards the empowerment of women and the eradication of injustice.

THE MESSENGERS

For those who search for a more expansive view of God,
I suggest you look at the works from these authors:

Bishop John Shelby Spong
Marcus J. Borg
Jean-Lves Leloup
Tikva Frymer-Kensky
Dr. L. David Moore
Geddes MacGregor
John Dominic Crossan
Deepak Chopra
Dr. Wayne Dyer
Dr. Rocco A. Errico
Louise Hay
Kristin Zambucka
Joseph Head
S. L. Cranston
John Temple Bristow
Sherry Ruth Anderson
Patricia Hopkins

For more information on this book, and to contact the author:

Scott Lindquist, c/o
Spirit Visions Unlimited, Inc.
4880 Lower Roswell Road, Ste. 165, PMB 303
Marietta, Georgia 30068-4385
Email: SL.thejesusfactory@gmail.com
Website: www.thejesusfactory.com

Other books written by Scott Lindquist:

Before He Takes You Out, The Safe Dating Guide for the 90's
(1990, Vigal Publishers, Inc.)

The Date Rape Prevention Book, The Essential Guide for Girls and Women
(2000, Sourcebooks, Inc.)

The Essential Guide to Date Rape Prevention, How to avoid Dangerous Situations, Overpowering Individuals, and Date Rape
(2007, Sourcebooks, Inc., Naperville, IL)
www.sourcebooks.com
ISBN-13: 978-1-4022-1022-8
ISBN-10: 1-4022-1022-1